THE
TRIAL
PERIOD

THE TRIAL PERIOD

AUBURN MORROW

wattpad books W

wattpad books **W**

An imprint of Wattpad WEBTOON Book Group

Copyright © 2025 Auburn Morrow

All rights reserved.

Published in Canada by Wattpad WEBTOON Book Group, a division of Wattpad WEBTOON Studios, Inc.

36 Wellington Street E., Suite 200, Toronto, ON M5E 1C7 Canada

www.wattpad.com

First Wattpad Books edition: February 2025

ISBN 978-1-99885-413-4 (Trade Paper original)
ISBN 978-1-99885-414-1 (eBook edition)

Library and Archives Canada Cataloguing in Publication information is available upon request.

Printed and bound in Canada

1 3 5 7 9 10 8 6 4 2

Cover illustration by Lotty Illustrations
Typesetting by Delaney Anderson

For Rebecca, for embracing me for who I am

PART ONE

Browsing the Internet

ONE

Parker

Two weeks, one day, and ten minutes is the longest I have ever officially dated someone. Or at least the longest I was able to stand being in a relationship. I always thought I wanted a girlfriend or a boyfriend until I had one, but after a while, dating was nothing but a chore, eating away at the few precious minutes of my day.

I was not a thing created to date.

As a girl, I was expected to crave things like relationships and romance. Sure, sometimes I felt the absence of intimacy and the hunger for a connection, and after a few mild spouts of depression caused by loneliness I'd step up to the plate yet again. I continued taking swings, but I always hesitated and ended up missing the ball.

Gross, a baseball metaphor. My dad would be way too pleased.

My friend Camille and I were stranded outside the grocery store I worked at, Frugal Finds. Camille's black Volkswagen Beetle sputtered its last breath by the cart return, marooning us in a sea of abandoned shopping carts and midsized sedans. Typical, getting stuck at work as soon as I was freed from it.

Camille's intention was simply to pick me up, but I'd doomed her to this capitalist limbo. We sat on top of the hood of her car, trying to soak up the residual heat from the engine. Her groan rattled her entire body, her short legs flailing in the crisp fall air. "I'm so bored! Do you think this is a bad omen? Like the whiff of death?"

"All bad things do come in threes," I warned her.

In my boredom, I opened my ex-girlfriend's Instagram. Emily was a blemish I couldn't stop picking at even though I knew leaving the scab alone would let it heal. I loved to scratch at it for the quick relief. After only taking a few scrolls on EmilybutSpooky's feed I lost all feeling in my fingers and toes from the cold. She hadn't blocked me yet on social media. I assumed it was because she'd miss the extra "like" on her pictures too much to kick me to the obscure void of being muted.

It had only been a week since Emily told me we were finished. I had innocently arrived late to one of our weekend movie dates and asked her what I'd missed, and she went off on me. You'd think I ran over her cat or told her print media was dead. Such an innocent little question wasn't grounds for a breakup. To me, the whole thing was blown way out of proportion and our relationship was ended too quickly.

I thought for sure she'd have come to her senses by now. I even tested the waters yesterday, sending her a text complaining about the way my dad had to make the same three jokes to every cashier he met, but Emily didn't respond. That was a bad sign. She used to respond immediately, as if she had been waiting for my texts the same way I was waiting on hers. I wondered what she was doing—if she was going to cool places or doing cool things without me. I always relied on the fact I could reach out to her whenever I needed her and she'd be right there.

Camille leaned in, wrapping her arm around me. With Camille, I was never alone. She was my lifeline, the one friend I would take with me to a deserted island. If she hadn't been the first person I met after transferring to Creekside High School at the tail end of last year, I might have gone crazy. We huddled for warmth against the autumn climate, but I knew her true intentions were to siphon the heat out of me. In her ripped black skinny jeans she was shivering as bad as a shy girl giving a PowerPoint presentation.

Clothes spoke to me. An outfit told me everything I needed to know about a person. Similarly, pairing my comfy, light-washed jeans and an oversized sweatshirt underneath a denim jacket told everyone that I expected a food baby later, and wanted to hide it. In this, I was comfortable. Approachable. Maybe down for a nap.

Meanwhile, Camille's clothing suggested that she awoke from her coffin in the morning with the intent to exchange people's deepest darkest desire for their souls. She was like my fairy gothmother with bangs.

"You know . . ." Camille said, stringing her words along as she pointed at Emily on my screen. "I could call Emily and ask her to pick us up instead of Lizzie. Her house is like five minutes away."

"I don't want to seem desperate." I grimaced, not sure which rescue option left a worse twisting feeling in my guts. Emily inspired nervous little butterflies in my stomach. Lizzie, Camille's cousin and the bane of my existence, curdled my stomach like I'd eaten a spoiled deviled egg.

Camille shrugged and then suddenly perked up, motioning to a woman pushing a cart full of groceries. We liked to play a game as we watched shoppers leave in their more obliging cars. "This lady hates feet. She bleaches her socks all the time." Camille snickered.

I nodded and stroked an invisible beard. "It's why she's afraid of clowns. Can you imagine the kind of feet on those things?" We didn't know if any of this was true, but it was a fun game.

"That guy"—Camille subtly pointed at a man walking out of the store with his arms full of canvas bags—"he's afraid of basements."

3

"Everyone is afraid of basements," I said. As if channeling an epiphany, I pointed my index finger to the sky and proclaimed, "He's petrified when he hears nursery rhymes." With a pitch of haughtiness, I glanced back at Camille. "Come on, I thought you came to play."

Camille narrowed her eyes, her lips picking up slightly in the corner. "Are you picking a fight with me? Because you know I would destroy you."

"Is that a challenge?" I pressed my nose against hers.

"It's a promise." She shoved my shoulder and jumped off her car. A jolt jumped around in my chest, and I grinned nice and wide, revealing every dimple in my arsenal. Hopping off the car and onto my feet, I lunged for her tiny frame, and she shrieked, dashing behind the car. I raced the opposite way, ready for a head-on collision, but she dodged. We bobbed. We weaved. We mirrored each other's moves to run around the car over and over. We wrestled the way actors did on stage, not a lot of action but a lot of drama. Ready for the grand finale, I grabbed Camille around the waist and hoisted her off the ground, whirling us around in a never-ending twister. She shrieked and kicked her legs in the air while I laughed manically.

Camille was my bridge to my new life here. She led me to find Emily, who had been Camille's friend before becoming my girlfriend. Camille's roads mostly guided me to sunny pastures, roadside attractions, and the best fast-food joints. However, at some point we swerved off the road into a ditch. Nothing could ever be perfect. Even Camille came with some baggage. She never returned the clothes she borrowed, always arrived late, and worst of all, her cousin was Elizabeth Hernández.

TWO

Lizzie

One week, two days, eleven hours, and not a second more was the longest anyone has ever held out to date me. Girls never thought I cared about them—texting made me anxious; making plans made me anxious. In a fight or flight scenario, I ran away. I liked staying at home. I liked being by myself. But just because I couldn't handle a relationship didn't mean my heart knew to stop having crushes.

Crushes were easy. They were little daydreams I could live inside while the terrible world burned around me. Girlfriends were too real, and while I always promised myself I'd do better the next time, I never did.

My van hummed around me as I kept my foot pressed on the brake pedal, waiting for my turn to drive into the Frugal Finds parking lot to pick up my cousin, but that flash of ginger hair made my stomach drop. Camille had failed to mention anything about Ashley Marie Parker being stranded too.

In the distance, Parker and Camille were making a scene, slapping and mock pushing each other around. Camille gave Parker one hard push, but with Parker's height and overall physique, she picked Camille off the ground as easily as I picked up a penny. I didn't have the strength to handle them today. Taking out my phone, I tried to find an appropriate playlist for this specific situation.

My playlists were more important to me than anything. They gave my feelings explanations when I couldn't find the words. With music, I was allowed to stay in the moment and live with my emotions. It was my only form of therapy.

Lizzie's "I hate my friend's friends" Playlist

Perfect. A bunch of songs wherein the instruments were louder than the singers, most of the lyrics were laced with sarcasm, and the frequencies made the car windows shake.

Parker had become Camille's best friend last year, to my horror. I had always assumed Camille was *my* best friend: we were cousins in a close-knit family, we were the same age, and we got along so well. I had a friend more instant than microwavable Easy Mac, which was nice for a shy kid like me. But once Parker entered the picture and I saw the way they talked, the way Camille screamed with laughter at Parker's jokes, and how it didn't matter if I joined their fun or not, I had my concerns.

If Camille had mentioned Parker would be here, I would have told her that I was too busy sticking my face into a vat of scorpions to come help her. It wasn't that Parker and I hated each other *per se*. It was that whenever I saw her face and annoying pretentious hipster clothing an itch consumed my entire body. I longed to reach for the nearest breakable thing and snap it over my knee. I wanted to scream into a pillow when she talked over or interrupted me. My heart pounded in her presence, ready for yet another fight. Being around Parker was simply exhausting.

"Let's get this over with." I grunted and tapped on my car horn.

They jumped at the sound and Parker dropped Camille like a goth hot potato. While Camille walked off her laugh, Parker's face fell. Our eyes met and my instincts pinched my chest, warning me to floor it in reverse and get out of here. My life might not be at stake, but my mental sanity around Parker was always threatened.

She grumbled something to Camille, who elbowed her before running toward my car. I got out, letting myself be swallowed in her arms. "Lizzie!" Camille gushed. "My love! The light of my eternal life—"

"Yeah, yeah, yeah." Despite being happy to see her, I gave her a halfhearted pat on the back. "You owe me, you know that? I wasn't planning to wear real pants today," I joked as Parker made a confused face.

"As an apology, I'll drive you to get some ice cream," Camille offered. She held out her hands, begging for my keys. I frowned at her terrible attempt to make it seem like she was doing me a favor. She always wanted to be the driver, even if it wasn't her car. Camille insisted like a toddler at a grocery store begging for candy. "Oh come on. You know I get carsick when I don't drive and it's not like I *crashed* my car. It spontaneously died on me. There's no way it'll happen twice in one day."

When I didn't budge, she added, "I'll splurge on a triple scoop for you."

I frowned. "But it's freezing."

"It's free sugar."

Sighing, I dropped my keys into her grubby little hands and she took off for the driver's seat.

"Shotgun," Parker said, already getting into the car.

"Hey!" I turned too fast and tripped into the nearest car, hitting the door hard enough with my elbow to set off its blaring alarm. My spine went stick straight as I whirled around to see if anyone noticed.

Of course the handful of people in the parking lot stared bullet holes right through me, and I flushed and glared back at Camille.

With a huff, I stormed to the passenger side of the car and knocked on the window, imagining what it'd be like to knock on Parker's head. Parker rolled down the window and Camille shouted, "Get in, loser, we have to leave the scene of the crime."

"But!" I looked at my cousin and then back at Parker. "But why is *she*"—I referred to Parker in the same way people talked about women who ate children inside of candy houses—"in the front seat? It's my car!"

Parker raised her hands in innocence as she yelled over the blaring alarm, "I'm sorry, I guess you don't understand the sacred rules of shotgun. It's a you snooze, you lose kind of game. You snoozed, Lizzie, so therefore you lose."

Camille nodded. "She has a point. Get in already, that alarm is giving me a headache."

"I can't believe this." Cheeks burning, I threw up my hands in surrender, feeling the ache of getting picked second hit me again. She wasn't always taking Parker's side, but she did it enough for me not to be surprised. I stomped to the back, got in, and slammed the door.

"You're gonna love it." Camille wiggled into place and started backing up.

I slammed my back against the seat and crossed my arms. "I'm being taken hostage in my own car."

Parker rolled her eyes. "Stop huffing and puffing. You don't have to spoil our good day because you can't keep your keys in your pocket."

Grabbing her seat, I pulled myself up and served Parker a sandwich layered with my favorite flavors of sarcasm and bitterness. "What a great fountain of advice you are, Parker. Oh! And by the way, you're welcome. Remember, I came down here to pick your broke ass up—"

"Sorry, sorry. I didn't mean to start something with you because you know I hate it when you do that thing when you move your mouth and that whiny noise comes out."

Camille reached for my phone and raised it like a white flag between us. She hit Play on a playlist that contained jams only.

Lizzie's "Songs you have to scream along with" Playlist

The moment the first song started blaring, the tension exploded, and we were wrapped up in the moment and the music. Parker and I might disagree about most things, but even she had to admit I had great taste in music. The lyrics were ripped right out of my lungs. Parker danced with her hands stick straight and chopped at the air like an idiot. We performed for the people at every stoplight. Camille sang a little louder, showing off that she was an actual good singer. It was a travesty she was stuck as Chorus Girl 2 in yet another school musical, but she was at least safe from mixing with the thespians who'd sooner laugh at me for falling down than help me back up.

Camille's laughter brought me out of the music video playing in my head. Parker had switched from robot dancing to an emotional ballad as she stroked Camille's face. Swiping at her, Camille was all smiles as she poked Parker's side. Parker nearly flew out of her seat.

"I surrender!" she squealed.

Still smiling, Camille patted Parker's head and focused on driving again. All of this just to pick Parker up from work even though they'd spent all day yesterday hanging out with each other. My hands fell to my lap as I kneaded the back of my fingers nervously, not really singing anymore. I imagined shrinking to the size of the pennies stuck between the car seats, where I'd be forgotten too. In the background. Hanging around. It hit me all at once that I wouldn't even be here if they hadn't needed the help.

It was becoming horrifically clear that Parker wasn't a passing interest of Camille's but someone who was going to stick around. This was all Camille's fault, putting a dog and a cat in the same room and not expecting them to snap at each other. Parker barks, I scratch, and Camille cleans it all up.

THREE

Parker

As gluttons for punishment, we were willing to withstand the cold for ice cream. Only Camille would have a craving for sugared ice particles at the tail end of September, when the leaves shivered and died off their trees.

Inside the small Bruster's hut, the lights were crisp and bright. Little bats hung from the red and white striped awning and squishy jack-o-lantern stickers clung to the glass. The smell of sweet milk made my mouth water.

The girl taking my order had a cute round face and dimples that appeared when she smiled. "Hey, how are you guys?"

I took a deep breath, preparing myself to be a cool and normal person. I had a deep need for all pretty girls to like me.

Leaning into the counter, I pretended to whisper to this girl like it was top secret information. "I don't wanna brag, but I just got off work."

The cashier's customer service façade instantly shattered, and she rolled her eyes. "If I were you, I would brag. I've got another hour."

"I hope it goes by fast." I raised my brows. "You know, I could set the trash can on fire. Get the fire department involved. The drama alone would eat up that hour."

With a laugh, the girl shook her head and sighed as wistfully as possible. "And they say chivalry is dead."

A spark ignited in my stomach, and that warmth spread through my limbs like wildfire.

There was a chance this girl was straight, but even if she wasn't, it was still fun to flirt with someone pretty. Girl or boy. Sometimes I glanced at Camille to see if she shared my appreciation. I wondered how other girls saw each other and if it was with the same chest-crushing feeling I felt, but I guess that was what made me bisexual and what made Camille, Camille.

Camille shoved me a little. "Can you order already?"

"Oh right." I laughed nervously. "One scoop of cotton candy explosion."

Hiding behind us, Lizzie piped up. "Um, same for me."

"You got it." The girl accepted the order, smiling the whole time.

I walked to the red picnic tables that faced the road and nabbed an empty one. I glanced at my phone, noticing a text from my dad, asking when I would be home. Since moving in with him, I was experiencing parental control for the first time and I was not a fan. Dinners together were excruciating when all I wanted to do was ask him which part of ruining my life did he like best: Was it being the reason I lost all my cool opportunities in New York or was it ripping me from my mother, who used to be my best friend?

His text was a part of our family group chat, which usually consisted of memes from my little brother and typical grocery-related questions from my stepmom, Debbie. Quickly, Debbie added that they'd ordered Chinese food and had even gotten me an order of rangoons. I texted:

Parker: I'll be back by curfew

Hayden: Sweet more for me

Next, I texted my actual mom about how this roadside ice-cream shop hadn't closed down yet. I didn't linger on the screen long. It hurt my eyes to see the stack of text bubbles from me and the lack of replies from her. Scrolling backward, I checked to see her last message and noticed she had promised to call. She was a few days late keeping that promise.

Everything changed last year when I was volleyed from my mom's concrete jungle to my dad's suburban hellscape. She lived in New York and worked as an editorial designer for a fashion magazine. With my parents' new custody arrangement, I was all hers during the holidays, though I was sure we'd spent it here anyway. Her family lived here, too, and it wasn't that my parents didn't get along, they just fell out of love and split when I was three, before things got nasty. She chased her dream job, and my dad chased the American dream, quickly marrying again and popping out Hayden to carry the Parker name.

Before I knew it, Lizzie was by my side and Camille was sitting across from us. Lizzie's black hair was compiled into a long braid down her shoulder like always. My eyes glazed over with boredom, seeing the same plain pair of jeans, the same yellowing Converse, and the same chunky gray cardigan every single day. It was always the same thing with Lizzie.

Sitting down, Lizzie practically bounced back up. "I forgot a spoon—" Turning around, she locked eyes with the pretty cashier and froze. "Um, uh, actually, I think I'll just eat it like this."

With a sigh, I rolled my eyes. "I'll get you a spoon."

Hopping up, I walked back to the counter, fixing a smile on my face. "Hi, sorry to bother you, but that girl over there forgot a spoon."

"Oh, no worries." The girl handed one over.

"Thanks. Don't tell anyone this, but you're my favorite cashier here."

The girl laughed a little, smiling wide enough to show off her dimples again. I loved women. They sparkled without doing very much at all. She said, "Your secret's safe with me."

Triumphant and with a little pep in my step, I sauntered back to the table and handed the spoon over to Lizzie. "You're welcome."

"How do you do that?" Lizzie grumbled, using the spoon to stab her ice cream.

"Do what?"

Flushing, Lizzie scrunched down to try to hide it. "Nothing."

"Well! Would you look at that." Camille motioned between our ice creams. "I'll add ice-cream flavors to the list of things you two have in common." Her shoulders wiggled in satisfaction at the matching ice-cream colors.

Lizzie snorted. "That's gotta be the shortest list known to mankind. I'm pretty sure Parker has more in common with that trash can."

The metaphor was not lost on me. I grimaced, feeling my voice rise with every word. "Tell me, Lizzie. Who hurt you? Why do you love sucking the joy out of everything? Let's make this a group therapy session. First one is free."

"God!" she huffed. "I was being sarcastic!"

"Hey." I raised my hands in surrender, getting a kick out of her neck and ears turning red. "My mistake. The missing posters looking for your funny bone are still up."

"*AAAAAHHHH!*" Camille threw her head up and unleashed a terrible gargling yell that attracted the attention of everyone around us and the cars driving by. "You guys are driving me crazy! Can't you do anything else besides bicker?"

I turned to Camille and tapped on the table between us. "You can add we like to bicker to your Parker and Lizzie Are Best Forever Friends list." Lizzie snickered and dipped into her ice cream, a real laugh. I had amused her, and something inside me ignited. My whole face brightened as I scooted against her until our knees touched. "Is that laughter I see? Did I crack the code?"

"Technically"—she rolled her eyes, even though she was still smiling. Lizzie's teeth were perfectly straight but stained from copious amounts of coffee that no Crest White Strip could fix—"you didn't see me laughing, you heard it."

"Zip it!" Camille snapped, glaring at us. This was the end of her patience. "Please, you guys were so close."

I was chuckling to myself when my phone buzzed. Whipping it out, I saw a notification on my screen. Another Instagram post from Emily. It was a selfie of her holding up a peace sign in front of her AP British literature homework. Her light-brown hair was piled up in a bun and I recognized her oversized sweatshirt from having borrowed it on more than one occasion. Sometimes a person is so cute you look at them and wonder how you're the same species. I read Emily's caption: *Things are about to get lit-erary up in here!* I snickered at the pun. I couldn't even remember why we'd fought so much in the first place. Maybe it wouldn't be so bad to make up with her. Unlike my mother, Emily was always good at answering my texts.

Besides, Emily never stayed mad long. I just needed to remind her of all the good parts about our relationship. Let her forget all the ugly stuff that turned people away.

Unable to help myself, I double-tapped the screen to like the post and commented *Careful. Don't have too much fun.*

"No phones at the dinner table," Camille said.

"Has Emily been talking about me?" I asked, leaning in closer.

Lizzie sighed and mumbled, "It always has to be about you."

I ignored her.

Humming, Camille took another bite. Her spoon lingered on her lips as she thought about it. "Yeah, I mean, that wasn't a fun fight for her either. She told me all about it."

"Why is she mad at me?"

"You were late."

"By like ten minutes."

"*Again*. Late again. You're always late. She said you got caught up on Cinderella's gown and lost track of time."

"She'll forgive me, right?"

"I wouldn't," Lizzie grumbled.

I snapped my head at her. "Well, I wasn't asking you, and you wouldn't understand. Emily is cool and chill and doesn't get too shy to ask cashiers for spoons—"

Lizzie raised her soggy spoon like she was gonna whack me with it and I jumped up, slipping out of the picnic bench to retreat to Camille's side.

Without us killing each other, Lizzie drove us back to Camille's car and helped jump us. Despite Camille's battery pleading for death, she was able to drive me home in time for everyone to be adjourned to their rooms. After nabbing some rangoons to help wash down all the ice cream, I hurried to my bedroom, locked the door behind me, and flopped into bed, planning to scroll away the hours on my phone starting with a new notification.

A reply on Instagram from Emily:

Emily: Don't tell me what to do 😝

My smile was out of control. If Emily didn't want anything to do with me, she wouldn't have acknowledged my existence. I still might have a chance.

FOUR

Lizzie

The swell of the last violin note trembled around my hands and inside my chest. My heart shook like a skinny tree during a storm, and a single tear slipped from my eye and down my round cheek. The world around me was a black void, and I stood alone with only that last note. That note meant everything. It meant spending the night in my human form before dawn, when I'd become a swan again, left to swim forever in a lake of tears. It meant that while I longed to be human, I felt more poised and beautiful as a beast than as a girl. It meant finding love.

Applause burst my bubble as the reality of auditioning in the school auditorium faded back in, leaving *Swan Lake* far behind me. I took a sharp breath, holding the nerves in my chest and keeping them down like a nauseated person with a full stomach. I refocused on the small audience of fellow band geeks who for the next hour were my competition for a chair in the symphony orchestra. Only a few seats were available, and all grades were welcome to audition. The Creekside band director, Mr. Burka, joined in with the clapping.

"Thank you, Lizzie," he said from behind his round spectacles.

He had thick coiled curls with hints of gray and eyes surrounded by impressive crow's feet from obviously not taking life too seriously.

"Uh, you're welcome. I mean, thank you," I said, immediately wishing I could suck the words back in like spaghetti noodles. Someone in the crowd snorted, making their amusement known, and suddenly I was no longer a violinist on stage, I was the clown.

He jotted something down on his clipboard and opened his mouth to say more, but all I could hear was the whispering. The crowded area of the brass section leaned into each other, eying me and saying whatever they wanted. Their whispers created weapons pointed at me, shooting bullets through my confidence. My face warmed, a wetness overflowing into my waterline, and I hiccupped.

"*Oh god,*" I whispered and hiccupped again.

"Everything okay?" Mr. Burka asked, the worst question in the world.

"Um, yes," I piped up, hearing the crack. Talking made it worse. Talking always made it worse. The pressure in my face pushed harder and my eyes burned, begging for tears to come and douse the fire. I gripped the neck of my violin the way someone would hold on to a friend for support. Keeping a handle on my emotions was harder than lassoing a bull.

"Now, let's go over the sheet music. Can you read me the first stave, please?" Mr. Burka asked. I looked at him, swallowing my need to make a face. We both knew I could read sheet music. I'm in his class every day and with him during band practice. It should be like reciting my ABCs and yet a lump formed in my throat, a high vault my words were forced to jump over.

"Yeah." I nodded and took a deep breath. Then a rush of whispers exploded from the corner of the auditorium. I heard my name. I heard the mocking sound of a baby crying.

Mr. Burka looked at me with a more encouraging smile. "Starting from the treble clef, Lizzie."

"I, um—" I licked my lips and tried not to focus on all the things that made me nervous, but that forced me to think of them more, and the first tear escaped my eyes. My emotions staged a riot and led to an entire revolt. "I'm sorry," I said, choking back a sob. I ducked my head and ran right off the stage.

"Dude." Andrea nudged me with her sneakers. I hadn't even heard her walk into the bathroom. The drama department had their own bathrooms in the large hallway that separated the choir room from the band room, which helped during shows. Even now it smelled like the sweet hair oils the other girls used to protect their hair from piping hot irons. Feeling sorry for myself, I sat on the cold tile, listening to Daniel Powter's "Bad Day" on repeat.

"Are you . . ." Andrea squinted through her round glasses. ". . . okay?"

"Yeah, I'm, like, jumping for joy." I ripped out my earphones. The music gently echoed against the walls now that it was free from my earwax prison.

"Whoa. The rage is spicy today, huh?"

"Maybe I'll get a muddy lake tattooed right over my face and disappear into obscurity."

"No, no, you might as well commit and tattoo the swan. She gets top billing."

Andrea was a second chair clarinet player. She owned every legging design known to man, as she believed jeans were a meat prison. She had dark-brown skin and most of her black box braids were piled on top of her head, except for two braids that framed her heart-shaped face. All my life I've gravitated toward people who were everything I wasn't, as if they could fill in my own blanks. Andrea wore what she wanted. Andrea didn't shy away from her curves.

I wanted a sliver of that confidence. I let my mom believe I was still the same little girl obsessed with horses and anything pink. She was still buying me Christmas presents I would've liked five years ago. Anything that deviated from the image my mother had of me confused her, and what confused her, upset her. Therefore, the real me would upset her.

"If it makes any difference, your audition sounded amazing." Andrea shrugged and joined me on the floor. "I always get goose bumps when you play. It's crazy. You lose yourself, like you're really there watching Odette transform. I was waiting for ballet dancers to pirouette or whatever on stage."

"And that's my problem," I muttered, and shifted my sleeves around my palms, bunching the cotton into my fist. Hiding my face, I pressed my hands against my eyes. "I want to rip out my tear ducts. God, I'm never gonna hear the end of this." I sniffed, feeling the pressure build again.

"Oh, Lizzie, you're allowed to be emotional. Don't let them take that away from you." Andrea sighed and wrapped an arm around my shoulders, bringing me into her comforting embrace. She had no advice, and maybe I didn't want her to say anything. I was sick of hearing the same thing I've already heard a thousand times.

Relax.

Why do you have to take them seriously?

Ignore them. It's okay to be emotional.

I scooted out of her arms and wiped the tears and sadness from my eyes. This serious talk was too much, and the tension felt suffocating. I wanted to brush today under the rug. "Man," I said, letting out a shaky laugh, "I'm so glad I didn't wear eyeliner today."

Andrea laughed, sounding relieved. "No way, can you imagine the drama? It would have been iconic." We both laughed and let the awkwardness fade away. My phone buzzed and buzzed again, letting me know it was a phone call and not a text I could ignore or read later. If someone was calling me, it must be serious.

A picture of Camille flashed on the screen. I answered. "Hey, what's up?"

"Tell me you're not busy tonight," Camille begged, and I could feel the ooze of her sickly sweet smile coming out of my phone. "Will you go to Olivia's party with me? I need a plus one!"

I looked down at my sheet music and my violin case. Camille was giving me an out, and I was happy to avoid more stares and mockery. With escape in sight, I replied, "I'm not busy."

"Great! I'll pick you up in a couple of hours."

"Perfect," I agreed, thinking that was enough time to shake off my nerves, or at least wash them off in the shower.

Andrea rolled her eyes. At once, we got up and I started shoving everything into my bag, maybe a tad harder than necessary. "Hey, if Mr. Burka asks about me," I said before Andrea made it out of the bathroom, "tell him dust got in my eyes."

"Sure, Lizzie." Andrea snorted and left me alone with Daniel Powter's velvety voice. "Text me if you want to hang out later, okay?"

"I will," I said, like I always do, but Andrea and I both knew this game. She always offered to hang out outside of school and I never followed through. I really liked Andrea and yet I couldn't seem to reach for anyone once I was home by myself. I was too nervous to ask, and once I'm out in the world, I'm too anxious to actually enjoy hanging out.

FIVE

Parker

"Mom, you need to write it down," I said as I adjusted my backpack over my shoulder.

"It'll be all right," she said, but I could hear the distraction from her end of the call. I recognized it from my own. "I'll remember."

"*You won't*," I insisted, passing an empty building and glancing at my reflection. Bethel's downtown square was an office building graveyard, and I studied my outfit as I passed every window. "I'm serious. The play is at the end of the month. Opening night is October twenty-sixth, so write it down on all twenty calendars you own and make plans to come. I'll email your assistant."

"Ashley, don't be dramatic. It's not twenty."

"Fine. All *ten* of your calendars."

My mother laughed and I let out a breath, relieved I still had the power to amuse her. Looking back, forth, up, and down the road, I waited for the coast to be clear and crossed. Downtown was all small brick buildings from the 1950s and skinny sidewalks. This was the closest hipster mecca to my house, a hub for local businesses and the best iced coffee in town.

I longed for the magic of New York. I missed being able to walk into a small coffee shop and the barista already knowing my order. I missed the freedom of my feet taking me anywhere I wanted to go. Even more, I missed not feeling alone on a Friday night. I had twice as many friends in New York and a house I called home.

"Okay, *mom*," my mother teased me. "It's written. I've even asked my assistant to remind me, all right? But now I need to head out. What about you?"

"I was supposed to go on a date, but we broke up," I said, thinking about Emily.

"The one-date wonder strikes again."

I tripped, quickly composing myself. "Now who's being dramatic?"

My mother laughed again, but it wasn't as fun this time. Going on a date didn't seem like a big deal, even if it was only going on one. "Oh," she said, "I'm getting another call. I'll talk to you later, Ashley. Love you."

"Love you too," I said, biting back my need to correct her yet again over my name. Ashley didn't suit me. Parker was unique, a little more standout, a little more me. Sighing, I looked up and remembered my lonely life again. Feeling somehow teleported to this town despite being here almost a full year.

It was odd seeing Bethel outside of the summer, when I was used to visiting my dad's house. With October so close, there were scarecrows stationed on every corner. It was kind of like a horror movie. Walking toward the square, I could feel their little beady eyes watching me approach.

I headed to the white gazebo. In front of it the Jensen twins had set up a small table with a handwritten sign that said hot cocoa and bad advice. It was a cheap plastic table covered by an orange Halloween-themed tablecloth with little cats and bats all over it.

"Hey, kids." I waved to them and to their mom, who worked at the front desk of the law office next door. I could only see their dark eyes and a hint of their chestnut-brown skin under the amount of bundling. They were both tiny, still young enough at eight years old to look a little alike, with cute, wild black curls. They only detached from their phones to acknowledge me.

"How much for a cup?" I asked.

"A dollar," Mitchell Jensen said, his hand out.

"How much for advice?"

"It comes with the cocoa," Crissy Jensen answered.

I exchanged the quarters in the corner of my book bag for a drink. They made a show of checking for counterfeits, but nodded in satisfaction. With the swagger of bartenders in New York, Mitchell poured some cocoa from a thermos into a flowered Dixie cup. Crissy tilted her head, eying me up and down. She stated with incredible conviction, "You should wear lifts. That way you can lord over the other high schoolers better."

"That is bad advice," I said, as the tallest girl in my grade. It was kind of freakish how tall I'd ended up, but my family paraded around the world as a band of giants. Back in the day I was scouted to play every tween basketball league, but I could never wake up on time for practice. Not that my mom ever had time to take me anyway.

"You'll stand out," Mitchell agreed. "Marshmallows?"

"Of course," I said. "Thanks, kiddos."

I went on my way, glancing up and down the street before I crossed. I took one sip of the hot chocolate, and its warmth spilled into my chest, pooling across my limbs, and I shuddered in delight. The chocolate was creamy and surprisingly thick, with enough sweetness to make me smile. Taking out my phone, I quickly sent a text to Camille:

Parker: Hey

Parker: Are you still busy? Wanna hang out?

As I glanced up, something in the window of Miss Patty's Salon caught my eye. The window was massive, lined with parted, sequined curtains. When the light hit the holographic sequins just right, it scattered rainbows across the floor. Twirling stars in rainbow colors hung like the window's bangs among other single strings of beads. This was all framing the same three mannequins stationed in the center. They were 1980s empowered women, with flashy eye shadow and bouncy, frizzy hair. Some faces had obviously chipped, but hearts and stars were painted over their scars.

I visited Miss Patty's Salon every time I was downtown. Miss Patty sold dreams. She sold the idea that you could do crazy things like purchase stuff from her shop and take it home with you and actually use it. Like I did every time I walked by Miss Patty's Salon, I firmly gripped the handle and yanked on the door only to find it locked.

Miss Patty's had no hours.

Miss Patty has never been seen.

But the mannequins did switch positions, draping themselves across baroque furniture in expensive satin with golden cord trim. One mannequin, my unbiased favorite, displayed a tiara. The perfect tiara. I wanted that tiara more than I wanted this year's sexiest man alive to wrap his muscular arms around me. It was the missing piece of the Cinderella costume I was working on.

Making the costumes for the high-school play was as close to my dream of going to an art school as I could get. There wasn't an option for me here, not like in New York. How else was I going to work on my portfolio?

Again, I thought about calling Emily. She was the one who had introduced me to Mrs. Donnelly and the theater department. If it wasn't for her, I would've never begged Mrs. Donnelly to let me take charge of the costumes for the fall musical, *Cinderella*. Emily understood that part of me. My desperation to always be producing. I hated to say it, but I wasn't happy with myself unless I was working on a costume or a new outfit.

Coming to this town as a junior in high school dropped me into a sea of fish that already knew everything about each other, and I was the weird squid that didn't fit. Emily was the first person I'd met who couldn't wait to get out of this town. She was the only one who didn't make me feel crazy.

After a few minutes of staring through the glass, I finally called Camille. The moment she answered, I said, "What's the punishment for looting?"

Camille had a voice like a fortune teller. There was something mystical about her. Something all knowing and powerful. "If you're in front of Miss Patty's Salon again, I'm gonna eat my shoe—"

"Add public vandalism to that mix." I touched the cold glass. My fingers tingled with want. My forehead smacked the glass as I tried to acquire the power to walk through walls. "I've got masks at home. I wouldn't drive myself here. How would they know?"

"Through wiretaps, bitch!" Camille shouted. "I've got your confession fresh off the iPhone. I've been watching you all year, waiting for you to slip up, missy. You're going down for this!"

"I would go to jail for something I didn't even do yet?"

"It's all about intent, Ashley Marie Parker." Her laughter faded. I could still hear her smile in her airy voice, but this sweetness had a sour aftertaste.

I sighed again, making my voice as pitiful as possible. "Hey. Come pick me up."

"I can't. I'm going to Olivia's birthday party with Lizzie."

My entire face scrunched. "Who's Olivia?"

"*Olivia*," she said, but I still blanked, so she said the name again, but louder. Regretting that I'd even asked, I stuffed my free hand in my pocket and took a sip of the hot chocolate. I immediately spit it out as someone caught my eye. The tail end of her long brown hair was the last thing I saw before she disappeared inside the coffee shop. *Emily*.

It was like I'd summoned her. Magic was real.

"No, no. Say it again and I'll miraculously know."

"It's Olivia! She's part of the ensemble in the play!" Camille insisted, and I had a vague squiggly face in my head. Something about a chunky blue highlight but not much else. I stalked down the sidewalk as Camille said, "The one who uses Sharpies to paint her nails!"

"Oh! Why didn't you say that?"

"You're impossible. Are you going?"

"Probably."

"All right, see you there."

Quickly, I hung up the phone and threw my half-drunk hot chocolate into the nearest trash can before walking into the coffee shop.

I hit the wall of noise upon entry—the chatter from fellow patrons, the high-powered steam from the espresso machines, and hum of today's indie music. It was all exposed brick and local art hanging on the walls, while also being so warm I'd never be able to bring myself to leave.

Like a true leading lady, Emily stood at the counter in her thrifted clothes, rummaging in a crocheted bag for her wallet. She was cool without trying too hard.

She hadn't noticed me yet. A wicked idea sparked like a match inside of me. Shuffling over, I leaned over Emily's shoulder as casually as possible. She jumped a little, snapping her head up at me, her hair brushing my cheek. Emily Kaplan was as pretty as a well-curated scrapbook; freckled, colorful bandages on her fingers, temporary tattoos under her sleeves, and notes of all the things she couldn't forget scribbled on her hands.

"Fancy meeting you here," I said.

Emily glanced around at me and rolled her eyes. "What are you doing here?"

"Haven't decided yet. You look pretty."

She whipped her eyes at me again, and over her shoulder I saw that smile, but she sighed and faced forward again. "I'm still mad," she said, but her tone was light.

I chuckled. "Good. I'm mad at me too."

Leaning around her, I spoke to the cashier, but kept Emily in the corner of my eye. She watched me in sparkly fascination, and I ordered my usual vanilla latte with oat milk. "I've got her drink too," I said, already taking out my wallet.

"You don't have to do that," Emily said, her dark eyes giving me a once-over.

"I know, but I want to."

She crossed her arms. "Did you know I was going to be here?"

"I know everything." I wiggled my eyebrows. "Would you like some company? I offer intelligent conversation, photography critique and praise, and a very long-winded apology for being an absolute ass." I smiled, praying she would take the bait and let me be around her again.

"I've had worse company." Emily shrugged, all coy, and we found a table in the corner. Thankfully, I had brought my backpack just in case no one was around to hang out. Now it looked like I hadn't done this on purpose.

In a corner booth, Emily worked on her Photoshop projects while I researched all the ways to ombre dye fabric and how to do it in the cheapest way. It was half an hour before I noticed how smoothly things were going.

We could do this. We could hang out and go back to the way things were.

"What?" Emily asked. Without realizing it, I had been staring at her, and Emily mirrored my body language, resting her chin in her palm and leaning toward me. "Do you see something you like?"

"Oh yeah," I said, scooting closer until our knees touched. I pointed to her computer screen. She was editing a portrait of herself in a field of sunflowers, dressed as a scarecrow. Our greatest common interest was not our love of art but our love of Halloween. My half-baked idea was quickly warming up and rising to the top. I said, "She looks cool. Would you consider giving me her number?"

"You don't have her number?" Emily posed back.

Half smiling, I admitted, "She told me she didn't want to see me anymore, but I have a counterargument."

"Which is?"

"She should go to a party with me tonight because we'll have a lot of fun together."

"Olivia's party? This girl"—she pointed to herself—"wasn't planning to go. She doesn't know anyone there."

"She'll know me."

Leaning back, Emily rolled her eyes again, but it did nothing to hide her smile or the blush on her cheeks. I knew I could put flattery on a hook to reel Emily back in. Emily took a deep breath before sitting back up and reaching over me for my phone. It was already open for her to type her number back inside. "It's a date."

SIX

Lizzie

I dropped my book bag as soon as I opened my front door, walked a few steps onto the carpeted hallway, and then, finally, collapsed onto the floor. The day's stress weighed my bones down and the unforgiving humiliation crushed my chest. Closing my eyes, I debated napping here. Fuck it.

My phone buzzed and I groaned against the rough carpet. The dust made my eyes itchy and watery. Living was exhausting, and I wondered if hibernating through the rest of high school was feasible.

The front door swung open, almost hitting my shoe. Peanut Butter and Jelly, our two Welsh Corgis, barreled into the house, barking their tiny heads off. They jumped around as my little sister, Gina, and her litter of sixth-grade friends also stepped over me, talking a mile a minute about their sleepover plans.

"*Gina,*" I groaned.

One pair of feet stopped halfway up the stairs before running back down. "What?" Gina asked, snapping at me. In these moments, with her thick brows, sharp eyes, and squared jaw, she looked so much like our mother. Gina was teeny but, like a small dog foaming at the mouth, she was a thing to fear.

"I just—what are you guys doing tonight?" I asked, wondering if I could trade my party plans for something closer to home.

"None of your business." Gina huffed and ran upstairs to join her friends, slamming her bedroom door to fully shut me out.

Poking his head out of the living room, my older brother, Danny, laughed when he spotted me. Home from college for the weekend, Danny lived easily, getting to leave whenever he wanted. He walked over to get a better look at me. "I think I've stepped on a bug in that position before, Lizzie. Are you alive or what?"

He was an all-American short king with his plaid shirt, cargo pants, and baseball cap. His big brown eyes sparkled as he laughed at my grimace and continued walking by. He yelled up the stairs at Gina, "Hey! If we're getting pizza, you gotta get something I like too! Something with toppings! If you want bread, cheese, and sauce, I'll make it for you at half the cost!"

"It's my party!" Gina shouted back from behind her closed door.

"And I get it, you'll cry if you want to!"

"I'm not crying!"

"It's a joke! It's my car going to pick it up, so it's gotta have toppings!"

Our dad had a strict policy of carry-out service only. He said the "convenience fee" on delivery was the worst criminal act someone could legally demand.

Danny bent down to my level. "Wanna help me do laundry?"

"No," I said into the carpet.

"Wanna get off the floor?"

"No."

Crawling onto his knees, Danny made old man noises until he

lay beside me. He turned onto his stomach and nudged me. "How's it going? Are you good? Bad? Medium?"

"How does one feel medium?" I squinted at his dumb, grinning face.

"You tell me." He smiled wider, coaxing my lips up. The best weekends were the ones when Danny came home. Despite a house full of people, Danny was the only one playing on my team. "We can hang out if you want and watch something. Helping me fold my laundry will be optional, I promise. We can just chill out and talk maybe?" His shrug didn't come off as casually as he probably hoped.

Talking was a dangerous thing. It didn't use to be dangerous. I could've gone to Danny for a soft place to land and be able to safely spill all of my problems to him without judgment, but there was one secret I wasn't ready to part with. So it was better to avoid talking to Danny about anything. Even the small stuff.

My small problems didn't exist without the bigger ones. All my struggles compiled into one giant trash mountain threatening to topple over and crush me. I'd start by telling him about the worst audition ever today, then I'd go off about our parents being too strict, about Camille liking Parker more than me, then say something about me being too shy to initiate new friendships, and then I'd end up blurting that coming out inherently comes with a risk of rejection that would destroy me.

I smashed my face into the carpet to hide my fear. He had been perceiving me too much lately, not just today. As the eldest, Daniel Hernández has watched me grow up, and was an expert in my likes and dislikes.

Danny witnessed my teenage rebellion as I gave up My Little Pony and became obsessed with music, and the time in middle school when I lied about losing an ugly jacket Mom bought me so she'd have to get me a new one. But this change wasn't outward like that. The difference lived inside of me. Unlike Gina, I wasn't drooling over boy bands and gushing over a male celebrity crush. Out of everyone else, Danny would be the one to pick out the lesbian needle in the rainbow haystack because I couldn't stop bringing up Reneé Rapp and other leading ladies. Always ladies. Only ladies.

And I could imagine it. Watching TV, folding laundry, and saying *Oh, hey, Danny. Um, by the way, I'm a lesbian.*

Danny would probably make a joke and lighten the mood.

He'd probably be cool about it.

He'd probably keep it from Mom and Dad if I asked.

But probably didn't make this easy.

"Isn't anyone going to ask what Lizzie wants?" Mom called from the kitchen before continuing her phone call in Spanish. It must have been someone from work because it was all medical jargon.

With a little shrug, Danny popped up first. I held out my hand so he'd help me up, but he gave me a low five instead and then disappeared.

Sighing, I worked up the energy to stand. I grabbed my bag and dragged it into the kitchen. The dogs followed, nipping at my heels. My mom sat at the table, slipping her work shoes off. She was wearing her favorite light-blue scrubs and her spools of dark hair were piled into a high bun, with a few rebellious strands framing her round face. My mother was all curves, with plump lips, and the only thing we shared was our sharp, dark eyes.

"All right," she said into the phone and sighed when her feet were free. "See you tomorrow. Okay." She hung up, looking up at me. "Are you hungry? How was your day?"

"I don't need dinner," I said and dropped my bag on the table. "I'm going to hang out with Camille tonight." This wasn't a lie. I was going to hang out with Camille and a house full of other people throwing a party. Did I know Olivia well enough to celebrate her seventeenth birthday? No. Did I want to be left out? Definitely not.

Mom freed her hair and ran her hands through the curls, making me a little jealous. My hair fought between being wavy, straight, and full-on frizzy. She sighed, studying me longer than I would have liked, making me feel like an ant underneath a vengeful magnifying glass lined up with the sun. She said, her words as tired as her bones, "Mr. Burka called."

I froze.

"He said you were very upset during your audition." She explained my own life back to me, a freak game of telephone. I grabbed the end of my braid, squeezing and twisting the dangling strands. "But when he tried to find you, you were gone. *Mija*." She paused, her eyes sympathetic. It was the exact way to make my heart all mushy. The word threw me back to sleeping in her arms after a nightmare when I was a kid. It was the equivalent of stroking my hair. She went on, "If orchestra upsets you so much, you should stop. You'll be a senior next year, so maybe you should focus more on school and less on music."

My mind blocked out the words. The idea of not being in orchestra wasn't something I could process or envision into reality. It was as unnatural as the sky turning green, chocolate tasting sour, or the entire plot of *Love Never Dies*. All my panic sat like congestion, burning inside my chest. Sniffling, I cut my mother off before I broke into a sobbing mess. "Can we talk about this later?"

"Okay, but look into other options for yourself," she said, standing from the table. Her back to me, she went to the pantry so she could pull out some food for the dogs. She was so casual and yet everything she said could be earth shattering. "You know, you can always keep music as a hobby while you go to college for something else."

"Sure, right." I nodded, but I would've said anything to end that conversation. Quickly, I grabbed my book bag and ran to my room. I locked the door behind me, pressing my back against the wood. Taking a deep shuddering breath, I looked up at my ceiling so as to not ruin my eyeliner. Telling myself to let it go, I pushed aside my mother's words and threw on a sweater because if I was going to suffer at a party, I was at least going to do it comfortably.

SEVEN

Parker

Sitting shotgun inside of Emily's red Toyota Corolla, everything felt right with the world. All the puzzle pieces in my life were being put back into their rightful place. Change was overrated. I breathed in the familiar and all my tension melted, making a puddle in the front seat.

"Thanks for picking me up," I said, rubbing the sleeve of my pink faux fur jacket to do something with all my nerves.

Her eyes on the road, Emily smiled. "You're welcome. Sometimes I think you only make friends with people who drive."

I feigned a gasp. "You caught me. Don't tell Camille."

"You're so dumb," she grumbled fondly, and turned into a neighborhood.

Happy with myself, I went back to fiddling with the side of the door. My finger brushed something soft, and I twisted my hand down, finding the pink scrunchy I'd left behind. I smiled. It was still here. I was still here.

"Are you hoarding my things?" I raised the scrunchie between us.

With her curly hair pulled back, Emily's bright-red ears were on display among the piercings but she pretended to be unbothered. "I think you're leaving your stuff behind."

"You could've given it back."

"Maybe I like your scrunchie."

"Maybe . . ." I said, and rested against the console between us, inching a little closer. "You like me."

Emily sucked in her lips, biting down on her smile so as to not let me win, even though I already felt like I had. She turned away, trying to fix her parking. I didn't speak, letting us sit in this silence and the sound of her not arguing with me. Two matching smiles and a crackle in the air. I had hope.

She parked at the back of the line of cars outside of Olivia's house. I got out of the car first, walking around to meet Emily as she stepped out, and she was even prettier this close. My heart did a little jig, hyping me up to say whatever I wanted to say. Even though my face was hot, I asked Emily with nothing but confidence, "How do you feel about forgetting about last week and us just having fun tonight?"

Her eyes traced the lines of my face, searching for any sign to trust me. I offered her my hand, and watched all her tension drop. She returned my smile and took my hand with a little squeeze. "It better be fun or you owe me a better date."

"Deal!" Grinning, I swung her arm around and dragged her up Olivia's lawn. We walked up to the house together and were greeted by ear-splitting electronic music as we opened the front door to a clogged house. Olivia must've invited the entire drama and art departments, with a few chorus and band kids sprinkled in.

"Hey, I'm going to run to the bathroom," Emily said. She squeezed my hand and pointed to the living room. "If you'll grab us some drinks, I'll meet you over there."

"Okay." I nodded. "You got it."

Letting her hand go, I let out a relieved breath. It seemed like everything was going to be okay. Glancing around, I took a swing and let my feet guide me to the kitchen. Beyond the threshold and behind a kitchen island, I caught the smallest glimpse of a cardigan, a long braid, and Lizzie's perpetual stink face, and swerved right back around.

They really let anyone come to this thing.

"Nope," I whispered and checked out the next room, glancing through the crowd.

"Parker!"

Someone called me, and I turned, noticing Ian waving from the stairwell. "Oh, hey," I said, swimming against the stream of people to meet him. Like a cartoon character, Ian sported his usual all-black uniform, complete with skinny jeans, Vans, a plain T-shirt, and a baseball cap that covered his white-blond hair. I locked onto the red Solo cup in his hand. "Is there anywhere to get a drink other than the kitchen?"

"There are some drinks on the porch," a girl beside Ian said. She had a cute, little brown bob and a bright-pink jumpsuit that I was kind of living for. "And if you can find a band kid, they have flasks."

Ian smirked. "It's a game of roulette. You get what you get."

"Thanks, um . . ." I said, peering at the girl and trying to place her name.

The girl's face dropped, and Ian curled his lips, hiding behind his cup. She grimaced like I'd kicked her in the shins. "It's Olivia. Olivia Barber, the birthday girl. It's my party, Parker."

"I know!" I spouted, my voice cracking. Panic zipped through me and danced nonsensically through my limbs. I used the first excuse that popped into my head. "I wasn't trying to place your name. The music distracted me, like, what is this song?"

"Whatever, Parker. Enjoy the party," she grumbled on her way past me.

I dropped against the wall, losing the feeling in my legs. Grabbing Ian's arm, I asked him, "How bad was that?"

"So bad," Ian said, laughing at me right in my face. "It's actually worse than you think."

He gave me an obnoxious, all-knowing look and led the way to the back deck. It was a huge backyard with a sizable in-ground pool. Olivia's father was grilling hot dogs at one end and a huge table of gifts stood at the other. There were balloons, lights, and pink streamers everywhere. I found the cooler and grabbed a Coke and a Solo cup. Ian helped me scour the yard for a band kid with a flask full of Jack.

Eventually, Ian and I found ourselves by the gift table, attempting to guess what was inside the boxes.

"Parker." Someone yanked on my sleeve, and I whirled around to find Emily, red in the face and narrowing her brow in a glare that wasn't messing around. "Where have you been? I've been waiting in the living room."

"Oh really? Did you run into someone you know?"

"No." Emily shook her head. "I told you I don't really know anyone here. I was waiting for you. We were supposed to meet in the living room, remember?"

I mentally kicked myself. "My bad. I forgot. Listen, I ran into Ian and got caught up with Olivia and—"

"It's fine," Emily said in a way that didn't sound fine at all. She crossed her arms. "Did you at least get me a drink?"

"Oh right, about that, it's actually really funny—"

She cut me off. "Just say you didn't get me one."

Shrinking back, I swallowed nervously. "I didn't. There are drinks in the cooler and band kids have flasks with all kinds of drinks. I think they're competing to see who can empty their flask first."

Not amused in the slightest, Emily stared at me, waiting for me to say something else, but my mind went blank. She finally huffed. "Fine. I guess I'll get it myself."

"Okay." I nodded and rubbed her arm. "That sounds good. We were thinking about going inside and finding a card game or something."

"All right," Emily said and tightly crossed her arms. We'd just gotten here but she already sounded exhausted. "I'll catch up with you."

"I'll try not to hide this time," I said as a joke, but Emily didn't laugh. My stomach took the silence like a punch to the gut. I opened my mouth to take it back or say something clever, but my throat had completely dried up. I hadn't said or done anything right since stepping into this house, so trying again seemed like a bad idea.

"Come on." Ian tapped my shoulder, and I gathered myself up. Still touching Emily's arm, I gave her one last squeeze and followed Ian inside.

EIGHT

Lizzie

Upon arrival, I lost Camille to the chorus girls loitering around the porch with their drinks and inside jokes. They threatened me with karaoke, but the idea of singing live in front of actual singers sounded as fun as bashing myself with the microphone. So I politely passed on the opportunity for torture and promised to catch up later. I found a safe zone in the kitchen.

Two kinds of people hung out in the kitchen: the people who only came for the food and the people who'd brought something and were obsessively checking to make sure others were trying it. My mom had bought me napkins to bring, but I wanted my pick of the pizza and the birthday cake.

I was getting the feeling that Olivia, the birthday girl, had caught on to my game of continuously refilling my red Solo cup with Coke and was a little miffed I was draining the household supply. My mom didn't let any soda, boys, or happiness into the house. Little did she know, I only wanted two out of the three.

Offering Olivia a tight smile, I said, "This is a really good party."

"Thanks," she said. Olivia wore a fresh bob that framed her face. My dream haircut, honestly. The pink jumpsuit and glitter makeup kind of hurt my eyes, but it worked on her.

"Seriously, like, I hate leaving the house and I came, so you know it's good."

"Cool." She raised her brows. "Thanks. It means a lot."

"Yeah, no, for sure," I couldn't stop talking and nodding. My motor functions errored, and my attention stuck on Olivia's confused face.

Thankfully, Olivia took me out of my misery and said, "See you around. I'm going to use the bathroom."

"Totally. Hey," I shouted over the music, unable to stop the verbal vomit, "don't fall in, all right?"

She didn't look back or acknowledge my existence, and I didn't blame her. I poured myself one more drink and stepped out of the kitchen. The music wasn't so loud that I couldn't hear myself think and all the lights were on (a rule from Olivia's mom), but it was still too crowded for me to relax. I peeked into various rooms on a quest for solitude, until I walked through the front door onto the creaky porch. Discovering Camille by accident, I scared her enough that she jumped so hard I thought she might've dislocated something.

"*Oh my god,*" she huffed, quickly using the porch railing to steady herself. "Don't scare me like that."

"Sorry," I said. The cool air hit my arms and a trickle of goose bumps made my hair rise. Zipping up my hoodie, I wondered how Camille could stand wearing a dress. Stuffing my hands in my pockets, I joined her by the railing. "I didn't realize you were in outer space. What are you doing out here?"

Her surprise fizzled out, leaving her like a deflated balloon on the porch railing. She looked out at the quiet street with the vibrant party behind us. She said, "I'm partied out."

I raised a brow. "We got here an hour ago."

"Is that a no to leaving?" she asked, as if I'd miss the opportunity to go home.

"It's a you're ridiculous—" I said, but I couldn't let this uneasiness go. Camille deflated when she paused for more than a few seconds. Sadness glazed over her eyes and the happy-go-lucky girl who'd come to this party had vanished. "You looked like you were having fun. Did something happen?"

"Nothing happened."

I nudged her, and she met my worried look, knowing she couldn't hide from me. Rolling her eyes, Camille straightened her arms against the railing. "It's actually dumb, we were all talking about the play and they started discussing going off book and how they're all stressed out and making jokes about how they're going to sneak cheat sheets everywhere." Her face fell. "I couldn't add anything."

"But you have to learn lines. You're an understudy." As soon as I pointed it out, Camille's frown deepened. Whatever nerve had been pinched, I'd just twisted it.

Camille rolled her eyes to the blackened sky. "I've been in theater since middle school. Next year is our senior year and I"—she sighed—"wanted a main role. Just once. But Mrs. Donnelly always casts the same people. The favoritism reeks."

"That's not true. Isn't the girl playing Cinderella a new student?"

"Right, but I can't compete with beauty and natural charisma."

"True," I said, and Camille snapped her head around, gawking at me, and I couldn't hold my smile back.

"Stupid!" She laughed and gave me a little shove. Her fluttering laugh made me more than a little relieved. "As punishment, come help me find Parker."

All the joy that existed in my body died. Grimacing, I asked, "Is she really here? Can't we leave her?"

"You find comfort in being alone. I find comfort in my two favorite people watching a bad movie with me while we eat enough pizza to make us puke."

"You have bad taste. Okay." I relented. "But I will not be nice."

"Then you better find her first, because I will be."

Sighing, I dragged myself back inside to look for Parker.

Parker

Nothing good happens at parties.

I was innocently playing cards with Ian and a couple of no-names at the dining table when Emily dumped her Jack and Coke right on top of my head and ruined my fluffy pink jacket. It was once 100 percent faux fur; now it was more like 25 percent faux fur, 25 percent sugar, and 50 percent rage.

"Ah!" Emily threw her freshly emptied red Solo cup across the dining room. In triumph, she placed her hands on her hips and glowered with a fiendish smile. "Now that I finally have your attention, I'm leaving."

"What?" I blinked, my brain not catching up fast enough to comprehend why she was walking away. Random people were handing me stray towels and napkins. I grabbed a handful of the offerings and dabbed at my wet-cat appearance. Somehow, I was the one chasing her down. I was the one getting the judging looks. I was the villain.

"You invited me," Emily stated in a huff.

"Uh, yeah, I know. I kind of have complete control of what I do. No alien body snatchers yet," I said, and it came off bitchier than I wanted, but it came out of me naturally.

"Oh!" she roared, her eyes big and wild like they'd pop out of her skull like a cartoon. "So you're purposely ignoring me! Okay, yeah, Parker, like that makes it better? Okay." She whipped her head back around only to nail me with her sharp scowl. It cut an ugly hole in my chest, and I flinched. That only deepened her grimace. She threw the back door open and a gust of cold air made me sneeze. "You're such an ass."

"Hey! That was a joke! And I think you're overreacting," I insisted, horrified by the commotion we were causing and wishing to disappear. As a redhead with pink undertones, anytime I blushed it might as well have been a blinking neon sign above my head telling the universe that I was embarrassed.

If this was another rejection, I wanted to be better prepared this time. My heart could only handle so much abandonment before it broke. "We're not dating anymore, which was your choice, by the way. I don't even understand why you're mad at me. You seem to be having fun—"

Those must have been the magic words because Emily finally stopped running away. She slammed her boots on the concrete outside of Olivia's pool. Half the party was out here, under the strings of Christmas lights tied between the trees with the grill and the hot dogs and now, a comedy show between two queer chicks as the main attraction. Emily whipped around, her fists curled at her side. She was so mad her nose flared, and I could swear I saw steam streaming out of her ears like a boiling kettle ready to serve some tea.

"I'm not surprised you don't understand. God." She shook her head, chewing on her anger. "I thought it was so nice you asked me out because—" She huffed and threw her arms out. "I thought you wanted to hang out with me! I guess I'm crazy!"

Sighing, I combed through my sticky, wet locks. "Okay, fine. I fucked up again. If you tell me how to make it up to you, I'll do it."

"If you actually gave a shit about me and my feelings, you'd know exactly why I'm upset. And there's no point in explaining it because you won't listen to me! Make sure you delete my number. Your little problems are your own."

A wave of guilt hit me hard and fast. I fell straight into the deep end of my own regret and reached for Emily to keep from drowning. My voice couldn't come out louder than a whisper. "Em—"

She twisted, snapping at me with her hand raised. Her voice was low and final. "No, Parker. That's it."

My entire life has consisted of watching someone walk away and slam a door in my face. I must've been as stupid as I looked, because the hurt was still the same. I still wanted to run after her and convince her that I was someone worth staying for. Someone had to believe me.

NINE

Lizzie

Parker had to be hiding. Hitting the ground floor again, I stumbled through the throngs of people and headed to the last place I hadn't checked. I was reaching for the back door when a girl nearly ran me over. "Whoa!" I gasped, jumping out of the way in time before she flattened me.

She was a streak of wild dark hair as she turned back to me. "Sorry," she mumbled, her voice breaking into a sob. It was Emily Kaplan. And I recognized that terrible expression, that tender look of a fresh wound.

"It's okay," I whispered, watching her run for the exit.

I stepped outside. The crowds were murmuring for some reason. I caught some girl whispering into someone's ear and pointing toward the pool. I followed their gazes to find Parker looking at the ground.

"Oh!" I straightened up and hurried across the lawn. "Hey, Parker—"

"God." Parker closed her eyes and raised her head to the sky. She raised her hand at me, and I realized her hair was wet. There were stains on her shoulders, bruising the faux fur forever. "Not you." Parker's voice was tight, as if I was distracting her from something more important, like she was an acrobat balancing on a tightrope. "I can't deal with you right now. Go away." She waved her hand at me.

"Jeeze," I grumbled, taking a full step back. We were two seconds into this conversation and I could already feel heat festering in the back of my head. I glared up at Parker. "All I said was hey. You don't have to bite my head off. I wanted to—"

"No! No!" she shouted, reaching for her own head with claws out. "I don't want to hear it, because I know you're going to whine more and I'm not in the mood—"

"Why are you being such a dick?!" I roared back, stomping forward. "Camille and I are leaving, and she wants to know if you want to come! That's all!"

"Fuck off, Lizzie! Emily ripped me a new one. Again! God, I'm so stupid!" She threw her arms out and her hands fell fast, slapping her sides. She yelled more at herself. "I didn't even know a person could get dumped twice, but I guess you can! I deserve it. I wish I wasn't so good at fucking up."

"What?" I choked out a whisper, struggling to remove the foot lodged in the middle of my throat. "How was I supposed to know?! You didn't tell me that!"

"I couldn't! Not with your whining!"

All my guilt burned away, and my fight or flight activated. I wanted to get rid of everything that had weighed on my chest since Parker had torpedoed her way into my life and blown it up. I wanted sweet relief, the kind I could ball up and throw at Parker's stupid face. "You know what? I'm not surprised that someone dumped you! How you even tricked someone into dating you is shocking! I can't stand being around you for more than a minute!"

"Then get out of my face!" Parker shoved me.

I shoved her back. We both swatted at each other, pushing and shoving like a couple of idiots. I gave her a great push on the shoulder that she attempted to dodge, but her ankle crooked and her combat boots squeaked. At her height, I'm shocked she didn't fall over all the time. She reached for me, grabbing a handful of my sweater and yanking forward. Gravity was a menace.

We both shouted as we toppled over, slamming into the pool. The water wrapped around me and I panicked, thrashing and kicking until my shoes touched the bottom. I shot up to the surface, hacking up a lung. Parker emerged next and I splashed her with a yell, "Why are you the worst?!"

"You pushed me!" Parker snapped, splashing me back. The cold water had a horribly sharp bite that burrowed deep into my bones, making me sore all over. The water had drenched my clothes, filling the cotton.

"You pushed first!"

We both roared at each other with now a lack of words; reduced to animals, we splashed each other mercilessly. People gathered around the edge of the pool with mixed reviews. I didn't care. I leaned back, floating on my back and kicking the water right into Parker's face. She grabbed hold of my ankle and yanked me under. I pushed off from the bottom and showed no mercy. This pool was going to be empty by the time we were done.

"*Oh my god!*" someone shouted from dry land.

I stopped. Parker stopped.

Together, we snapped our heads to the side to find Camille with her arms crossed and her black-painted lips thinned into one small angry line. Shouting at us, she slammed every word out like a horrible clap. "What. The. Actual. Fuck?" Before we could get a word in, she snapped, "I've had it up to here"—she threw her hand up, making it higher than Parker—"with the both of you! Out of the pool. *Now.* We're leaving."

TEN

Parker

Lizzie and I had been reduced to children. No, less than children. Camille sat us both in the backseat, where all children deserved to sit. My clothes clung to my body. Water trickled from the top of my head into my mouth, and I knew my mascara had run down my cheeks like I was the runner-up on *The Bachelor* who had tried to steal the last rose from the winner before being escorted out by security.

"I can't take it anymore," Camille bellowed, tightening her grip around the steering wheel. No music played. The windows were shut tight. The heaters were blasting, becoming miniature hair dryers to keep us from dying from pneumonia. However, a slow weakening death might be better than the excruciating pain of dying from embarrassment.

Camille shook her head, glaring at us from the rearview mirror. If anyone was more done than Camille, they'd be straight-up dead. She zoomed through the neighborhood, past dozens of houses that looked the exact same. "I can't keep babysitting you and expecting you to not kill each other."

"She started it!" Lizzie cried.

"I was upset!" I snapped, feeling the itch in the back of my head return. With her, these feelings festered inside of me like maggots in rotted wood. "Emily broke up with me again." The hurt was still fresh, and I wanted to spend the remainder of the night rocking myself in the fetal position.

"I didn't know!" Lizzie shouted, growing louder and louder. "I didn't know!"

Camille rolled her eyes, but once we started going, there was no stopping us. We were two people in the middle of a forest fire, splashing gallons of gasoline at each other. "God!" I huffed, and tried to squeeze the water out of my hair like a wet rag. "The category of people who are attracted to you must be the smallest faction in history."

"Oh, I'm sorry." Lizzie raised her hand, her voice gritty. "Give me a second to process this, I didn't realize I was in the presence of perfection."

"Why are all your insults compliments?"

"It was sarcasm! And it's not my fault your dates can't handle five minutes being around the real you."

My face grew hot, but before I could whip my own comeuppance sandwich and stuff it in her big fat mouth, Camille snorted. She laughed high and pitchy, and I took it like a slap with her underhand. "You know, Lizzie, that's not actually too far off."

"Camille!" I gasped, aghast that she'd dare pick Lizzie's side. Camille never picked sides at all. She played referee, blowing the whistle and dealing out yellow cards. Her joining the fight was unprecedented.

"Oh, don't 'Camille' me! What's your longest relationship? A week? Oh, sorry I didn't mean to confuse you with Lizzie. Parker, you can last two weeks, right? You can point out each other's flaws until your faces turn blue, but that doesn't mean either of you is going to change.

Ever. You two never even try to be better. You both stay in this realm of mediocrity and think you're satisfied, but I know you're not. You're miserable—*god*." She rolled her eyes. "Why the fuck am I even bothering? You two would never last long enough to go for it."

We'd done it. Lizzie and I had finally broken Camille.

"That's not true." Lizzie sat up. She grabbed the driver's seat, trying to creep into Camille's vision. "I'd try! And I'd last longer than two weeks."

I jumped up too. "I could last a month!"

"Fine!" Camille roared and slammed her brakes at the stop sign. She whipped her head around and snapped, "Do it then. I dare you, you cowards. Date each other for—" She chewed on the idea, spitting it all out without a second thought. "Date for thirty days! And then I'll stop giving you so much crap. I'll even stop making you two hang out! And, hey, if miracles exist, maybe you'll even fix your shitty dating habits. A thirty-day trial of what a real relationship is like. The whole nine yards! Dates! Hand-holding! Fighting and then apologizing! All of it!"

Lizzie glanced at me in the quiet, her brown eyes shining in the lamplight. She was busy searching my face for a reaction, for a gauge of the situation, but it didn't read like an outright refusal. I didn't want to admit that for a second I considered it, if not for the fact that I could finally hang out with Camille without Lizzie being the third wheel. Emily's voice egged me on too:

You're such an ass.

She'd said it, tattooing it across my heart, and I still didn't understand why. I didn't have the answers, but maybe if I studied, if Lizzie was my experiment, I could create the right solution and Emily wouldn't block me out like everyone in my life has.

"Forget it." Camille turned and rolled her eyes. She finally left the four-way stop. "You'd never do the whole thirty days. You don't have the guts. Ugh!" she roared, slamming her hands on the steering wheel. "Dammit! I need to get home. I think I started my period. You two made me so mad, I started my period."

We drove the rest of the way silent, and for the first time since I've ever been in a car with Lizzie, we listened to the radio. Camille reached my house first and had to come inside to steal a few tampons. Lizzie reluctantly followed us in.

All the lights were off but I could hear Hayden playing games on his PC upstairs. Camille headed to my bathroom as I led Lizzie to the guest bathroom, which was drenched in the fragrant musk of potpourri. Debbie had been bitten by the decorator bug, engrossed in some demented need to create a home from all these misshapen human pieces. It was more like she made our house look like a hotel, decorated with beautiful works of art, surrounded by classy furniture. This had the opposite effect. It looked nice but was shallow at the surface. At my old house we had a table that I'd carved my initials into. There were pictures of me along our old hallway. I was nowhere in this house.

Bending down, I opened a cabinet with stacks of maroon towels and tossed one to Lizzie.

She blinked. "Thanks."

"Sure." I shrugged. I glanced at her again and said something other than what I was thinking about. "I could get you some clothes too. Uh, something to get you home."

"Oh, that's fine. Um." She pressed the towel into her face, muffling her voice. "I only live a few minutes away."

"Right." I swallowed. My nerves bubbled inside me like a raging pot of boiling pasta, making a mess all over my life.

Lizzie sputtered into laughter when she noticed the eyeliner on the towel and scrubbed her face. "Camille is insane. A thirty-day trial period? Am I supposed to swipe right on you too?"

"I know, right?" I laughed and hopped on the counter, crossing my legs by habit. "It's like I asked YouTube for a tutorial on how to fix my intimacy issues."

I got her to full-on snort. Leaning against the counter, she nudged me. "So dumb."

We paused, sitting in silence and waiting. It was the first time I've ever had a silent conversation. I could feel the want radiating from her edges in waves, crashing into me. At the same time, we locked eyes and burst into laughter again. We were both blushing and slightly mortified by the events of tonight.

"No, no way." She shook her head.

"Yeah." I laughed, still feeling uneasy. "No way."

All my thoughts clogged my brain and my IQ dropped lower than the earth's surface, so I had nothing to say. It wouldn't make any sense. None of it did. Camille had challenged us out of anger. She'd said all that to laugh at us.

But what if?

What if Lizzie and I dated and she ironed out the wrinkles from my messy dating history. What if I learned how to keep a girlfriend? Maybe learned how to keep people from leaving me all the time. What if I could win Emily back? End the breakup cycle.

Glancing at Lizzie again, I watched her standing in front of the mirror, squeezing the water out of her hair. Sighing, she unraveled her braid to reveal long black waves that nestled right below her elbow, and wrapped her hair up instead. "Can I get another towel?"

"Oh, uh, sure," I said, and handed her another one. She grabbed it, but I didn't let go. Meeting her eyes, my face warmed as I admitted, "Hey, sorry about the whole pool thing. I really didn't mean to push us in."

"It's whatever," Lizzie said, budging only an inch. She wrapped her body in the towel with a huge sigh. She leaned into the mirror, scrapping off the last ruined mascara off her under eye. I caught the little smirk of hers in the mirror as she said, "It means I get to push you into a pool next. You know, to make it even."

"*Okay.*" I snorted and rolled my eyes, but surprisingly, my smile stayed. I looked Lizzie over again, still wondering about all the possibilities of a trial period. Spending thirty days with Lizzie wasn't so crazy out of the normal for me. Who knew? If I couldn't learn a thing or two about romance from Lizzie, I'd at least practice patience and temper control.

"Hey!" Camille popped into the doorway, and I plopped down on the toilet, putting another foot of space between me and Lizzie. "I'm ready to go." She blinked, glancing between us. "What?" With a huff, she dropped her arms. "What now?"

"Nothing," Lizzie hissed, brushing past Camille on the way out.

Camille shook her head, grumbling on her way to give me a quick hug before she left. "Some sort of moon is in retrograde or something because you two are going insane." I hugged her tightly, not moving from my porcelain throne. Once they were out of sight, I didn't stop thinking about Camille or Lizzie for the rest of the night.

ELEVEN

Lizzie

Someone took a picture of Parker and me climbing out of Olivia's pool and it had been circulating all weekend. My sports bra and wet T-shirt were on full display clinging to my back. I might as well have been naked. There were no more secrets.

I yawned, letting my backpack slap the concrete school tile. Our school had long strings of green lockers and a speckled floor that might have once been white but was now aged to a dingy yellow, complete with scuff marks and scratches. No high school would be complete without the cement walls. Every now and then you could spot the white patches where a janitor had painted over someone's artistic rendition of genitals or their favorite curse word. It was wall-to-wall chatter right before class started with everyone crammed into these few halls.

"Whoa!" I gasped, surprised at Parker's face as I slammed my locker shut. Immediately, I clocked that her oversized pink-rimmed glasses didn't have glass in them. Her trench coat–length cardigan hit the floor, like her flowy striped pants. Her ginger hair was up in a messy bun. It was a casual look in comparison to her other costumes.

That was Parker, always putting on a show. She had to dress the part.

Sometimes I imagined Parker diving headfirst into her closet and emerging as the fashion creature from the overpriced thrift lagoon.

She leaned against the other locker, crossing her arms. "Let's pretend we agree to do it."

"Huh?" I yawned again. "It's too early. Speak human."

"The bet." She whipped out her hands, waiting for my reaction. When I didn't, she rolled her eyes. "The thirty-day trial period."

To mock her, I rolled my eyes too. "Oh, that. What about it?" I started for my first period British literature class.

"We're talking only in hypotheticals," she said. "Let's say we have a relationship, our first long-term relationship, for a thirty-day period. What would be the big deal?" She raised her hands in a shrug. "It's only thirty days."

I considered it. We're the same, but so different. Like me, Parker was perpetually single. But with her unearned confidence, she has also been on a lot of dates. She's been with multiple people. The tips and pointers she could give me could lead me to a real relationship. I might actually get to French kiss a girl once in my life.

I nodded, unsure if my stomach was bubbling from the coffee I'd drunk this morning for breakfast or if it was from the bet itself. "It's only a month."

"Yeah, only a month. What harm could we possibly do in a measly little month?"

"Yeah." I eyed her.

"We might even grow or something."

"Sure. Maybe."

"Yeah." She eyed me cautiously back. I stopped at my classroom door and Parker awkwardly fidgeted. As she opened her mouth, the first bell rang and she huffed instead.

"I'll see you later?" I asked.

"See ya." Nodding, she skulked away, leaving the conversation in the air. I watched her go for a few seconds before she ducked into her classroom. Even then, I lingered. I wanted to talk to her more.

Parker

By the time my biology class ended and I had all my stuff packed up, Lizzie was by the door. She held on to her backpack straps, pursing her lips. She wore her usual uniform, the lightly colored jeans without holes or any flare. The mom jeans for the everyday teen. And the usual chunky sweater and white button-up underneath. Lizzie did everything I expected her to do.

Except for today.

Lizzie picked the topic back up from where we'd left off. "So, we would date like *date* date? Hold hands and go on dates and all that. Would we tell people?"

"I think so," I said.

She leaned in a bit closer. Her breath smelled like soured anxiety and Altoids. "Would we have to kiss? If we date, would that make it mandatory for thirty days, I mean."

"I don't think we have to, but let's be honest, we're gonna end up kissing after dates. No offense, but I'm guessing you'd like a few tips on kissing anyway."

Not wanting to lose to me, she rolled her shoulders back and held her head high. "And I could help let some of that air out of your ego before it explodes and kills us all."

"Exactly." I grinned.

"Exactly."

We weren't only agreeing on something, we were joking around.

We were bantering in a way that didn't make us want to throttle each other. Hell was freezing over. But not before she back stepped. "If we were being serious."

Forcing it, I snorted and rolled my eyes. "Yeah. If."

"Yeah," she said, but hesitated. Those big brown eyes searched my face for an extra moment, deciding which thing I'd said was true and which was a lie. Whatever she found didn't inspire confidence. She left with this big question mark in her eyes, and some kid had to shoulder check me to finally get me to move.

I arrived late to my next class and then spent the entire period wondering how far we could take this joke.

Lizzie appeared at my locker. She must have bolted down the hall, knocking all the freshmen out of the way, to meet me here before the next bell and class started again. The thought alone coaxed a smile out of me despite my love of arguing with her.

She was still slightly breathless. "We'd need penalties." She shook my arm and I blinked stupidly. "Knowing me and knowing you, we're going to try to bail before the thirty days are over, right? So we need a penalty if we try to back out of the deal."

"Like the terms of the agreement."

"A contract." She smiled as I got it. This was the most comfortable conversation we'd ever shared. "But what would it say? Can a person choose their own punishment? We can't go too easy, or we won't be afraid to break the trial."

"We could ask Camille!" I clapped, getting too excited and too ahead of myself. A small blush crept across my face. The heat pricked the tops of my cheeks, and I wished I had control of my own face's thermostat. "I mean, we'd ask her if we were serious."

"*If.*" Lizzie nodded, as strange and noncommittal as I was.

The tip of my tongue tasted like sweet temptation. There was a buzz, an electric spark that bounced off me and crashed into Lizzie's sparks.

I didn't want to end the conversation here but the bell rang, summoning me to my final class of the day. The bell and I were gonna have a fight today.

I thought about her for the whole period, thinking of all these ways to ask Elizabeth Hernández out. I debated the age-old classic note with two boxes to mark off *yes* or *no*. I wrote with my blue gel pen:

> Lizzie, make me the happiest bisexual in the world and become my fake girlfriend for thirty days.

It might be cute, or it could be a good place for Lizzie to stick her gum before throwing it in the garbage. Maybe I wasn't created to be a romantic thing. My limbs were not meant for climbing into my crush's window, past curfew, against our parents' wishes. My lips couldn't possibly perform a passionate confession of undying love during a rainstorm. At best, I had a little sheet of paper covered in a lame joke.

I guess the real joke was me.

I crumpled the paper and shoved it in my pocket.

Lizzie

Somehow, instead of doing their busy work during class, my fingers opened Instagram. Possessed by some malevolent being, I scrolled right to Parker's page. The first few pictures were her hanging around backstage as the cast of *Cinderella* rehearsed in the background. In one, she was sewing her initials inside Cinderella's hem.

Leaving my mark, the caption read.

It was beautiful. Who would have thought Parker could make beautiful things. I scrolled farther down, past the funny-faced selfies she'd taken with Camille and people at her work. It was odd to see her in a uniform. She could still stand out, though, with those shiny eyes and goofy smile. She had plenty of dimples to go around.

I scrolled farther down again without really paying attention until a pattern appeared. Emily Kaplan. She was the sole constant addition to Parker's Instagram for a short amount of time. I scrolled back up, realizing Emily was in every picture until she wasn't anymore. She disappeared out of Parker's life, just like that. A trail of goose bumps appeared down my arms. It looked too easy for Parker to erase her.

My curiosity got the best of me. I found the first picture Parker had taken with Emily. The date read *September 3*. I scrolled right through until I found the last picture. "September eighteenth," I whispered. This was Parker's longest relationship. She wasn't even the one who had ended it. All I ever heard was Parker ending relationships, but if it was up to her, she would've continued to date Emily. Thinking back to that party, I could picture Parker's flushed face twisted in frustration. No wonder she was such a mess. If I didn't know better, I'd say Ashley Marie Parker had a heart.

A text appeared at the top of my screen from Camille.

Camille: Are you down for McDonald's? I'm craving some fries

I was texting back when a thought tugged at my mind. I typed something only to delete it, write it again, delete it again, and write the same thing one more time, but with the shrugging emoji at the end. I had to play it cool. For once in my life.

I texted Camille:

Lizzie: Sure. Can Parker come?

TWELVE

Lizzie

It was difficult but I managed to avoid Camille's suspicious looks. She attempted to dissect the situation. I could feel her eyes pinning my limbs down like they were chaotic butterfly wings and trying to pick apart the answers.

She took a swing. "It's nice that you invited Parker." It could be my own nerves or Camille's particularly sharp black eyeliner today, but she was extra-intimidating.

"My socks keep slipping down my foot. Hold on." I bent down, untying my shoes and fixing my socks back into place. We were in the student parking lot, watching everyone else escape. Camille leaned against my van, boring a hole through my skull with her judgmental eyes. I took my time, waiting for Parker to show up. This girl needed a new hobby, one that didn't involve driving up my blood pressure.

More unsatisfied than Angelica Schuyler, Camille crossed her arms and tried again. "I thought I saw you two walking together, but I assumed the school had a gas leak. Did I miss the reconciliation? You know, I would have sold tickets to that. I mean, who doesn't want to witness a live miracle?"

I couldn't tell her.

I couldn't possibly tell her that I wanted to take up the bet, that I wanted to pretend date Parker, whom I might dislike more than any person on the entire planet. In a lot of ways, it was like admitting to still using training wheels on a bike or that I needed a night-light to sleep.

Parker dashed out of the school from the arts department, drawing our attention away from Camille's comments. She lugged a huge plastic bin full of pieces of the *Cinderella* costumes. Unlocking the van, I opened the back door so Parker could drop it with a dramatic sigh. She raised her hand for a high five. "Go, team."

I rolled my eyes and slapped her hand.

Camille's eyes peered harder, as if she could somehow see through me. Parker was smart, maybe even aware of our awkward situation. She dashed for the front seat, going on and on about the behind the scenes of *Cinderella*. With nothing else to do, Camille and I followed her inside the car. Camille sat in the back with her arms firmly crossed.

"I swear, Camille," Parker exclaimed, "Jordan needs glasses. He's supposed to be Prince Charming, but I don't know what's so charming about a guy squinting all the time. But anyway! He walked right into the stepmother's table and took the whole thing down! Mrs. Donnelly nearly had a heart attack! Jordan has no understudy either."

"That feels like bad planning," I stated.

"It's so hard to get new guys interested in joining. We're always left with dozens of girls auditioning for the same character. Meanwhile, the boys basically get to pick who they want to play."

"Careful." Camille finally spoke. "I'm one of those girls."

Parker rolled her eyes. "You're different."

"Not really." Camille's frown deepened into a grimace.

"Seriously, you are. Have you met the new girl playing Cinderella, Norah Brady? She's so obnoxious—"

I spoke before I could stop myself. It was too easy. "Pot, meet the kettle."

"Fuck off." Parker laughed and even nudged me a little.

It was like getting the okay to go ahead. Parker had finally granted me permission to make her laugh. I kept going. "She must be a true monster if you're the one calling her obnoxious, Ms. I'm Wearing Glasses without the Glass."

"It's not fair I was blessed with twenty-twenty vision."

"I happen to be wearing contacts, you ass. Do you write this shit down at home? Do you have a list of things to say that will drive me crazy?"

"Now, Elizabeth." Parker grinned as if giddy from the accusation. "It's poor taste to peek inside someone else's diary."

Unable to help myself, I smiled—until I caught Camille raising a thick brow in the rearview mirror. A blush slapped me across the face, and I snapped straight ahead at the road, gripping the wheel a bit tighter. We were caught. In what, there was no way Camille would know, but we were obviously up to something.

I avoided all eye contact until we arrived at McDonald's. Camille held her place behind us, where she could keep watch. She waited to call us out until we'd ordered and were seated in one of the crumb-laden booths.

"All right, all right." Camille spoke up, raising her hands. "I love a good mystery, but none of the clues make sense and I have a feeling I'm the dead body in this scenario, so if you two could please get it over with. What's going on?"

"Um." My instinct was to deny everything, but I didn't. Parker didn't say anything either. We looked at each other for a moment, measuring the other's expression. We both toed the starting line, itching for someone to say GO. I wanted more. I wanted to change. I didn't want to be the girl who cried, the girl who was afraid of everything. I wanted to be the girl who could be loved. I needed to do this trial and learn how to be that girl.

So I looked at Camille across the table. "Camille, if we were to do a thirty-day trial period . . ."

She jumped on the thought like a cat finding its favorite prey. "What do you mean *if* you were going to do the trial period?" Her whole face brightened, her jaw dropping as she pointed between us. "Is that why you wanted to invite Parker?" She gasped, really working all those dramatic bones in her body. "You're really going to do it?! Listen, I'm in favor. It sounds so fun."

"We're thinking about it." I seethed, nudging Camille under the table. My face was already burning, and she was bringing too much attention to this table.

"We're speaking hypothetically." Parker agreed with me, and I wished she wouldn't. "What do you think should happen to us if we break up before the end of the trial? Like a punishment type thing."

"*Hmm.*" Camille dropped her back into the squeaky cushion. Sneering, she rubbed her grimy hands together as she spun her evil plot. "That's tough. It'd have to be painful enough to scare you into commitment, but it can't be illegal."

"Preferably."

"And let's say we start tomorrow?" Parker added, a bounce in her seat.

"Right." Camille nodded. "It would end around Halloween—" It was then that her eyes sparkled. The light bulb flashing above her head nearly melted my retinas. "I've got it. It's so easy. I know you both well enough to know your nightmares. If either of you ends the trial before thirty days, you must go back and find all your previous girlfriends—or boyfriends"—she nodded at Parker—"and apologize to them for being a terrible girlfriend."

I jumped in as my eyes popped out of my head. "You're crazy."

"But some of mine are in New York," Parker argued, her face pale.

Wiggling her shoulders, Camille was having more fun than cats toying with their prey. "Have you never heard of a phone call?"

Parker's jaw dropped so fast it almost snapped off. "That's even worse."

Camille grinned, her excitement bubbling over like a shaken soda bottle. "Imagine! You have to find these people and explain that you were awful, are still as bad as ever, and have zero plans to change. Would either of you want to do that?" she asked, already knowing the answer.

"Yeah," I said, "that's a big fat no for me."

"Pass." Parker frowned.

Camille sat up primly. "It's the perfect punishment then, though I'd love to see you two try it anyway. I'd sit in my car and eat popcorn. Oh!" She laughed. "But there's no way you two are serious. Lizzie can't even commit to cutting her hair."

Before I could defend myself, Parker said, "I want to do it."

Camille was taken aback. She blinked. "What? You do?" She whipped her head back and forth. Even I stared at Parker, overwhelmed by her confidence. I looked for that strong foundation to crumble, but Parker appeared unruffled. She stared straight ahead with a small nod. Everything about her seemed indestructible, and I wished my bones held half of that strength. Her confidence was like this bulletproof armor, while I spent every day dodging only half the bullets aimed at me.

"I like the challenge," Parker said and eyed me. "And I'm not scared. What do you say, Lizzie? How would you like to make an honest woman out of me for thirty days?"

My mouth went dry. This was supposed to be my cue.

Yes or no.

I wanted to be a better person. Everyone does, or at least they should. I wanted someone to love me, and that wasn't weird either. But no matter how much I wanted to change, I had no idea if I could trust Parker with something as precious as my truth, my pure self. She was going to learn all my faults and my insecurities. It was like handing my enemy the map directly to my weaknesses. If we're going to date, even in a fake way, I had to stop imagining Parker as my opponent.

"Okay," I said, ignoring the lump in my throat. Camille leaned over the table and nabbed one of the napkins. She took out a pen and scribbled some stuff down. Parker's eyes trapped me, and my resolve slipped through my ungraceful fingers.

Like jumping into the deep end, I closed my eyes, held my breath, and took the plunge. "Yes, I'll do it."

When I opened my eyes, Parker was smiling.

Camille squealed. "Awesome! Oh man, this is gonna be fun." She slapped the McDonald's napkin on the table in front of us, sliding it closer. Some places in the napkin had torn from Camille's pen pressure. I could identify with the struggle and the mess. "Sign here and you'll officially start dating on Monday, October the first! And you have to actually commit, all right? If anyone asks, you two started dating naturally."

In Camille's decent handwriting, the napkin read:

As of October 1st, Elizabeth Hernández and Ashley Marie Parker hereby agree to date as totally cute girlfriends for thirty days. The trial ends October 30th. If one party decides to end the trial early and "break up" with party two, they must undergo a horrible punishment designated by Camille Hernández.

At the bottom, Camille wrote two *X*'s in front of dotted lines.

Camille held out the pen to us, right in the middle. My palms were already sweating.

There was no way in hell I was going to go for it first, so I silently demanded Parker to take it with my eyes.

Parker got the message.

She took the pen and signed her name in a very Parker way, with flourishes and a dot at the end. She handed me the pen. I muttered a few curse words under my breath, having no idea what I was getting myself into, and initialed the open line because it didn't seem like anyone else was exactly lining up to be Parker's fake girlfriend. I held the pen and glanced from Camille to Parker.

My stomach squirmed. Parker had graduated from my worst acquaintance to my girlfriend. My heart skipped more than a beat. It jumped a full flight of stairs. It dashed headfirst off a cliff. The reality of the situation caught up to me. When I thought about having a girlfriend, from kissing to hand-holding and more, I suddenly placed Parker in that role.

Getting struck by lightning would've been easier on my heart. I fidgeted with the pen, rubbing it between my fingers. All I could look at suddenly was the stupid contract. Wanting to fill the silence with anything, I admitted, "I suddenly feel crazy awkward, oh my god."

"Maybe we should flirt a little, so the progression into dating is more natural," Parker suggested. She laid her arm around me and I got a whiff of whatever shampoo she used, a sweet homemade vanilla frosting scent. She wriggled her eyebrows. "You could seductively feed me a french fry."

"Yeah, I'm already regretting this." I groaned and dropped my head onto the table.

PART TWO

The Trial

THIRTEEN

OCTOBER 1

Parker

My alarm went off, jolting me out of my pleasant slumber. Groggily, I lifted my heavy body out of bed and staggered over piles of clothes to my alarm across the room. If I could turn it off within an arm's reach, I would never get out of bed. I had no impulse control and would hit snooze until late afternoon when my internal alarm clock (my stomach) woke me.

I picked up my phone and stared at the date. October 1. The start of the trial. Rubbing my face, I sobered myself up enough to write a text:

Parker: Good morning

Parker: Let me be the first to commemorate October first as the day we started going out

Parker: Please be gentle with me

I dropped my phone on my desk and proceeded to get ready. Clothes were as important to me as someone else's morning prayer, first cup of coffee, or morning jog. Today, I wanted to look fun and flirty. "I guess Lizzie and I are technically in the honeymoon period," I mumbled, glancing at my mirror like I was Mary Poppins, and my reflection was going to give me a thumbs-up.

Today I would wear my white flouncy shirt, which was a mix between pirate and Shakespearean (something romantic), and my bell-bottoms covered in bleached white stars (something fun). This paired well with my tan ankle boots and a beige coat. In the middle of fixing a top knot, I strolled back over to my phone.

No messages.

Maybe Lizzie didn't wake up as early because she didn't have to catch the bus. This inspired me. With a smirk, I texted her:

Parker: Hey

Parker: If you pick me up on the way to school, I'll buy you coffee. If you don't, I'll tell Camille you're a TERRIBLE girlfriend!

For the last hour of my morning routine I worked on the *Cinderella* costumes as much as possible and didn't obsess over the fact Lizzie still hadn't texted me back. In classic fashion, the evil stepsisters' costumes were outlandish, overbedazzled, and the prettiest eyesores in the world. Feathers and beads were unavoidable on these things. However, not a single bauble would be able to match the classic beauty of Cinderella's gown. Norah better be a good actress or this wasn't going to work.

A knock on the door made my head pop up.

"Yeah?" I paused the *Cinderella* soundtrack on my phone.

"Hey," my dad said, easing into the room. He narrowed in on my open tubs of design supplies and the scattered reference pictures. He raised a brow. "How do you walk around this stuff?"

"Carefully," I muttered, and picked up the dress, slipping it back over the form. "Did you want something?" I asked, my hair prickling. He wouldn't stop staring like all my things were trash, but all the scraps, excess fabric, leftover buttons, and bits and bobs were my witch's ingredients to make magic. A finance guy like him would never get it.

Dad shrugged, and then adjusted his glasses. "Just checking if you wanted something specific for dinner. We're thinking about watching a movie tonight, too, if you want to join. Maybe you can even bring some of this stuff into the living room and work there."

Stuff.

He always called it *stuff*, like it was junk or nothing important.

"I'm actually going to hang out with Camille," I said and walked to my closet. "I'll probably spend the night."

"Oh, okay." He nodded with a smile that didn't meet his eyes. He couldn't decide what he wanted more, time to hang out with me or that I was willing to make friends here. Of course, I already knew what I was going to wear, but I still hummed and moved hangers to the side like I was deep in thought.

Finally, I asked, "Did you need something else?"

"No, uh, have a good day at school. Call me if you need anything," he said, but still lingered a few more beats. He closed the door behind him with a long *click*. My quiet room wasn't as comfortable anymore. The air thickened with lingering tension, making it harder to breathe. It was annoying that I had to feel guilty for not wanting to hang out with my dad. I hadn't forgiven him yet. Not for taking me out of New York. Not for turning my whole world upside down.

I'd spent a lot of time by myself in my mother's apartment, so it was weird to go to the kitchen and always see someone who expected me to start a conversation. I couldn't find my place in a house that didn't want me in the first place. During the summer, when I visited my dad, I stayed in the guest room. I was a guest then, and still felt like one now. At any moment I could be ripped away again and sent back to New York. It wouldn't be my choice. It never was. In the back of my closet was one suitcase I hadn't unpacked because I wanted to be ready to go back home.

I laid my phone down again and finished my hair and makeup. There was a celebratory pimple on my chin that might make Lizzie so grossed out she'd immediately break the contract, so I did my best to smother it in my stepmom's foundation. She had no concealer. I hated covering my freckles.

My phone buzzed and relief flooded my veins.

"Finally." I let out a breath and hurried to my phone, eager to see Lizzie's reaction. An Instagram notification popped up instead. I assumed she'd send at least an eye-roll emoji or something. She hadn't. Lizzie hadn't sent anything. My stomach twisted. Maybe I'd annoyed her too much.

Backtracking, I texted:

Parker: Just kidding! I'll see you at school!

And to further embarrass myself, I quickly sent a thumbs-up emoji too. That uneasiness sat in the pit of my stomach as I went to my bus stop. Meanwhile, my phone remained silent.

Lizzie

In the parking lot at school, I checked my appearance like it was picture day or something. With a sigh, I slammed my forehead on my steering wheel.

A knock on the window saved me from myself.

Andrea waved, a look of mild worry behind her glasses. Her braids were down today, her leggings of choice were black, and she wore a rainbow blocked hoodie underneath a jean jacket. Her clarinet was strapped to her back. She opened the door for me. "Need help?" she asked.

I grumbled and slipped out of the car. We headed toward the school, squirming through the sea of cars and people. "I think I'm getting worse."

"I think you're spending too much time with Parker. You're being so dramatic," she teased, and my whole face flushed. The heat rose to the top of my ears and my chest squeezed a Venti triple shot of fear. Today was the first day of the trial and I wasn't ready. Parker had sent me a text, but I was too nervous to read it, dreading what it could say, and I didn't want to sweat through my deodorant so early in the day.

"Whoa, don't flip." Andrea blinked. She touched my arm, a comforting gesture. "I know you can't stand Parker. I'm only kidding."

"I've made a mistake," I said as we entered the building.

"When do you start making sense?"

"I'm dating Parker."

"What?!" Andrea jumped back, her eyes popping out of her head. We stopped traffic. The people behind us nearly crashed but managed to stumble past. They snapped at us to watch out and cursed our dumb legs. Andrea didn't care about snapping back. The spotlight blinded me. "Start over. Start way over. Is Parker threatening you? How— When—" Her brow narrowed the way one would when solving a difficult math equation.

"It's recent. Really recent," I explained. "We, um." I couldn't tell her about the bet. Thinking it over, it sounded so dumb and so weird. She wouldn't take it seriously. Instead, I said, "We kind of bonded, I guess."

"Since when?"

"Since Olivia's party."

Andrea glowered. "You mean the party where Parker pulled you into a pool?"

After a lull, I said slowly, "Yes?"

She seemed unconvinced, but before she could interrogate me for details I heard Parker's voice bounce down the hallway.

"Lizzie!"

I could see a splash of her ginger hair among the drab crowd. Suddenly, I didn't know how to hold myself with her attention aimed at me, and made myself busy rolling my shoulders back and fidgeting with which side to lay my braid. I was so aware of even how I tipped my chin up to avoid neck rolls. I should've skipped school with a phantom stomach bug.

Andrea rolled her eyes. Raising her hand, she could hardly even look at me anymore. "I'm not ready to see this. My heart needs to be prepared. I'll meet you in biology."

"Hey, you!" Parker came at me hot, guns already loaded and ready to shoot a hole through my confidence. I was taken aback, searching my brain for the cause of the fire. "Why haven't you texted me back?"

I blinked, letting my brain buffer. "Oh shoot! I'm sorry," I mumbled. "I was going to reply."

Parker huffed and crossed her arms. "So, you knew I texted you?"

"I saw the notifications—"

"That sucks. I was really hoping you didn't notice, but you were *purposely* ignoring me." Parker dropped her eyes to the floor and kicked at it. She sounded wounded. "Great, that really sucks."

"Parker." I spoke up. "Do you want to know what happens when I have to text?"

"No," she grumbled. "Not if it's gonna hurt my feelings, like,"— she popped her palm against her forehead and mocked my speaking voice—"oh, a text from Parker. She's annoying, I'm gonna ignore her."

"That's not it!" I snapped. "I look at it." I gave her a demonstration, looking at my phone and setting it down like I actually do. "But I don't want to reply too fast and look desperate. I don't want to be the annoying one. So I think about my answer for a while, something worth texting and then I text something."

"Well, how do you think I feel?" She stretched out her arms. "You left me hanging. I thought I'd *already* screwed up. It doesn't have to be the next great American novel, Lizzie. I just want you to acknowledge my existence."

The subtext twisted my chest as I remembered Emily had dumped Parker, which was her last relationship. If we were keeping score, Parker was the one starting way more fights than me. All the tension in Parker's shoulders deflated. She sighed. "Please, text me back."

"Okay, okay," I said, whinier than I wanted it to sound. I didn't want to be so defensive but I couldn't easily unzip the layer on my own. Still, I said, "I'm sorry."

We stood in the humming hallway in silence.

"Okay, I'm going to class," Parker said, and lifted her hand. I stared at her open palm with a quirked brow. It hung in the air like an unsolvable riddle. I needed a hint.

I pointed to her hand. "What's this?"

"Well." Parker shrugged, her hand still up. "Usually, when I'm dating someone, we hug or kiss or something, but we're really not there yet."

My heart thumped against my chest ready to reach out and high-five hers. In middle school, Andrew Walton asked me out on the bus. I said yes (because all my other friends said yes when boys asked them out) and then we very romantically high-fived.

Camille still hasn't let me live that down.

Parker's eyes were pinned on mine, and in that small moment with that one honey-glazed look and that little genuine smile on her lips, I was tricked into understanding why so many people dated Ashley Marie Parker. I slapped her hand.

"Hot," I muttered with a crucial eye roll to distract from my blush.

Parker snorted, but it was enough. She eyed me as she turned with a smirk on her pink lips, and I couldn't unglue my Converse from that spot. Yesterday was a different world. This new one had me questioning everything, and I wasn't sure if I was brave enough to explore it.

FOURTEEN

Lizzie

My phone buzzed in my pocket, making my bones jump and hit the ceiling of my body.

Camille snickered behind her hand. "Chill," she whispered. She stuck out, the only student in class wearing spikes on her shoulders. All in black, you'd think she was on her way to a funeral, mourning the death of a good time.

We sat in our British literature class, listening to the audiobook for *Pride and Prejudice.* I scribbled down notes and theories as I listened along, even though I've already read the book and made three different playlists for it (my favorite being a Lizzie Bennet playlist titled *Mrs. Bennet's least favorite daughter.* Its album cover is a vintage drawing of Lizzie Bennet with photoshopped sunglasses and explosions in the background).

A knot formed in my chest and tightened as the seconds went by. Totally defeated, I slipped my phone from my pocket and glanced at the screen. Parker's text sat at the top, beckoning me. She needed a text from me.

Eyeing my teacher, Mr. Nelson, I brought my phone's screen light down to minimum. Not that Mr. Nelson ever had to worry about me, but I wanted to be safe. I opened Parker's text. She'd sent me a secret selfie at her desk, giving herself at least four chins, a derp face, and crossed eyes. I snorted, quickly hiding it with a cough. My phone buzzed again.

Parker: plEASE tell me your class has spots open I'm quitting mine. Should we switch? Would anyone notice??

I curled my lips to keep down my smile. Thinking over my response, I debated holding off. Maybe I'll text Parker back in my next class, but she said to text her. This wasn't a big deal, I had to tell myself. Maybe that was my new mantra. It wasn't a big deal. It was just a text.

Flipping on my camera, I did my best to outdo her four chins with five and flared my nose to create peak horribleness. I twisted my face back and forth and back and forth and up and down and threw out my tongue, too, for some flavor. Camille slipped her middle finger into the screen, and we both sputtered into a flurry of giggles.

"Lizzie. Camille," Mr. Nelson said, an edge to his voice, and he stopped the audiobook suddenly; it was jarring to be slapped with silence. "I know you're not laughing at something Mr. Collins is saying." In my panic, I tried dropping my phone into my bag, but it missed and clattered to the floor. Mr. Nelson sighed. "Bring it to me. You can have it back at the end of the day."

My heart sank. Everyone either laughed or made a face that looked as uncomfortable as I felt. A teacher asking for my phone? That has never happened to me in my life. I couldn't believe it. I never got in trouble. I never got singled out. No way. My heart inflated to max capacity and threatened to pop and shatter my insides. This had to be a heart attack.

"This century, please."

"Sorry!" I squeaked, heat rising from the pit of my stomach to the tips of my ears. I fumbled around to pick up my phone and quickly stood on my weak, jellified legs. My shoulders raised on their own as I transformed into a turtle to hide my shame. Mr. Nelson took my phone and dropped it in his bottom desk drawer, with the rest of his treasures. The loss of my phone wasn't bad. Camille's secret giggling didn't hurt. But the look in Mr. Nelson's eyes stung. Getting in trouble gave me hives, like someone with a mild peanut allergy, but it felt like disappointing someone I respected could throw me into anaphylactic shock.

I was never going to listen to Ashley Marie Parker again.

Parker

The school day ended.

I stormed through the halls directing myself to Lizzie's locker, which I could find with my eyes closed at this point.

She stood at her locker, two inches shorter than usual, with her shoulders slumped. That wasn't a new look or anything, but the way Camille grinned up at me was kind of odd. The words flew out of my mouth before I gave any of them a second thought. My big mouth was the authority of my existence, not my head and not my heart.

"Hey," I said, crossing my arms and leaning against the locker next to Lizzie. "You didn't text me again. What do I have to do to get you to text me? Sacrifice Camille to Satan?"

"Leave me out of it," Camille said.

"Are you even gonna take this trial seriously?"

"I am!" Lizzie snapped, taking her binder and smacking me with it. It didn't hurt as much as it surprised me.

"Whoa!" I fumbled, my arms slipping from their hold.

"I got into trouble because of you! I'm so stupid for listening to you!" Lizzie shouted, hitting the meat of my arm with her binder. Her little heart-shaped face burned the brightest red I had ever seen, like the light from an electric burner. If she could, soon she'd boil my blood.

"Because of me? What'd I do?"

"I did try to text you!"

"Nu-huh!"

"Yea-huh!" She lifted her binder and my hands whipped up to the sky for mercy. "I tried to text you and Mr. Nelson took my phone!"

My lips curled.

"I've never gotten in trouble during class! And during *Pride and Prejudice* of all things! He probably doesn't think I care! UGH!" she roared.

"It'll be okay," I said. I tried to stifle my laughter as best as I could, but Lizzie's darkening glare told me I had failed. Still, I smiled at her like she was the cutest cat with her claws out in the world. "You just need some practice."

"Practice!" Her eyes widened in shock and awe. "You expect me to try again?"

"You're going to quit? What are you? A quitter?"

"Don't call me a quitter." She pointed a warning finger between my eyes.

I smiled wider. My face was going to break. "What do you want me to call you then? A stopper?"

"You're impossible." Lizzie huffed and slammed her locker shut. "I'm going to get my phone. I'll meet you at the car," she told Camille, not me. She breezed right by my shoulder, leaving it cold and prickly.

I looked at Camille. "Am I dumb?"

"Are you seriously asking me that?" She blinked.

"I don't know." I shrugged and held on to my backpack. "I thought we got past the whole let's fight until our last breath thing?"

"Honestly, I think this whole bet is going to transform into a murder trial. There's no way you two aren't going to kill each other by the end of it. You may have to beg her to drive you home today."

"Thanks for the vote of confidence," I muttered, and we walked to Lizzie's car.

Lizzie

I didn't acknowledge Parker or make conversation. I directed everything I said and did to Camille, who was sitting in the backseat of my van. I made it a point not to glance at Parker, but every time she moved I could feel the air shift. When she spoke to Camille my chest squeezed and my body locked up.

Unfortunately, Camille's house was first on our way home.

She got out and knocked on my window, signaling me to roll it down. With a knowing smile, she said, "Time for your first lesson, ladies. I'll never be able to keep you from fighting. You need it like oxygen."

I shifted uncomfortably, rubbing the steering wheel and looking at the road.

"Now's when you learn to make up," Camille said, pushing off my door. She walked away, throwing back a little wave as she hurried up the steps to her house. By accident, my eyes met Parker's, and my instinct was to whip forward. Sighing, I put the car back into Drive and got back on the road.

Out of the corner of my eye I watched Parker's face. Her mouth spent a lot of time coming up with bullshit, but her face stayed honest. It twisted back and forth as her brain tried cooking up something to tell me.

After I already shut her down.

I didn't know how to fight. Actually, I knew how to fight. I could fight Parker anytime, anywhere, and over anything, but I guess I didn't know how to end a fight. We never apologized to each other. Not really. Was fighting like a dance? Was someone supposed to be leading? Was the other person supposed to apologize first? If we were both wrong, did no one apologize?

Parker hadn't looked away, her resolve staying firm. Finally, she spat out, "Hey, I'm sorry I yelled at you. I'll try not to fly off the handle at you anymore. I know you're trying. I didn't mean it when I said you gave up."

My chest squeezed, compressing my organs like a book preserving wildflowers. Summoning my courage, I tightened my grip on the wheel and confessed, "I get nervous." A shaky breath escaped my lips. "All the time. About everything. I regret more than half of every conversation I ever have."

At the next stop sign, I met her eyes, and realized I'd given her all the ammunition she needed to put me down. Instead, she said, "As your girlfriend, I won't make you text in class if you don't want to do that. I still might text you, but I don't want you to feel guilty, like you're not doing a good job." She smiled weakly and shrugged a little. "All I wanted to do was talk to you. It's not always the worst to talk to you."

"You're not so bad yourself." I chuckled a little and started driving again, not feeling the usual defensiveness she inspired within me, but something lighter. Happier. "I won't ignore you. I want to know you better."

"*Dangerous.*"

Rolling my eyes, I bit down on my smile and this time, when it was quiet, it was comfortable. It was like the butterflies in my stomach had escaped and were happily fluttering around the car. I stole a glance at Parker. Even though she wasn't looking at me, a bright and shiny smile hung from her lips. I hadn't ruined anything. If anything, things were going well.

"Do you need to stop anywhere?" I asked.

"No, but thanks," she said, still smiling. It might be her longest smile in my presence. I thought about timing it and reaching out to Guinness World Records to claim the record for the longest period without Ashley Parker and Elizabeth Hernández fighting. The longest I've gone, making her happy. And I planned to go for longer.

It had been almost thirty seconds, and Parker was still smiling. Forty-five seconds. One minute passed. Half the ride home, and even after I dropped her off. Still wearing the prettiest smile as she waved goodbye.

Rationally, this was all fake—we were just pretending. And yet I couldn't deny that my heart had skipped a beat. I couldn't fake that.

FIFTEEN

OCTOBER 2

Parker

Play practice after school had the theater buzzing, from actors practicing lines, to musicians tuning their machines, to the backstage crew arguing over who was doing the bulk of the set change and who was pretending to hold up their side of the fake trees.

From the wings, I peeked around the heavy red velvet curtain to wave at Lizzie in the orchestra pit right in front of the stage. She jumped, realizing my existence, and glanced at her fellow bandmates, but I was only looking at Lizzie. I blew her kisses. She gave me the finger. The romance was palpable.

"You're ridiculous," Ian said from the floor as he shoved batteries into the microphone packs. He was all limbs, like a spider, with bony joints. His white-blond hair sat hidden underneath a baseball cap with the *Zelda* logo.

"Since when were you and Lizzie tight, anyway?" he asked, and I briefly eyed Camille, sitting close by on the full stage, and humming the prologue's melody. I knew better than to try to joke around with Camille while she worked, so Ian was my practice buddy. I sat next to him and started helping, like I'd promised.

"I'd tell you about our torrid love affair but I don't want to make you jealous."

"Whatever." He rolled his eyes, but I couldn't stop smiling. "I give you guys a month."

Oh, he had no idea.

My phone buzzed.

Lizzie: How about you get some work done?

I chuckled and tapped out a reply.

Parker: How about you come make me?

My entire existence wanted to jump off stage and be next to her, because I could get a better rise out of her in person than over text, but our director, Mrs. Donnelly, called for our attention as she walked onto the stage. She was a woman made of soft, round edges with bohemian drapery waterfalling down her curves and a short blond bob that never had a hair out of place. I adored her costume jewelry and smoky eye shadow.

"I hope you all had a great weekend, but it's Tuesday and you're all on my time now. We have plenty of work to do." She bit her lip. "Honestly, we're running a little behind."

"I wonder whose fault that is?" I whispered to Ian, nudging his foot. I motioned to the pile of actors surrounding Norah.

Norah Brady, the bane of my existence. Gifted with the face of a cherub and heart-shaped lips, Norah had golden-brown skin, big russet eyes, and the kind of smile a toothpaste commercial would cast. I hated to say it, but I liked her style, too, with her black curls wild and free, and she wore a lot of vintage '80s inspired clothes.

"I mean," I said, "they act like it's the first week of practice, like no one knows their marks or their lines. It's a place to hang out for them. If it was me, I'd recast the whole thing. That's just me, though."

"*Ssh.*" Camille shushed me, her eyes flashing red.

"What?" I whispered back, then looked around and realized I was using my slightly louder stage whisper, not the one reserved for shit talking and secrets. The acoustics in this theater were good. Too good. Norah locked eyes with me and gifted me the meanest grimace I had ever seen stain her pretty face. From my chin to the tips of my ears my skin caught fire like a witch who'd pleaded guilty during their trial.

"Uh, carry on?" I suggested and Mrs. Donnelly sighed.

After the talk, we all broke apart to our designated tasks, and I gathered the box of shoes I still needed to bedazzle, planning to find a spot behind the orchestra so I could bother Lizzie some more, but Ian asked, "Hey? You wanna go to the audio booth with me?"

"Yeah." I nodded. "Let's do it."

I was halfway across the stage when I heard someone say, "You know, if all I had to do was glue some cheap costume crystals to some clothes, I'd have enough done to outfit the whole student body by now. She's probably going that slow for attention." I whirled around to spot Norah shrugging and walking away with the stepsisters. Norah muttered, "That's just me, though."

My stomach twisted as their stifled laughs heated my cheeks back up. I watched Norah walk up to Camille and say something, somehow funny enough to make Camille laugh. A horrible thought ran through my head, and I wanted to know if the joke was about me. No. No. Camille wouldn't let anyone make fun of me. No way.

The bin of shoes somehow doubled in weight.

I turned to the crowd of empty seats and the band warming up. Lizzie was sitting at the piano, and when she met my eyes, she made a twisted goofy face and stuck her tongue out at me. My heart wasn't in it anymore. I half smiled, bowing my head to the floor. Until rehearsal ended I stayed hidden in the audio booth. Not one person noticed I was gone, and if they did, they didn't care to find me. Usually I liked being proved right, but this time it made me the loser.

Lizzie

Camille and I went back to my house after rehearsal under the guise of studying, but we hadn't opened our backpacks once. Parker still hadn't replied to the texts I'd sent at the end of rehearsal, which was especially strange given all her commotion about the necessary evil that was texting in a relationship. I checked her Instagram too. Usually she posted something about play practice, but there wasn't anything, and rehearsal had ended hours ago.

When I asked Camille if she'd noticed anything weird about Parker, Camille shrugged. "Parker works today." Camille rifled through my dresser drawer.

"Is that so?" I glanced in the mirror, holding my chin up to form more of a jawline with these apple cheeks. For no reason I flipped my braid to my other shoulder and then shrugged my hair onto my back with a sigh. I hadn't even taken off my shoes yet. I couldn't get Parker and the sad smile on her face out of my mind, so I snatched my jean jacket from the closet. "I'm starving," I said, before I could overthink my way out of it. This anxiety wasn't going to go away until I asked Parker what her problem was. "I'm gonna run to the store and grab snacks, do you want me to bring you anything?"

"Yeah." Camille chuckled. "Sure."

"I could go for anything."

"How did you know anything is now part of my top ten favorite snacks?"

"Oh, shut up," I grumbled, and snatched my backpack. I told my mom the briefest goodbye and climbed into my car. Shoving the key into the ignition, I caught a glance of myself in the rearview mirror and frowned.

A ghost took over my body. My hands unraveled my braid before I realized what I was even doing, and I let my dark hair hang loose and wavy, a little frizzy but free. The strain of the braid relaxed, pulling at my head. Still, my stomach didn't settle. I moved my hair over one shoulder and then the other.

I started the car, blasting my emo rock playlist, which contained every screamo song ever created, and drove to the grocery store.

I dashed through the front sliding doors of Frugal Finds, keeping my chin planted on my chest. It would look way cooler if I didn't spot Parker on the way into the store and only happened to run into her while checking out.

Because everything about this screamed cool.

I decided on purchasing some Flamin' Hot Cheetos and a random can of spaghetti off the shelf. I debated grabbing more, but that made me wonder how much visiting Parker at work would cost on an allowance of twenty dollars a week that was supposed to be for gas money. Being crazy was expensive.

"Lizzie? What are you doing here?"

I jumped, fumbling with my stuff. The can of spaghetti slipped from my hands and smacked the tile floor. Parker was standing right next to me. I blinked, almost not recognizing her at all, as if I needed to wait for my eyes to adjust in a dark light. It was definitely Parker with her freckles, hair piled into a messy bun, and every single one of her nails painted a different color, but seeing Parker in the most unflattering navy-blue polo in the world tucked into plain black pants, black ruddy shoes, and a belt gave me the same level of alarm as a jump scare in horror movies.

"Uniforms don't suit you," I blurted before I could stop myself, despite there being one of Parker's co-workers right there. They were dressed the same, but this girl with a JULIA name tag wore a huge puffy black coat. She had cropped blue hair with a shaved side and more piercings than I thought a person could have. The nose ring alone would make my mother faint.

Parker snorted. "Right?" She raised her arms to show the true horror of the outfit. "I'm dressed like my father. Can you believe they wouldn't even let me put pins on the apron?"

"There's an apron added to this mess?"

"It can always get worse." She chuckled and picked the can up for me. She rubbed her finger over the dent and replaced it with a nicer one off the shelf. I smiled, feeling a bit shy all of a sudden. My cheeks warmed as I accepted the new can.

Julia nudged Parker and it suddenly dawned on her that she needed to make introductions. Parker motioned between us, and I fixed my posture to come off at least a little equal to Parker. I wanted us to make sense as girlfriends, even if we were a lie. "Lizzie, this is my co-worker Julia, and Julia, this is Lizzie."

I waited for her to say more, but a title never came. Julia smiled and waved. "Hey! Nice to meet you."

"Hi," I said, shrinking in size. Suddenly, I was just Lizzie. Camille is her best friend. Emily is her desired ex-girlfriend. Even Julia gets to be a co-worker. I'm nobody.

Parker asked again, "So, what's up? Why are you here?"

The truth would sound something like:

I was worried about you.

You seemed upset earlier, and I wanted to make sure you were all right.

I've come to offer you snacks in exchange for a smile.

Instead, I told Parker, "Camille demanded chips. Are you on break?" I remarked on the bag hanging off her shoulder.

Parker shook her head. "Nah, I don't clock in for like an hour, so I'm loitering. Do you wanna hang out? We could go check out the decorations downtown."

My heart thrilled like a hand raking across the full length of the piano keys. I loved downtown; it let me pretend to be from a place bigger than me.

"I'll see you later," Julia said and shrugged off her jacket, handing it to Parker. "You can have this. If I freeze to death in the dairy cooler, I can get off early."

"You'll be missed," Parker joked back, and my hand itched to go ahead and punch her in the arm. My face must've said it all because she froze halfway through putting the jacket on. "What? What did I do?"

"Is that really how you introduce your girlfriend?" I asked.

"Huh?" Her brows flew up.

"Shouldn't you introduce your girlfriend as your girlfriend?"

Slowly, Parker finished putting on her coat. "I don't know. I've never really thought about it. Does it really matter?"

"We're not just friends, Parker. A girlfriend is more than that. They're special and that should be acknowledged. I mean, when you have a girlfriend, isn't it because you like her more than anyone else? Isn't it because you think she's special?"

Parker blinked and I was caught in her brown eyes, forced to hold my breath as I waited for her reaction. My heart thrummed, wishing she'd say the right thing for the first time in her life. Flushed, Parker's brow narrowed as my words really seemed to affect her. "I don't know."

What were once butterflies shriveled into worms at the pit of my stomach. "So you don't think your girlfriends or boyfriends are ever special? More special than friends? I think that's mean, Parker. I think it would hurt their feelings to hear that."

Parker curled her lips, obviously unsure what to say. She nodded.

"I'll, uh, keep that in mind. Introduce girlfriends as girlfriends, thanks. Let's grab some hot chocolate," she said, and guilt landed in my stomach like a bolder. I'd come to her work to make her feel better. Not worse.

Still, Parker drove us downtown, about ten minutes away, and instead of pulling up to the coffee shop that houses the best iced coffee in the entire world, we walked to a homemade stand covered in a Halloween tablecloth with a sign taped to it: HOT COCOA AND BAD ADVICE.

"Hey, kiddos." Parker greeted two bundled-up little kids at the table. "I thought you guys would be closed by now. Lizzie, this is Crissy and Mitchell. Kids, please be nice. This is my girlfriend, Lizzie."

Almost on command, I stood straighter as if to make a good impression. Parker must've noticed, based on her pinched smile, and I flushed instantly.

These kids sat in front of a plastic table, wrapped in more layers than I had layers of deep-rooted anxiety. They had big adorable brown eyes and little button noses that barely stuck out from their chunky scarves.

"We're always here," Mitchell stated as fact, without an ounce of sarcasm. He came across as a spiritual deity that was merely borrowing this child's body.

"And we're always nice," Crissy added matter-of-factly. She had more confidence in her words than actors reading their lines. I've never been that sure about anything.

Getting it together, and pretending I didn't care what small children thought about me, I asked, "Do we pay for the advice and the hot chocolate separately?"

"The advice comes with the hot chocolate," Crissy explained.

"Two cups, please," Parker requested, handing them a five-dollar bill.

I could only see her eyes, but I could tell Crissy grimaced. She said, "We don't have change."

"Put it on my tab," Parker suggested. The twins looked at each other and through telepathy seemed to come to an agreement that this would be acceptable. Mitchell jotted something down in a *Bluey* spiral notebook as his sister poured the cocoa into Dixie cups and dropped little marshmallows inside.

Mitchell picked his head up and told Parker, "We think you should start screaming at the top of your lungs before every conversation, so you have complete attention."

"Don't encourage her," I begged, and accepted my cup of cocoa. Parker smiled, bumping me with her hip.

Crissy cocked her head, giving me a second glance over. She said with all the confidence in the world, "You should shave your head, paint it blue."

"And cover it in glitter," Mitchell added. "Freshen up your look."

"Well, that is advice." I nodded, conscious of my free-flowing hair. The exact moment my hands were free, I was braiding it all.

"I like your hair," Parker said inside her cup of cocoa. "It's really pretty down."

A fire burned in my belly, and the way Parker looked at me caused a dozen embers to fly through my body. My fire reflected off Parker's eyes, and if we didn't stop staring at each other, I'd be reduced to ash.

Self-consciously, I touched my hair and mumbled, "Thanks. I'm, uh, thinking about cutting it." To avoid giving these kids a show, I started walking again.

"Do it!" Parker said, following me like a little puppy with her damn sparkly eyes. "It's hair! It'll grow back."

We crossed the street side by side. Our reflections from the shop windows kept an even pace. One week ago if you'd told me I'd be here with Parker and we wouldn't be fighting, I might've passed out the way Victorian women loved to dive for lounge chairs.

"My mom would never take me to a salon," I insisted and finally took a drink. The hot chocolate soothed my shivering bones. The chocolate was savory while the marshmallows were light and sweet. Those kids were magical, I knew it.

"I'll cut your hair," Parker suggested, and I sputtered into a belly laugh.

"Oh yeah! Sure!" I gasped. I couldn't even breathe I was laughing so hard. My face hurt. "Parker, like I'd let you anywhere near my head with a sharp object!"

"Hey! I'm handy with a pair of scissors!" Parker insisted.

"The day I let you cut my hair is the day I've totally lost it. You might be talented at cutting fabric but that's not the same as cutting hair."

Parker blinked before her face twisted into something wicked and hungry. She nudged me, leaning in closer as she begged, "Tell me how talented I am, Lizzie. Go on."

"Sure, you're really good at being an ass." I smiled, properly snuffing out her fire.

"Walked into that one," she admitted, but her frown didn't last long.

As she looked down the street, something caught her eye. "Lizzie, come here, I wanna show you something." She tugged at my jacket and I mirrored her smile. Her excitement infected me and made my heart thrum. She jogged down the sidewalk like a little kid, and I fast walked to keep up with her. I wanted to laugh and tell her it would still be there, but she was so cute I didn't want to spoil the moment. Maybe it had been a good idea to come. Her spirits seemed higher than earlier.

I did wonder what had happened, but I didn't dare ask and ruin the mood.

"This is Miss Patty's Salon," Parker said and waved her arm,

showing it off. I peered through the window at the handful of mannequins lounging on a velvet sofa and mismatching armchairs. If we
turned away, I was sure they'd go back to gossiping and chattering
about the people walking by them. Parker gaped. "It changed again."
She cupped her hands over her eyes and spied through the glass. It was
impossible to see anything on the shelves. She started muttering about
how she'd missed the owner again.

I walked to the door and went for the handle but it resisted.
Cocking my head, I tried to find a sign for the store hours but received
only disappointment. "When does it open?" I asked.

Parker slumped, resting her head on the window. "Never. Probably
the moment before I die so I can choke on the irony."

"Okay." I rolled my eyes. "*Dramatic.*"

Peering inside, I struggled to find shapes inside the shadows. There
was an appeal to the mystery that there could be anything lurking
beyond the glass. "Why do you want to go inside?" I asked.

"There's a tiara. It'd be perfect for the show and I honestly can't
get it out of my mind."

I looked over at Parker, at the determination in her eyes and the
weight of the entire show hanging from her brow. She didn't just like
making costumes, she loved it. A strange tight feeling coiled around
my heart like a rattlesnake and I let out a shaky breath. This trial was
going to swallow me up.

"How often does the window change?" I asked.

"Every week."

"What day?"

Parker didn't lift her forehead from the glass when she turned to
look at me. "I don't know." She blinked as if asking that question had
never occurred to her.

"We could come back every day and wait to see which day the

décor changes. Then we could stake it out and wait for Miss Patty to show up."

"Ooo," Parker cooed as her grin grew fiendish. "Nobody's ever asked me out on a stakeout before."

"And I've never asked, consider us both special."

Parker finally lifted herself off the glass. She put her arm around mine, still grinning. This plan ignited life back into Parker's stride as she went through her illustrious history with Miss Patty's Salon on the way back to the grocery store. I parked in front of the doors, letting Parker off.

"Thanks," Parker said, unbuckling her seat belt. The car engine hummed lightly, underneath the sound of the radio and the hiss of my struggling heater. I didn't care about putting on a playlist, not when I wanted to talk more. Not when we were about to separate and I still hadn't asked Parker about her troubles.

"Um," I said as Parker opened her door. She turned back around and I needed to suck in a breath, filling my chest to maximum capacity. If I didn't say something, I knew I was going to go home with Cheetos and regret. Times like this, I was usually worried about speaking my mind, about being honest with my feelings and coming across as stupid, but Parker didn't make it so scary. She had already seen all the ugly sides of me and still wanted to talk to me.

"Parker, you can talk to me, if there's something on your mind. I noticed you were upset earlier, and we can really talk about anything. I won't even talk. I'll just listen."

Parker nodded. She smiled a little and said, "Okay."

"Are you okay?"

"Yeah." She shrugged. "It isn't that big of a deal."

"No, it matters if it mattered to you," I insisted, speaking from experience. Still fresh in my memory, I could hurl thinking of all the times people have told me to get over it or that I'm making something small into a bigger deal. I never wanted anyone to feel that way, not even Parker. "And I'm the expert on being emotional, so you have to listen to me."

That made Parker chuckle, and seeing that smile again made it all worth it. "Yeah, I kind of had a shitty day, but you already made me feel better, Lizzie. So, thanks."

"You're welcome and . . ." I gripped the steering wheel. "You really can come to me."

"I will," Parker told me like a promise, and it'd be one I intended her to keep. She hesitated in her seat with her hand still on the door. She didn't move. She only studied my face. Her eyes flickered from my eyes to my mouth. Shyly, I sucked in my lips, retreating from that small flicker in Parker's eyes.

And yet Parker smiled and said, "I'll see you tomorrow."

"See ya," I said, my voice shakier than intended.

She hopped out of the car and I watched her walk back into work, stuck inside a daze until a car behind me honked their horn. "Oh!" I jumped and put the car in Drive. I waved and apologized even though they wouldn't hear me.

I drove the long way back to my house as my mind wandered and my thoughts traveled anywhere and everywhere. I put on one of my favorite playlists with the longest songs possible for an even longer drive.

Lizzie's "Let's drive around a while and maybe get lost" Playlist.

My car somehow ended up back at my house. I returned to my room to find Camille cuddled up to my old teddy bear as she read one of her mystery novels. She perked up, half dazed and with one foot inside her book world.

She turned her head, looking at my alarm clock. "That took a while for just grabbing 'anything.'"

"Yeah, sorry, I ran into Parker," I said, and started shedding my fall layers.

"Hmm." Camille hummed knowingly, and my face was already hot. "That's not surprising. You did go to her place of work."

"Yeah, turned out she hadn't started her shift yet." My phone buzzed and interrupted me. It was a text from Parker, telling me good night, and I grinned and sent her a good night text back. I told Camille absentmindedly, "Uh, we went downtown, and I met the kids with the bad advice booth."

"It's a hot cocoa booth, the bad advice is a bonus."

"Right, well, then she showed me Miss Patty's."

"Really?" Camille sat up in bed. "She let you see that much crazy?"

"I don't think she's crazy." I looked up, protectiveness flaring up inside of me. "She's excited. I mean, she has a vision for what she wants the costumes to be, and she needs that tiara."

"I didn't mean anything bad." Her eyes dropped to the phone in my hand, me in the middle of texting Parker back. "You guys are getting along and that feels weird to me. You're actually acting like a real couple."

"Isn't that what you wanted?"

"I said I didn't mean anything bad by it," Camille snapped, her voice raised louder than usual, and we both froze. The tension in the room rose. If we continued, this was going to end in a fight. I knew how to fight Parker. I knew how to fight my siblings. But I wouldn't know what to do if Camille was ever mad at me.

"Well, anyway." I quickly jumped topics. "What do you think about me with short hair?"

Camille laughed and the tension eased in the air, even if the anxiety tumbled around my chest like loose coins in a dryer. Camille and I debated how bad the punishment from my mother would be versus how cute a bob haircut could look on me.

Camille posed a good question: "But do you want to change your hair because you want short hair or because you want to change?"

"I want short hair," I answered matter-of-factly, but immediately got the feeling it was really the other way around. I didn't admit that to Camille. Even before the trial everyone had acted like they already knew what I was going to say or do, as if I was so predictable.

I kept my thoughts secret as Camille and I watched a dozen videos of girls cutting their hair at home and watched enough fails to make me second-guess this plan. Still, I sent one video to Parker, and she sent back:

> **Parker:** I'm so proud of you. Did you figure out how to share a link all on your own?
>
> **Lizzie:** Fuck you

In the corner of my eye, I caught Camille looking at me. "What?" I asked, realizing I was grinning my face off.

"Nothing," Camille mumbled and looked back at the video.

SIXTEEN

OCTOBER 3

Parker

I yawned as I walked up to Lizzie's locker in the morning and found she was halfway inside it. Her braid dangled down the middle of her back. When she finished putting her stuff away, she slammed her locker and turned around with two iced coffees in her beautiful hands. I went all bug eyed and stupid.

"Is that—" I blinked. "Is one for me?"

"Yeah," she said, like it was nothing, like she wasn't gifting me with the nectar of the gods. That gesture alone almost brought me to my knees to worship her.

"Thank you," I said, clearing my throat and my nerves. "You're my favorite."

"Don't lie to me."

I wasn't.

"*Anyway*, I was downtown this morning—" Lizzie started to explain, as I slipped my hand into hers. She pulled her hand back and away from me like I was trying to give her a rash. Her brow narrowed. "What are you doing?"

"Holding hands," I said, stating the obvious. Glancing down the hallway, I knew this was around the time Emily would be at her locker, and I wanted her to see me holding hands with another girl. The old jealousy trick was lame, but it was effective, and I was past caring about my dignity. "It's for practice. PDA is an easy way to show affection. Isn't that your problem?"

"You're my problem."

A huge sigh rattled out of me as I sat my hands on my hips. Tilting my head, I raised my brow and asked her, "If you don't want to practice holding hands, then what should we do?" The moment the idea hit me, I grinned. Leaning in closer, I kept my voice nice and low and just between us. "Should we practice kissing?"

"You wish." Lizzie grimaced and held out her hand. I took it, holding my head high. Winning felt as good as the rumors promised.

"Anyway, you were saying," I prompted, as I pulled her forward to walk in step with me.

She huffed and adjusted her book bag over her shoulder, changing our hand position from pressing our palms together to intertwining our fingers. "I checked out Miss Patty's shop and it was the same as yesterday. I even asked the baristas at Good Beans if they knew anything about the shop."

"You really asked?" I blinked, waiting for the second head to sprout from Lizzie's neck.

"Yeah." Lizzie's eyes narrowed. "Or were you not serious about figuring this out? Because I'm supercommitted. Seven-dollar coffee committed." She rattled the ice in her cup.

"No, I'm serious!" My face burned, but Lizzie didn't seem to notice or care.

"Anyway, they didn't know much but they once saw the lights on at night. The building has been occupied for like ten years or something, so we should really do some googling later."

"Another date, huh?" I grinned, biting down on my straw. Little butterflies were throwing a rave inside my stomach, dancing to the heavy thud of my heart. "God." I rolled my eyes. "You're so obsessed with me."

"If you think me accidentally visiting you at work was a date," Lizzie said, "then you need more help than I thought." She shrugged, sticking her nose in the air. "But I guess I'll let you have a win. I mean, it's pretty pathetic that you've never even thought to ask the coffee place next door about Miss Patty's. I'd be embarrassed, too, if I were you, *Parker*."

My jaw dropped, stunned by this Patron Saint of Sass.

Lizzie sighed. "My hand is sweaty. I don't like this."

"You'll find anything to complain about," I said.

"You need to be more considerate," Lizzie argued.

I huffed and let her hand go, changing position and sliding my arm around her shoulders. Lizzie tensed, her brows flying up as she waited to feel the wrath of our fellow teens. Some habits die hard, and I couldn't help myself, adjusting my arm around her to bring her closer to me. "Is this what you wanted?" I tilted my head. "If not, kissing is still on the table."

Getting elbowed by Lizzie was absolutely worth it.

"Hey," Camille said, appearing next to us in a strappy black jumpsuit. I dropped my arm off Lizzie's shoulders. Camille's thick black brows scrunched together as if our two coffees were actually venomous snakes.

"You didn't get me one," Camille pointed out, staring at the coffee in my hand. Not an accusation and yet there was still something there, like a tiny splinter inside my palm that I could scratch at but couldn't quite find.

"Sorry," Lizzie said. "I couldn't remember your order and I was in a rush. Are you mad? You can have the rest of mine." She offered her half-slurped latte.

"I'm not mad," Camille said, like she was tired of saying it. She focused on me, tension clinging to her shoulders the way ice clung to my dad's car windshield in the morning. "Mrs. Donnelly wants to see us in the auditorium before class starts."

"Okay," I said. "I'll meet you there."

"Hm." Camille glanced at Lizzie and me as a unit, and then turned, muttering something in Spanish that made Lizzie roll her eyes.

I waited for her to be out of earshot before I reached for Lizzie's arm and asked, "Is everything okay? You two aren't fighting are you?"

"No," Lizzie said a little too quick, a little too loud. "No. We don't fight."

"Okay." I nodded, despite the fact no one got that defensive over nothing. For once in my life, I wasn't going to argue.

Like that, we separated, and I headed to the auditorium. The stage looked different every time I entered the theater. It had started out as a wide place for dust to land, but now there was a cottage, a corner of Cinderella's own little world. I walked the dimly lit path to find Camille planted between two girls already, Kara Harris, who played one of the stepsisters, and Norah Brady. Norah Brady sitting in *my* seat.

I couldn't stop the scowl forming around my face.

Camille smiled with a squeamish little shrug. "Sorry. It filled up fast. We can go to the back if you want?"

Norah sat up, without acknowledging my existence. "Wait. Stay here. I wanted to talk to you about going to the bookstore later." Camille had Norah's complete attention, and I could see Camille being hypnotized by it.

"It's fine," I grumbled, and sat behind her, unnerved by the idea of Camille making plans with Norah, by the thought they'd already talked about it and I had no idea. Thankfully, Ian showed up and saved me from my spiral.

He grumbled and pushed his glasses up like a headband, to make room to rub his eyes. "Didn't they do a study about how our brains can't function before nine or something? Why can't educators listen to studies? They want us to trust the educated, but they don't even do it."

"My brain can't even handle what you just said," I told him, and handed him my iced coffee. He sucked it down faster than a baby did a bottle. Camille twisted around, eyeing me with an amused look. Good. She hadn't forgotten about me. Norah's light hadn't overshadowed my presence.

"What do you think this is about?" Jordan Thompson, our Prince Topher asked from the front row. Jordan had all the qualities of the boy next door with his soft brunet curls, big brown eyes, dimples, and even that squared jaw thing. There was one glaring problem about him: he was squinting so hard at us that his eyes disappeared in the wrinkles, and he still wasn't looking directly at us.

"You need glasses, Thompson," I yelled.

"Olivia, I told you I don't need glasses—"

"You're talking to Parker! If you don't need glasses, I will eat Ian's glasses! Ian's sitting next to me, if you can't tell."

"Oh, that—" His frown deepened like he couldn't tell it was me. "That doesn't prove anything."

I threw my hands up in defeat.

"You're killin' it, Thompson!" Ian called, as an agent of chaos.

Mrs. Donnelly saved Jordan as she appeared from stage left. She walked to the edge of the stage, the fabric of her caftan wafting behind her like the tail of a ghost. Pushing her large, square glasses up, she projected her voice and said, "Good morning, everyone."

A low rumble of hellos replied.

"Okay." She chuckled. "A sleepy morning to everyone. Well, this will surely wake you up. If you haven't already heard, Caroline will not be joining us for the rest of the production."

I sat up straight. Caroline was the other stepsister, Charlotte. A huge role.

"What happened?" I straightened my arm out and dropped it.

"Does it matter?" Norah asked. "Maybe it's not our business."

"No, no." I raised my hand again. "I want to know."

Mrs. Donnelly raised her hands. "All I can say is that Caroline wanted you all to know that when a sign tells you not to pet a giraffe, don't do it."

I raised my hand again to ask more but Mrs. Donnelly ignored me and went on with her announcement. "So, obviously this means we need to make some changes. Camille, if you're up to the challenge, how would you feel about taking on the role?"

"Really?" Camille asked breathlessly. I snuck my hands through the cracks between the seats and squeezed her shoulders. This would be her first title role. She'd have her own solo.

"You'd save the production." Mrs. Donnelly smiled. "And you deserve it, my girl."

"I'll do it!"

Everyone applauded and high-fived the closest people around. Norah leaned in and said something that made Camille laugh and hug her.

Oh.

I never realized they were that close. Seeing it in person was a worse wake-up call than a splash of ice water to the face.

I reached for her, ready to congratulate her, too, but she grabbed Norah's arms and jumped up and down. My chest tightened, shrinking to the point of collapse. It was weird, being forced to wait for my turn with my best friend. I had used so much energy worrying that Camille would drop me for Emily that I never considered someone else coming along to take her away. Norah wasn't someone I could compete with, but someone I'd be compared to, and my odds didn't look good. I could feel my existence fade away, like I was standing in an elevator going down but everyone else was going up.

We wrapped up the meeting and everyone shuffled out of the auditorium, heading to first period. I clung to Camille, despite my class being in the opposite direction.

"Now I get why the thespians suddenly wanted to sit with you." I laughed, annoyed with how shaky I sounded. Everything was fine. I wasn't bothered. I didn't know why my hands were sweaty or my ears were on fire. "They could probably sniff the title role on you. Are they going to let you fraternize with the lowly dressmaker?"

"They're not that bad," Camille insisted. "Norah—"

"Oh, don't get me started on her. I think all that spotlight has fried her brain."

"Hey." Camille raised her voice and the tension in the air went from zero to a hundred. "I'm an actor too. Just like them."

"No, you're not. Trust me, you're never going to be one of them."

Camille's face burned bright red. Her brows narrowed. "Why? Because it's the first time I've ever gotten a big role?"

"No, because your personality isn't totally heinous."

Camille's jaw tightened and she looked away.

"You're gonna kill that solo, Camille."

"Yeah, thanks." She checked her phone, and I spotted a text from Lizzie. A little jealousy flared up in me. Lizzie never texted me first or ever out of the blue. Camille suddenly looked at me and I jumped, ready for a lashing. "Do you still talk to Emily?"

"Huh?" My eyelids fluttered. That was random. "I look at her

Instagram sometimes." I shrugged, not really seeing the big deal. "But that's it. Why? Besides, I'm dating Lizzie right now."

"Right. I'll see you later."

She left me lost at sea. It was like two different conversations were going on and I couldn't translate either of them. I fiddled with my sleeve, going over every second of the morning. Somewhere along the way, I had done something wrong, but I couldn't figure out what. Maybe Lizzie would know.

SEVENTEEN

Lizzie

Out of the blue my brother texted, asking if I was quitting band and saying that he would come home on the weekends more to help me study. It didn't make sense until Mr. Burka pulled me aside to make time to discuss an email my mother had sent. Then all the puzzle pieces fit into place. My mom had told everyone I was quitting orchestra.

Gripping my backpack straps, I closed my eyes and counted my breaths. The buzz of the hall slowly died as the next class was starting. My anxiety wouldn't let me wait until the end of the day to talk to Mr. Burka. It was easy sacrificing my lunch period when I couldn't eat anyway. Fifteen breaths went by before I dared to glance through the classroom door into the band room and saw Mr. Burka at his computer, his glasses halfway down his nose. He looked busy. This was his planning period. I shouldn't bother him.

There was a tremble in my hand as my blood ran thin, and I tried to pass it off with fussing with my hairband, untying it and retying it. I couldn't believe my mom had talked to him. Behind my back. Without my blessing. She had her own life, she didn't have to go around controlling mine. I touched my hair, cooking up a few bad ideas of my own that I wasn't planning on getting her blessing to do.

"There you are." Parker appeared around the corner, joining me in the empty hallway. "Hey, like what's Camille's deal? You'd think she'd be happy that she got cast, but she's snapping at me." She stopped by my side, following my stare into the band room. "What are you doing? The floor's not lava, you can go in."

"I don't want to," I muttered.

"Why? Who's in there? Do I need to rough somebody up?"

I snorted and some of my anxiety flew away the way surprised birds jumped from tree branches. "Sure, if you wanna rough up Mr. Burka, be my guest. Maybe you can knock him on the head so hard he forgets every single embarrassing conversation we've ever shared."

"Whoa, whoa. You're fighting with Mr. Burka?"

Squinting at the teacher, I dropped my braid. "It's not really fighting if only one person has a problem and the other one is oblivious."

"Oh." Parker nodded as if understanding. "Been there." She crossed her arms, dropping her shoulder against the wall to face me. "So?"

"So?"

"So, what's up?"

My stomach twisted, tucking itself into a tiny ball. "My mom thinks I should quit orchestra. I, um . . ." I adjusted my bag, looking down at my shoes as if I had never seen a pair of Converse before. "I sometimes cry on stage, so my mom thinks I don't like it, which isn't true." I shrugged my shoulders up to my burning ears. "I have stage fright. I get so embarrassed when I notice people are staring at me. I think I look stupid and then I start crying, and once I start crying I can't pull myself together."

"You're not stupid, Lizzie," Parker said. "That's all in your head. What you do is cool."

"I guess," I said, not sure if I could ever convince myself of that. "Anyway. My mom emailed Mr. Burka about it but I don't wanna quit. What I really want is another chance to audition for the spring symphony again with ninety-five percent fewer tears."

"Say all that then, you're rehearsed." Parker grinned. She walked behind me, putting her hands around my arms.

"Don't push me," I grumbled, and tried retracting my neck inside my chest like a little turtle before a speeding eighteen-wheeler crushed it.

Parker pushed a little harder. Her breath tickled my ear. "Get in there."

"Don't push me," I said again, losing this battle. My sneakers squeaked as they slid over the linoleum.

"Speak your truth," she said, and gave me one last hard shove and I tripped, stumbling into the band room. Behind me, Parker slammed the door. I jumped, snapping my head around at Parker waving behind the window, where she was out of my reach and safe. For now.

Before I could fight back and tear that door, and her, open, Mr. Burka looked up from his desk. "Lizzie? Is everything okay? Is that—" He pushed his glasses up his nose. "Parker?"

"Uh, yeah," I grumbled and walked a little closer. "She'll be fine after a lobotomy."

"Sorry? What did you say?"

"I said, yeah, everything's fine." I scratched the side of my face, picking at a zit, and slowly approached Mr. Burka's desk. Glancing behind my shoulder, I could see Parker waiting by the door. She threw a thumbs-up and I took a deep, quivering breath.

"So, um." The words tumbled out of my mouth like a box of Legos scattering down some stairs. "Well, I, uh, think it's a misunderstanding. My mom's email, I mean. I'm not quitting band."

"Oh, good." Mr. Burka let out a huge sigh. "That's good. I was worried. You're so talented, Lizzie, I'd hate to see you give up. Sometimes performing is difficult, sometimes life is difficult, but you'll regret the things you don't do more."

I nodded. "I know."

That was always easier said than done.

"I also wanted to ask you something else." I stole a glance at Parker again, feeling the corner of my eyes pool. I took a deep breath and returned her little smile. "I kind of bombed my audition, right?"

Mr. Burka's face softened. "You didn't bomb, but I do wish you'd stayed after. We could've talked."

"I know." My face was breaking records with how hot I was blushing. "I was wondering . . ." It was like the words carved pieces out of my chest, leaving me completely hollow. "Is it possible to get another chance? I really don't want to miss out, and I know I ran, but you know I can sight-read and—"

"Lizzie, Lizzie." Mr. Burka raised his hands. "I wish you'd stayed after. I already filled all the spots for orchestra."

"Oh." I deflated. My voice came out so small. "I understand."

He smiled. "But I could always use someone on the piano. Now,"— he rubbed the scruff around his chin—"I've never had an assistant before for symphony. Have you ever considered trying to conduct?"

I blinked. "Oh, um, I haven't."

"You might like it. I know it's not playing the violin but—"

"No!" I shouted, stopping him before he could talk himself out of it. I half raised my hand. "I'll do it!" This was a second chance and I wasn't going to waste it. I had to remind myself that something new wasn't immediately terrible. It was just new.

"Great. Practice starts after we're done with *Cinderella*."

"Thank you. You won't regret it!"

Before I had the opportunity to screw everything up, I ran back outside and wrapped my arms around Parker, whirling her around the hallway, making my backpack slide off my shoulders. It wasn't an easy task, tossing around the resident giant. "I'm in! I'm in!"

"Of course you are! He'd be crazy not to let you in."

Before I realized it, we stopped moving and Parker was grinning. Ashley Marie Parker. She may have been more than I bargained for. A smile pulled up my cheeks and I said, "This is exciting. I don't know what to do with all these feelings. I've never felt this good after a serious conversation. I feel like I could lift a bus over my head or skydive or . . ." I grinned wider. "Cut my hair. Would you really cut my hair?"

"Are you sure you don't want to skydive?"

"No, seriously. Let's cut my hair. I feel like I'm finally taking control of my life."

Parker laid her hands on my shoulders as if knighting me. "Elizabeth Marie Hernández."

"That's not my middle name."

"Everyone's middle name is Marie until proven otherwise."

"Okay, that's weird, and still not my middle name."

"Lizzie, I would be honored to cut your hair. You tell me the time and the day, and I'll be there with a pair of kitchen scissors," she said, giving an overly confident thumbs-up. Without taking her eyes off me, she walked backward down the hall. Her voice echoed, tinged with excitement.

"How about tomorrow?" I blurted, my chest getting crushed by my own expectations.

"Tomorrow it is. I gotta go." She flashed her pearly white smile at me and I had to look away like her face was the sun. "See you later, okay?"

"Okay." I nodded eagerly, and couldn't look away from Parker's shine. No matter how big or how small, everything Parker did and said, she did like it was the greatest thing in the entire world.

EIGHTEEN

OCTOBER 4

Lizzie

I texted her first.

Lizzie: **Do you want to go to practice together?**

"Trouble in paradise?" Andrea asked when I stalled a little too long at my locker. I kept expecting Parker to pop up and start talking. She usually approached new conversations like a jump scare.

"No." I glared at her and pretended to shift through the horde of papers at the bottom of my locker. "I think I'm getting a taste of my own medicine."

Andrea rolled her eyes and laughed. "Okay, well, do you want to mope more here or do you wanna walk to practice together?"

"Mope." I frowned, dropping all my weight against the lockers.

"Have fun." Andrea sighed, raising her hands in defeat. She left me alone again.

Only my own reflection stared back at me from my phone, not a response, not a single sign of life from Parker. Maybe she'd died. I hadn't seen her all day. I almost messaged Camille, who at least had two afternoon classes with Parker.

But before I could message Camille, my phone dinged.

I jumped, holding the screen up.

Parker: Sorry. Not going to practice. Talk later

Lizzie: What about my haircut?

Parker: We'll do it some other time

My shoulders deflated. All the air was knocked out of my lungs. That cleared that up. She really had no time for me. Parker's mind was on a track with one destination. No stops. Today, it was all about *Cinderella*. My grimace twisted into a scowl, and I chucked my cell phone into my backpack.

"What's the point of teaching me how to text all the time if you're not even gonna text me back?" I grumbled, so angry I could taste it. She gave me so much shit for ignoring her and she couldn't even spare two seconds to reply? And she canceled on me!

I pulled out my phone again.

Hiking my bag up my shoulder, I started drafting a huge paragraph about how being a hypocrite definitely got her dumped and how I wasn't going to stand for it, but changed my mind. Instead, I did one of Camille's old tricks and simply texted:

Lizzie: fine.

One-word responses were regarded as a bad sign, at least that's the impression Camille gave me. Parker was going to need some ice for the burn of that ending punctuation. Camille would be proud. Feeling satisfied with my text move, I continued walking, my nose in my screen, when someone appeared next to me.

"Whoa," I yelped, ramming my shoulder right into someone. I sent a girl stumbling to the side and panicked, grabbing her arm to keep her from totally eating it. "I am so sorry. Oh my gosh, I'm so sorry!"

The last apology lodged in the middle of my throat.

My eyes widened as Emily Kaplan tossed her dark curls out of her face. "It's okay," she said, clutching the expensive-looking camera that dangled around her neck. "No harm. I'm more durable than I look," she joked, and an uncomfortable laugh flew out of my mouth.

Camille never forced us to hang out, so I've never really met Emily before. No one ever talked about how gorgeous she was. Gorgeous wasn't the right word, though. She didn't look like any of the girls from around here. She had big doe-like eyes and a small face, all cheekbones, and sharp lines. She looked like a girl from another time. I noticed something scrawled on her right hand that slipped underneath her sleeve, surrounded by little black doodles. This looked like Parker's kind of girl and my eyes slightly burned.

"Sorry again," I mumbled, tipping my face to the ground. I made a move to dash down the hall, but Emily moved the same way. She laughed.

"Looks like we're going the same way," she said.

"Are you heading to the theater?" I asked, praying she'd say no.

"Yeah, actually."

Damn.

"Are you a part of the play?" she asked, opening her camera. She fiddled with the settings. "I'm taking pictures for the yearbook. God." She rolled her eyes, laughing again. She had a deep voice, surprisingly gritty and a little flat. Even her voice was cool, like she didn't care about being perfectly understood, like an indie pop singer with a folky aesthetic. "I'm Emily."

I knew that.

"Elizabeth." I caught myself, flinching at my own stupidity. "I mean, Lizzie."

"Oh!" Emily spouted. "I do know you! You're Camille's cousin, right?"

"Yeah," I said carefully.

"Then, you must be friends with Parker."

"Actually, we're dating—"

I physically stopped, wishing I could stuff the words back into my mouth. Wide eyed, I met Emily's dumbfounded look. I was the kid who got caught red-handed swiping something from the store. Except in this scenario, Parker was the thing and Emily was the store.

"Huh." Emily blinked. Her demeanor cracked, as if the gears inside her brain malfunctioned. She shook her head, shaking her curls too. "Dating? Like dating, dating?"

"Yeah, unless there's another meaning to dating."

"Sorry. I'm just surprised. I haven't seen you guys together on Instagram or anything."

"No, I'm sorry. I know you two dated." I shut my eyes and fought back against the foot I had firmly shoved into my mouth. "I could've been more delicate."

"How long?"

"Since the first."

"Oh, wow." Her eyes widened. She mumbled the way I chewed through tough meat. "That was fast."

"It all happened really fast."

Emily didn't respond. She took a scrunchie off her wrist and tied her hair out of her face. We began walking again, this time with a third wheel I liked to call my social anxiety. Emily fiddled with her camera settings more, and I looked at the walls like I'd never seen concrete before.

"Is Parker going to be at practice?" she asked.

I straightened. "Um, no, but I'm not sure why. She hasn't texted me much today." The more I said, the more I wished this stupid mouth had a reverse button. Why didn't my brain understand that I didn't have to tell her everything?

That made Emily chuckle. She let out a relieved sigh. "She's probably busy with the costumes, then. Until the play's over, you might want to get used to getting ignored." She gave me a knowing look and walked ahead to slip through the auditorium doors. I caught the edge of a smug little smirk, like she had our relationship all figured out.

"Emily!" I called, not really caring about being nice anymore. "Is that why you two broke up? Because she ignored you?"

Her expression darkened, but her lips twisted into a smile. She looked at me much differently now, with daggers aimed to kill. "Let me warn you, *Lizzie*. I always came second to Parker's work, so don't expect much more. It's best to try again when there's no production going on."

She let the door close behind her, in my face. I tried to get over this feeling of wanting to knock that girl's lights out. She thought she was better than me, but Emily didn't know a single thing about me. I wasn't like her. I wasn't going to let Parker get away with ignoring me.

I pulled out my phone and dialed Parker's number.

It rang until her voice mail came on, so I called again and again and again.

Parker finally answered. "Okay! What? What? Why couldn't you text me? Who calls people anymore? I don't even call to order a pizza."

"I can't believe you're blowing me off after you ignored me all day! Why didn't you text me earlier? Why did I have to get my hopes up?" I shouted, guns blazing. My whole body tingled as my heart thrummed. This was taking all my courage, and I was already exhausted.

"I was busy! I lost track of time working on the costumes."

"You didn't have time to send me a quick reply? Why should I have to hear you're busy from Camille? I'm not asking for your whole day. Just a second. Give me a piece of you, Parker, and I'll be satisfied."

The other end of the line went quiet. I got a little pissed, thinking she hung up on me.

"I'm sorry," she said.

"You're sorry!" I guffawed, still steaming like a teapot, but then I actually listened to what she said. I did a double take at my phone, double-checking I was talking to the right person. That apology came too easy. "You're sorry?"

"Yeah, I shouldn't have canceled on you like that."

"You're the one who made me feel bad about not texting you, remember?"

"Right, again."

"Well." I spoke softer, walking aimlessly in the empty hallway. I reached the white concrete wall and jabbed my Converse against it. "You know, if we we're keeping points, I'd be winning in the girlfriend department."

"It's a bet. Not a contest."

"Why? Because you're losing?"

She laughed and I looked up with a smile. I said, "We're cutting my hair tomorrow at your house, understood? You're not allowed to cancel."

"I won't, okay? I'm sorry."

The double doors opened and a few band guys walked outside. One shoved the other as they let the doors go. Still, the music trickled outside. Norah was singing about a lovely night and a charming prince she definitely didn't meet at a ball that she definitely didn't attend.

"Okay." I looked back at the maroon theater door, imagining Emily there. I was a little relieved Parker hadn't shown up. I don't think I could stand watching them interact. Hopefully, I'd never see the day. Instead of confessing about our little meeting, I told Parker, "Practice is going to be boring without you."

"You mean more peaceful?"

My brow scrunched. "No. I mean, no one there can make me laugh as much as you." She went quiet again, but this time it didn't sit well in my stomach. "Are you okay? Why are you so distracted?"

"I get like this sometimes," she said, which wasn't really an answer. "I'll see you tomorrow at school and then after we can go to my house. Do the finishing touches on your Pinterest board, Lizzie, and say good-bye to those split ends."

"Tomorrow, then."

"Tomorrow."

I hung up the phone and walked into the auditorium. I took my place with the others and spied on Emily all practice.

NINETEEN

OCTOBER 5

Parker

Debbie and my dad didn't know how to deal with the idea of a girlfriend coming over to the house. They went into a tizzy about cleaning and making sure there were snacks and drinks. To be fair, I had never brought Emily over. I had never even had Camille over when anyone else was home. I guess this was a big deal to them.

While I sat on the kitchen counter, Debbie was at the table, scrolling through pizza deals on her laptop, getting insecure and opening more tabs with different takeout options. "Does she have dietary restrictions?" Debbie asked. "What does she eat?"

"Food," I answered.

"Thank you. Very insightful. I was about to order kibble."

"She's not picky," I said, hoping that would be the end of it.

"I want her to have a good time." Debbie's brow furrowed, and she clicked away. At this point, we were going to have Chinese pizza fusion. "I don't get to host often."

"It's fine." I sighed, wishing I could avoid having Debbie fuss over me, but at the same time, I didn't want to squash her good mood. For whatever reason, I could tell Debbie was excited to have Lizzie over. I tried to assure her. "Lizzie's really nice. You won't have to do much."

Debbie glanced at me over the laptop screen. "She's nice?"

"Yeah." I shrugged, opening my phone to avoid her curiosity. To my stepmom, I wanted to remain an unreadable mysterious teen. "She's great."

"She's great?" Debbie smiled wider. "You must really like her."

"I do," I said without thinking, and could have kicked myself for it. This woman. She was good.

Hayden wandered into the kitchen with his Nintendo Switch hanging by his side. In some ways, we did look alike with our stick figure frames, tall height, and freckles. Hayden had ended up with Debbie's brown hair and curls though. They both had thick brows and square jawlines. He came home and threw on some basketball shorts and a huge sweatshirt, seemingly unruffled by my "girlfriend" coming over.

He glanced at me from around the fridge door.

"Shut up," I said.

Hayden's brows narrowed and he shut the door, having secured a bottled water. "What? I didn't say anything."

"It's your face. It's very loud."

"Behave," Debbie said without looking up.

Hayden rolled his eyes and passed my dad on the way out. Dad pushed up his glasses, which outlined the one feature we had in common: a pair of tired eyes. My grandmother used to say we had the eyes of dreamers. He looked at me like he had something to say. Instead, he smiled and walked over to Debbie.

"How many people are we feeding?" he asked, leaning over her chair. Debbie backhanded his chest, still consumed by the many options.

I jumped down from the counter and wandered upstairs to my room, checking out the mostly halfway finished costumes hanging on a rolling rack. Dragging my hands over the fabric, I went through the endless lists of tasks I still needed to do and sew and pin and design and bejewel and embellish and embroider.

On my desk, a few videos on how to cut someone's hair at home were open on my laptop. My stomach tightened. Sometimes I regret making plans with people the second after I've made them. I get lonely and crave human interaction, but then I crave being alone with my work.

Still, I wanted Lizzie here. My stomach twisted, juicing out a hearty cup of guilt. Not even a week into this relationship and I was sure Lizzie already wanted to dump me. We should've put a clause that said if one of us was an unbearable ass the other person could dump the jerk without consequence—a Parker clause. But it wasn't over, and I was relieved.

Funny, when this bet started I didn't think I had anything to lose. I never considered Lizzie could be someone worth keeping around.

A knock on my bedroom door made me jump.

Hayden smirked. "You didn't hear the door, did you? Your girlfriend is getting grilled right now."

Cursing, I flew past, listening to probably the worst conversation I've ever overheard in my life.

Debbie asked, "Where did you two meet?"

Lizzie's soft voice barely made it up to the second floor. I only heard pieces like "I'm Camille's cousin" and "It's kind of hard not to meet her" and then my dad saying:

"Well, we're so glad Parker met you. She's never brought anyone over before, so you must be really special."

Lizzie

As I moved my mouth my heart was busy doing gymnastic stunts. Parker's parents were all smiles and asking the normal parent questions. It hit me that these people knew I was gay. Not many people knew that. My hands tightened around my backpack straps. Not being out increased my awkward meter, and I suddenly forgot how to be myself, which somehow translated into:

What does a lesbian do with her hands?

How does a lesbian make eye contact? Do they?

How does this lesbian make a good impression?

Should I have worn plaid?

I took a deep, needy breath and tried to will Parker into existence. Things weren't going badly, but I wanted her to get here before I said something stupid.

As if on cue Parker skittered into the foyer. "I'm here!" she shouted. "Please stop what you're doing!"

We locked gazes as I stood between her parents. My eyes sparkled, and I felt better already. She smiled when she saw me, and violin covers of love songs blasted in my mind.

I was in trouble.

Smiling wickedly, I turned my attention back to Parker's dad, who had the same brown eyes and poor posture as her. "No, this is great. Talk to me about what Parker was like as a kid, was she any different? At all? I need to know. Pull out the embarrassing baby pictures." I rubbed my hands together, eager to dive in.

The happy atmosphere faded out of the room. Disappointment flickered across Parker's dad's face, but he recovered quickly with a lukewarm smile, kind of like a forgotten mug of coffee.

Parker appeared by my side. "You're out of luck, we don't have any," she said, surprisingly nonchalant. She grabbed my arm, dragging me deeper into the house and up some stairs.

Parker's stepmom called after us. "I'm gonna order the pizza!"

"Get cinnamon bites too!" Parker shouted.

"Try not to get hair everywhere!" Her father warned us with a twinge of amusement.

"Okay!" Parker shouted, and pushed me into what I could guess was her bedroom, where a lo-fi beats playlist was playing.

It was a mess, but a Parker kind of mess, so it looked on purpose, like it was a choice to leave her fabrics and bins open everywhere. She had a moving rack full of *Cinderella* costumes and a mannequin form, currently sporting Camille's showstopping ball gown. Even paint speckled her floor. It was like I'd knocked on Parker's skull and she'd invited me into her brain's chaos.

The most surprising thing was the walls were bare, like she compiled a nest on the ground and forgot about decorating the rest.

Before I realized it, Parker had helped me out of my backpack and had tossed it on the floor. My stomach hadn't settled. I studied Parker's face, trying to figure out how badly I'd crossed the line back there. Not having baby pictures? That sounded strange. I mean, I'm the middle child and my parents still had enough pictures of me to fill my own album.

"Sorry about that," I mumbled anyway, even if Parker's face was a stone fortress. I couldn't move away from the door just in case I was no longer welcome.

"That? Oh." Parker sputtered her lips and shrugged. She moved over to her bed and dropped onto the mattress. She pulled her laptop onto her lap, snapping it shut and cutting off the music. "It's nothing, really."

Still, my brows wouldn't relax. I fussed with my sleeves, eager to ask more and press on. Parker was still a person, and I've watched her smile enough times to know that wasn't a real smile. I couldn't imagine living in my own home without a single picture of me as a kid, or a single picture of me at all. That would bother anyone, but if she didn't want to tell me, I wasn't going to force her to spill her secrets.

"My parents got divorced when I was a kid," Parker said softly, and caressed the smooth front of her pink laptop, distracting herself. "But when I moved here, after all the fighting and the moving and the mess, they'd lost most of my pictures." Parker smiled tightly as she thought about her choice of words. "It was all kind of rushed. A bunch of my own stuff got left behind." She sighed, looking off into the distance, as if she could see her old room in New York. "I've got the best sewing machine back home."

So she still referred to New York as home? A pang of jealousy punched me in the stomach.

"Why did you move here?" I asked, realizing I didn't know.

Shifting uncomfortably on her bed, she tried to explain, her voice soft and fragile, like brittle flower petals. "Well, last year in New York I fibbed about my age and got a job at a theater, and I stopped showing up to school. My grades plummeted and I couldn't really catch up. It's not my mom's fault. She didn't realize what was going on and . . ." She licked her lips. "Eventually my dad couldn't get a hold of me or my mom, so he called our housekeeper. She told him what was going on and he flew to New York and raised hell. He really blew everything out of proportion. I could've gone to summer school or something."

"So he brought you here," I inferred. I imagined her dad, the man downstairs, freaking out, being so scared for Parker's safety that he'd travel to New York for her to come home with him. They didn't seem close, but he really loved his daughter, I could tell.

Parker nodded, trying to comfort me with a soft smile, as if I was the one who needed it. I tore myself from my spot, no longer collecting dust. I approached Parker with caution and took the laptop out of her hands and placed it on her pile of scraps. Joining her on the bed, I slipped my fingers through her hand. Her brow twitched. One stone fell from her wall, and she laid her head on my shoulder, dragging her thumb up and down my knuckles. Her hair smelled like honey.

"Do you and your mom still talk?" I asked, because now that I'd had a glimpse inside the pages of Parker's history, I wanted to stay up all night, past my bedtime, and read her story from cover to cover.

Parker nodded against my shoulder. "Yeah. Not a lot, but I invited her to the musical, so hopefully she'll be able to come."

If I still hated Parker, the hope in her voice would have melted my icy heart.

"I'm sorry," I said because there wasn't anything I could do to change her past, and I couldn't go back in time and be the person who cared about her, who noticed her in New York.

"Don't be. I'm fine," she insisted, glancing at my face. She sighed, glumly smiling back at me. I wasn't exactly an expert at hiding my emotions.

"Yeah, you say that a lot but I'm still sorry. New York sounds lonely." I stared into her eyes and traded her hand for a hug. She chuckled, holding me back, and I existed snugly inside her arms. I closed my eyes, my lungs filling with the smell of her shea butter lotion, and it drove my heart crazy. It hit me all at once that I was in the arms of a beautiful girl, and I was sitting on that girl's bed. People went insane for less.

She leaned side to side, forcing me along with her, and a laugh tumbled out of my mouth. She squeezed me before breaking away and jumping up. Nabbing her laptop, she motioned me. "Come on. Let's go chop that hair off."

"Oh," I mumbled, shuddering a little. "I almost forgot." I met her at the doorway, looking up at her and wondering why she'd stopped. I swallowed, my eyes flickering to her lips and back up to her questioning eyes. That sultry look posed a question to me, asking for permission to act on our impulses. The moment was right. The feelings were there. If I let her, Parker would probably kiss me. But in the moment I never knew how to respond, not when I could be wrong about her feelings for me. I hated being wrong.

Parker smiled a little, a real one this time. She rested her hand on my shoulder, which was still warm from her forehead snuggled against my neck. All my baby hair stood on edge, waiting for whatever was going to happen next. Parker leaned in closer, and I held my breath, stiffening straight, like a stick. I shut my eyes, totally ready for whatever. Parker pressed her lips to my cheek and whispered, "Thanks. The bathroom is this way."

Popping my eyes open, I watched Parker strut down the hallway, her ginger hair waving back and forth. She might as well have covered me in gasoline and thrown a lit match at my feet. It was more than a heat flash; it was a fiery car crash, and I was trapped underneath five eighteen-wheelers. My knees gave out and my back hit the threshold.

Dropping my face into my hands, I wrapped my mind around kissing Parker's pink lips. God, her lips looked so soft. I really wanted to kiss Parker, and I didn't know how to tell her that without risking looking like a total idiot. This wasn't real, not in a way that mattered. I covered my screams of agony inside my hands, quiet enough that Parker couldn't hear me freak out.

"Yeah," someone said.

I looked up at a preteen guy who kind of looked like Parker. He moved the flop of curls out of his eyes and said, "Parker gives me stomach cramps too."

I sighed.

TWENTY

Parker

"Ah!" Lizzie released a rattling yell as I doused her head with bath water. "I'm drowning! I'm definitely drowning!"

"Drowning people can't talk," I informed her as I moved my laptop a little farther down the counter and away from the tub. Streaming the *Hamilton* soundtrack was the perfect way to avoid brief spouts of awkward silence, since every theater kid knew the words.

Somehow, we'd already soaked the dark-blue bath mats. She shook her head back and forth as she leaned underneath the faucet. Debbie had permitted us to use the big master bathroom, which had a double sink and enough legroom to bring in a kitchen chair.

Peering at her, I said, "Maybe I should have given you a towel first."

Lizzie yelled again, squeezing her eyes and twisting her face against the power of the water. With a laugh, I reached into the towel cupboard and grabbed one of the older towels Debbie used to dye her hair. I turned the water off and Lizzie gasped, making a series of groaning noises as I tried not to laugh more than necessary. She sounded like a dying cat caught in the rain. I carefully moved her hair and slid the towel around her shoulders.

The lump in my throat swelled.

Somehow I had become more aware of Lizzie than ever before, the way she constantly rolled her shoulders and cracked her back, the way she curled her lips and concentrated on the words she wanted to say next. Her mere presence gave me a ticklish feeling in my stomach as I waited to see what she did next.

When she took my hand in my bedroom, the tears had nearly leaked out. I hadn't talked about leaving New York since I sat in a car for fourteen hours with my dad as he moved me down south. We had tried moving as much of my stuff as we could, but I could list all the things left behind. Including Mom.

I could still feel the shape of Lizzie's warm hands on mine. Her hands were calloused around the edges and worn from playing music. Every curve and edge were like the deckled pages of a conductor's score, and my ears itched to hear more.

Lizzie flipped her head up, lashing me with her mop of wet hair.

"Watch it!" I cried, shaking off the droplets from my arms. Luckily, I was wearing an old T-shirt underneath a huge plaid thermal jacket and my most comfortable pair of leggings. She groaned, her shoulders high and perpetually cringing. Flopping down on the chair, she sighed and moved the rebellious wet strands from her face, spitting some out of her mouth.

"So," I said, slipping a few hairbands around my wrist. "You have thick hair. I think I need to make a couple of ponytails."

I hesitated as I debated how much Lizzie would let me touch her hair or her skin, which was ridiculous since I'd kissed her cheek a few minutes ago.

What was I doing? Was I a chaste maiden from another century? Next thing you know, I was going to call Camille and ask her to chaperone all of our dates and ask Lizzie's father for permission to take her hand in marriage.

I should've planted one on her lips.

Not her cheek, like an idiot.

"Awesome." Lizzie rocked in her chair, hyping herself up as I sectioned her hair into long black pillars with a few elastics wrapped around each bundle. Gripping her thighs, she said, "I'm ready. Let's do this thing."

I peered at her reflection in the mirror, noticing her tight jaw, despite all the big talk. "Before we do this, should we discuss why you want to cut your hair? Are you mad at your mom for talking to Mr. Burka behind your back or do you really want short hair?"

"I need the change," she said, a burst of flames lighting up her eyes. "I want to change. I can't be run by fear anymore. I want to run my own life. Not my mom or Camille or anyone, but me."

"Starting with this haircut?" I took up the scissors and held one of the sections, thinking I should say a few words of respect for the strands we were about to sacrifice.

"Yeah." She nodded and smiled at me through the reflection. "I want short hair so I'll get it. No matter the consequences."

"Here we go," I warned Lizzie, and started chopping.

The scissors made a surprisingly satisfying crunching noise as I sawed through the thick strands. Pieces feathered to the floor and all over my hands. Once I had a handful of Lizzie's cut hair, I met her eyes and we both unleashed an excited scream, as if we were going down the first drop on a roller coaster. We'd never screamed and laughed so loud at the same time before.

"Here." I offered her a clump of her own hair, excited to chop off the next one.

"*Oh my god.*" She held up the bundle, held together only by the elastic. She made a long squealing noise, shaking it around. "I can't believe it! *Oh my god.*"

With a laugh, I leaned over her shoulder and asked, "Should we stop?"

She smacked my hand and rolled her eyes. "Shut up, I hate you. What am I even paying you for?"

"You're not paying me at all."

As I finished laughing long enough to start hacking at the next bundle, Debbie walked into the doorway and froze. Her eyes widened suddenly. That split second was all it took to compose herself. With a sigh, she dropped off our box of pizza and said, "I really hope you got permission." She leaned against the counter and tilted her head. She smiled. "That's a good length on you."

"Thank you," we said at the same time.

Lizzie hit me again. "Why are you thanking her? It's my hair."

"It's my handiwork, and stop moving so much."

Debbie helped dole out the pizza and napkins before leaving us again. In between a few bites, I finished my masterpiece.

"There's definitely no going back now," I said and plopped four bundles of black hair into her hands.

Lizzie's jaw dropped as she quietly screamed like there was a broken squeaky toy lodged in her throat. She shook her head from side to side. "This feels crazy!"

It looked slightly crazy in a few places, and it was slightly uneven, but Lizzie looked happier than I'd ever seen her.

"Wait. Don't look. Sit back down," I insisted, and trimmed the uneven ends. She giggled, wiggling in her seat. We started discussing hairstyles that she could try, and we talked about Camille's reaction. We talked about everything and nothing, going back and forth about the play and upcoming movies Lizzie was dying to see. I almost offered to take her when it hit me.

We wouldn't be dating this time next month. The trial would be over. A horrible nausea clouded my mind.

Now that I thought about it, I hadn't spoken to Emily since Lizzie and I started dating, but why? Wasn't Emily the reason I agreed to this trial? She'd vanished from my thoughts.

I smiled through the upset feeling in my stomach and grabbed the blow-dryer. Lizzie closed her eyes. "I want to be surprised by the end result."

"I love that," I agreed, and dried her hair. I took the scissors and trimmed a few more not-quite-even ends. Lizzie's hair was everywhere. It was like glitter, easy to scatter and impossible to clean up completely.

I walked around to stand in front of her. I grabbed the two pieces framing her face. My thumb grazed her soft cheek. Her eyelashes were thick. There was no way she was wearing makeup. It would've melted off from sticking her head under the faucet. She sat there with her eyes closed, begging me to kiss those pouting lips.

Swallowing my nerves, I removed the towel from her shoulders and managed to say, "Okay. You can look."

Lizzie's eyes popped opened, and she squealed.

"I love it! Oh my gosh! I have short hair! It's so cute! It's so short! Oh my gosh!" She jumped up again and ran her fingers through the strands. It wasn't a fancy cut. Her hair hit below her jaw, framing the heart shape of her face. Now her neck looked twice as long.

Nothing had really changed about her, except that smile, and that was what was beautiful.

"Thank you!" She cheered and wrapped her arms around my waist. She swung back and forth. I put my arm around her back, burying myself against her neck. I closed my eyes as I smiled and let her body burn against mine, like two stars colliding. I could've spent all night holding her. The butterflies in my stomach danced at the thought.

We ran to my closet and had a dance party, trying on all my clothes and a few costumes I'd made in the past. I gave her an old color blocked sweater of mine. Then we cleaned the bathroom and rewarded ourselves by going to the kitchen to make cookies. As I was eating cookie dough and getting reprimanded by Lizzie, who swore she had a cousin who'd gotten salmonella poisoning, I realized I needed today. It was the best day I'd had in a while.

TWENTY-ONE

OCTOBER 6

Lizzie

Today was the worst day of my life.

Gina hid in her room while my mother's shouting rattled the house. My dad sat across from me at the kitchen table. He crossed his arms, rubbing his jaw and saying nothing. Occasionally he'd cock his head to one side then the other to examine my face while wearing an expression void of any readable emotion. Antonio Hernández was a fortress.

My mother on the other hand was an overflowing tub of emotions that was quickly filling up the room and would drown us all. She broke out of Spanish to snap at me, "Elizabeth, you're grounded. You're so unbelievably grounded. I can't believe you would do this."

My dad started in on me too. "Why did you do it without our permission?"

I stood my ground, keeping my head up as I refused to cry. "It's my hair," I said.

"That's not a good enough answer."

"You're sneaking around." My mom added fuel to the fire. "You're lying to us. Telling us you're with your cousin when you're not. Instead you're letting some stranger cut your hair in her bathroom. You're never home anymore. I don't know what's going on with you. This isn't like you at all."

I dropped my shoulders, looking up at the ceiling. No one wanted the power to teleport more than me. Curling my lips, I swallowed the need to burst into tears. If I spoke one word, the floodgates would open. I refused to give my mother the satisfaction of being right that I couldn't handle things when they got tough.

"What's done is done," my dad finally said. "I don't know if I like this Parker or her parents for letting you do this. You're definitely not going to their house again."

Turning my cry face into a scowl, I nodded.

They couldn't even spare me one compliment. For the foreseeable future, this was my haircut. The least they could do was say it looked nice. My stomach twisted. My braid, my safety blanket was gone. I didn't know what to do with my hands, and I could no longer shield my face.

"Okay." My Dad nodded, reflecting on the moment. "Go to your room. You're not going anywhere this weekend and leave your cell phone on the counter."

I resisted chucking my phone and sat it down on the counter. Putting my head down, I stormed out of the kitchen in time to catch my mother say, "I can't believe it. I never thought Lizzie would act like this. She used to tell me everything. What is going on with her?"

I ran upstairs and slammed the door behind me. I fell back against my bed, bobbing up and down. A trickle of tears slipped out the corner of my eyes but I quickly wiped them up.

Thankfully, my parents were more clueless than me about social media. From my computer, I opened Instagram and messaged Camille first because her mom had the power to cool my mom off. Then I messaged Danny. Finally, after trying and failing to coherently text out the novel-length update about my personal hell, I called Parker through the laptop and immediately turned off the camera.

I figured she wouldn't answer. I did burn a lot of her time yesterday, so she had to be too busy for me. The phone line clicked, and I sat straight up, hearing Parker reply. "Hello? What's up?"

Her voice sounded distant, like I was on speaker and had to compete against something playing on the TV.

"Hey," I said, my voice already tortured and strained. Tears pricked the corners of my eyes, and I took a deep breath. "I know you don't like talking on the phone but typing it up was so frustrating and I'm—" My voice broke, and I sucked in my lips and shut my eyes, keeping the ferocious emotions at bay. My face burned. The ache in my chest reduced me to a little girl who'd only scraped her knee. Sticks and stones broke bones, but words hurt me the worst.

I sobbed through the needle-sized hole in my throat. "I'm sorry."

"Hey, hey." Her voice only weakened my resolve. I wished she was here so I could have a soft place to land when I crumbled. "What's wrong? What happened?"

"I'm sorry," I said again, unable to stop myself from crying my eyes out. My tears dribbled down my cheeks, making my face sticky and hot. "This must sound so ugly."

"Now, you stop that." Parker's voice lowered. "There's no way you could ever be ugly, Lizzie. You let it out. If you need to cry, cry."

I chuckled a little. "I thought you hated it when I whined."

"Did I say that? No way, whoever said that was an asshole."

I laughed again, but the tears didn't stop. I sniffled and pulled one of my pillows to my chest. Backing against my headboard, I tried not to speak too loudly, so my mother wouldn't hear me. "My mom flipped on me about my hair. I mean, I knew she would but . . ."

I expected Parker to interrupt me with some snide remark, but she didn't.

"They act like I'm a total monster now, like I've ruined my looks. If they can't even handle a hair change, how are they going to handle—" The words caught in my throat. I really didn't want to imagine telling them I only liked girls.

"Don't go down that path," Parker warned me.

"I'm such an idiot."

"You're not an idiot, Lizzie. They probably have no idea what cutting your hair meant to you, but I do, and you should still feel proud of yourself."

I swiped at my tears.

"You look good by the way, that's not something you have to worry about," Parker said, and I was so happy she wasn't here with me so she couldn't see my dumb cheese-ball smile.

"I don't want to talk about me anymore," I said, and crawled underneath my blankets. I kicked my shoes off, letting them tumble to the floor. Snuggling inside my nest of comforters, pillows, and plushies, I asked Parker, "Tell me what you're doing. Are you working on costumes?"

Parker didn't speak at first. She could be debating if we really did need to pin this conversation for later versus her inherit need to gush about her projects. "Well," she began, and I lost myself in her voice. I closed my eyes as if I was floating in the pool on my back and was slowly drifting to the bottom, like in one of those sensory deficient chambers.

Suddenly there was a knock on the door, and I slammed my laptop shut, shoving it underneath my covers. Gina poked her head inside, letting all the tension outside leak into my room. "Hey," she said in the softest voice I had ever heard.

"Hey," I said, all hoarse and pathetic.

Gina shuffled inside like there were trip panels that would set off land mines. "I wanted to check on you. I mean, I know this is the first time you've ever gotten in trouble."

"I've gotten in trouble before!" I insisted, a little irritated that her approach was to remind me how much of a loser I am.

"No, I mean like actually in trouble." With a sigh, Gina waltzed over to my bed and joined me. She grabbed a squishy pillow and gathered her legs up. "Not just a bad grade on a test, forgetting to do the dishes kind of trouble. I mean, like real trouble. Remember when Mom caught me stealing change out of her purse?"

I nodded.

"Or when I got caught sneaking out to go to my friend's birthday party?"

It suddenly dawned on me that my fifteen-year-old sister had lived more of a life than I had, which somehow made me feel even worse. "Where are you going with this?"

"Mom and Dad are dramatic." She rolled her eyes at them and not me for a change. She pulled the pillow to her chest, making herself comfortable. "I guarantee you that they're more bark than bite. We'll put on one of Mom's favorite movies. Have a girl's night, and all will be forgiven. Works every time."

"Okay, thanks." I nodded. It was good to hear, though my stomach still hadn't settled. I didn't know what to say and Gina didn't draw out the conversation either. She patted my leg and left. Once she disappeared, I opened my laptop back up to a new notification from Danny.

Danny: Your haircut is sick. Maybe even contagious. Should Gina and I get bobs in solidarity?

A surprised laugh flew out of me. Looking at his words, I shook my head. Both of my siblings had said what I needed to hear most.

One day I was going to know exactly what to say too. My words were going to come out poignant and clear and whoever was listening was going to listen in awe. That future Lizzie was going to be much cooler than this one. More honest than this one. Braver. I couldn't wait to meet her.

TWENTY-TWO

OCTOBER 8

Parker

Over the weekend I knocked out a couple of ensemble costumes by refurbishing gowns from last year's spring production of *Phantom of the Opera*. I brought my completed work to the theater for cast fittings. Ian helped me tote the supplies from my house to here using his mom's minivan.

I'd spent the entire weekend brainstorming a solution for Lizzie's problem. I couldn't find words to act as an ice pack for the ache. By now, in my typical relationship, I would've ghosted my girlfriend and gone on with my life guilt-free, but this wasn't any girlfriend. This was Lizzie. Lizzie was unlike any girl or boy I had ever dated in the past.

Iced coffee alone wasn't enough to fix things this time.

The trial was meant for this. How could I improve myself the next time I needed to console my girlfriend? Above all, I didn't want Lizzie to be upset with me. I should've been there and taken the blame for Lizzie. I was the one who egged her on. Hell, I was the one who held the pair of scissors. What was wrong with me?

Since moving in with my dad, I hadn't really gotten into trouble over anything. Nothing to the degree of getting grounded. My dad and

I walked on eggshells around each other. Being with my mom was the same. She asked nothing of me, so I couldn't be punished for breaking rules that didn't exist. I guess no one really worried about what I was doing.

"Are Lizzie's parents strict?" I asked Camille during lunch. She sat across from me at our usual table. It was crammed with other students, hundreds of conversations happening at once, and ours was a blip on no one's radar.

Camille's thick black eyeliner–rimmed eyes flicked up at me. "Oh yeah, I could've warned you of that if you'd told me about your little salon day."

"Shit. Did you want to come?" I blinked, my stomach immediately twisting. Sitting up, I softened my voice, hoping it would rub off on Camille. "I'm sorry. I didn't know."

"I texted Lizzie but she didn't reply until way later."

"That sounds like Lizzie." My smile took over. "Don't worry. We're working on it."

"Right." Camille took a deep breath. "Since the trial started, we haven't hung out."

"Well, Lizzie and I only have a month," I said, trying to keep it light. Every fiber, cell, and piece of my soul needed to make Camille laugh. If I could still make Camille laugh, I could smooth everything out. A good laugh equated to total forgiveness. "And we're really starting from the bottom. Honestly, we'd need more time to fix all this." I gestured to myself. "We need like a century. Minimum."

Camille didn't laugh.

"It's fine." She shrugged, obviously a little miffed. "I hung out with—oh!" Camille's entire demeanor switched from a dark and dreary night into a bright, summery day. Her eyes twinkled as she waved her hand like a crazy person. "Hey! Over here!"

She stood up slightly, still motioning to someone. I followed her gaze to see Norah Brady walking through the cafeteria. I tried leaning to the side to find the person behind Norah Camille must be waving at.

Camille turned around and spoke quickly. "Okay, so I know you and Norah haven't gotten along in the past, but she's really cool, and I think you should give her another chance."

"Another chance?" My jaw dropped. My eyes nearly popped out of my head into my mac and cheese. Suddenly, it was like sitting on a raft at the mercy of a violent rapid. If I looked forward, I could see the oncoming edge, where I would fall down a waterfall to my untimely death. "Is she coming to sit with us? She can't sit with us."

Camille rolled her eyes. "Okay, Regina George. Well, I already told her she could, so you better be nice."

"I'm nice—" I said, then I noticed Camille's unimpressed glower. My face went hot. I insisted. "I'll pretend to be nice."

"Great." Camille smiled and stood up. She gushed over Norah when she arrived, pulling her into a big hug like they were old friends. Their energies bounced off each other and got in my eyes. I groaned internally, quickly surveying the cafeteria for a friend and a new spot to sit. Norah eyed me, and I fastened the biggest grin to my face.

"Hey, Parker," she said in that annoying fake nice way.

"Hey," I said.

A lull overcame our table and I grabbed my phone out of awkwardness. I pretended to text, pressing random numbers into my calculator. Norah took the opportunity to talk to Camille. I smiled and nodded along because they always said if you couldn't say anything nice, then don't say anything at all.

The back of my neck burned as my jaw set. Most of the time I didn't know what Norah and Camille were talking about. Then Camille asked Norah about track and I totally spaced out, their words turning into white noise. It was painful to sit there and not matter. This would be Camille's daily life if I'd never come to this school.

I didn't even leave a blemish on her life.

"Oh, Parker!" Hearing my name nearly scared my bones out of place. Norah's focus was totally and completely on me. "You're a busy lady. I saw Lizzie's haircut. It looked awesome. Are you taking clients?"

"Why?" I peered at her and braced myself for the punchline. I said it first before she could smack me in the face with it. "I know you don't think costuming is hard, but it is, and I'm sorry I haven't had time to perfect a new hobby."

"What?" Norah blinked. She eyed Camille awkwardly and shrank away. "No. I thought she looked good."

"Oh. Thanks," I mumbled and picked up my phone again, deciding that if I couldn't look at how awkward this situation was, then it wasn't awkward. That's how life worked, right? If I closed my eyes, then nothing could happen.

"It's a cute thing to do," she kept going, trying to revive this already long dead conversation. "I mean, you guys are pretending to date or whatever, but I still think it's really sweet."

I looked over at Camille, who refused to meet my eyes, but her hands were red.

"You told her?" I finally remembered how to speak.

"Were we keeping it a secret?" Camille said, but she winced, obviously guilty.

"Uh, it kind of defeats the purpose of this thing if everyone thinks it's fake. It's supposed to feel real, Camille." The anger bubbling inside my stomach was real. This conversation or argument or whatever felt real. Too real.

"I won't tell anyone." Norah spoke up, her hands raised in surrender. She seemed worried enough that I could believe her.

"All right," I said, pointing a dangerous finger between Norah's eyes. I warned her, "Don't say anything to Lizzie. My girlfriend will implode if you tell her you know. She wouldn't recover."

Norah's anxious look melted like icicles disappearing as spring arrived. "You two really are cute, though. Have you thought about"—she studied me, debating if she should ask me this question—"actually dating? For real? After this whole bet is over?"

A part of me never wanted the bet to end. It took the pressure off things, still gave me room to be my total fuckup self and still get to have Lizzie at my side. If it was real, she'd be something I could really lose.

"No way." Camille spoke before I could. "I'm an expert on Parker. She's going to crawl right back to Emily when this is all done. She can't let Emily dislike her."

"Crawling back is a little much." My brows narrowed. "And I don't know what's going to happen."

Emily's face popped into my head, and the guilt bloomed in my stomach. The last time I saw her was at that party where I got her hopes up, dashed those hopes, and ruined her night. I owed Emily an apology. I owed Emily a lot of things.

"Emily was asking about you at practice the other day," Camille said.

"Why?" I asked.

"I don't know." Camille shrugged.

"Hmm."

I knew Emily. She didn't ask questions for no reason. There was always an underlying agenda behind her words.

Noticing the time, I picked up my tray and stood from the table. I dumped all the food I couldn't eat and got in line to add my tray to the stack of dirty plates. Glancing around, I watched Camille and Norah carry on. They picked back up easily. A pang echoed in the corners of my chest. In a crowd of thousands, I was alone.

TWENTY-THREE

Lizzie

A headache knocked into the front of my skull, forcing me to realize my jaw was clenched too tight. I was warped. Coming back to reality, I locked eyes with Andrea. We were back in the auditorium again with the house lights on, sitting in the orchestra pit as we waited for play rehearsal to get started.

Andrea sighed. As the queen of athleisure, she wore a sage-green jogging set and bright-white shoes. "As my incredible mother used to say, if you keep making that face, it's going to stay like that."

"What face am I making?" I squished my cheeks, feeling an army of pimples awaken.

"Like you've killed before and you'll do it again."

I smiled and dropped my hands. "Don't tempt me."

She chuckled a little and I reached back, rubbing my neck. I'd been doing it ever since my mother dragged me to the hair salon for a touch-up and a more symmetrical cut. The lady had brought an electric razor out and shaved my neck. Rubbing the little hairs soothed me and I understood the joys of being a house cat.

That happy little feeling disappeared as I glanced up and saw Emily taking photos on the stage. Her presence made my claws come out. How many pictures did this girl need?

She spent most of her time sucking up to Camille and flirting with Parker. God, Parker laughed at everything she said. She had hearts for eyes and a stupid look on her face. She never looked at me that way.

As Parker turned, I attempted to capture her attention by waving, but Emily tugged at her shirt before Parker could find me.

I closed my hand, bringing it quickly to my chest. Not a great start. But I was new Lizzie. Lizzie with short hair. I even rolled up the bottom of my jeans for more of a "look," like I was going for "something." Was this Lizzie going to put up with Emily openly flirting with her girlfriend? Jury was still out.

Emily's laugh trickled into the orchestra like roaches scurrying from the light. Everything in me screamed to get up and go be a part of the conversation, but my feet felt like cinder blocks. Why was I such a coward?

Then, as if she heard my cry for help, Parker's searching gaze from the stage found me. She smiled.

I smiled back. Everything in me lit up. Taking a deep breath, I shook out my shoulders and slipped past my fellow band geeks. My Converse caught on someone's instrument case and I nearly dove face-first into the sticky floor but luckily, I caught myself on one of the empty orchestra chairs.

"You okay, cousin?" Camille called from stage left, crowded by the ensemble who all looked up from their scripts to watch my impromptu slapstick comedy.

"Yeah!" I yelled back.

"That was a great action shot." Emily chuckled as she waved her camera. Plastering a smile on my face, I pretended I wasn't burning to a crisp and approached the stage. Quickly, Parker stood up and met me the rest of the way, leaving the rest of the girls behind.

Emily made a face like she smelled something rotten. Maybe she finally caught wind of her attitude.

"Hey," Parker said, slightly breathless. "How are you?" Her words stopped, along with her feet. She did a double take at my hair and my new pair of dark jeans. Something wicked sparked behind her eyes and ignited her smile. "Wow, you look awesome. I feel like you're about to tell me about the trendiest coffee shop and about the albums I'm missing out on."

"That was the plan," I said, smiling again. It gave me the strength to speak over my thunderous heartbeat. "I need to grab something from my car. Will you come with me?"

"Of course," Parker said without hesitation.

"Um." Emily spoke up, edged with a gritted annoyance. Hurrying to the edge of the stage, she had her hands on her hips and I swore that her hair stood up like I'd rubbed a balloon hard enough against her head to get a spark. "Parker," she said, "I'm not done with you yet."

Yes, I thought, feeling my jaw clench. *You are.*

Parker waved her hand at Emily dismissively, without a care in the world. "Text me the questions and I'll answer them later." I walked toward the exit and Parker followed me. Two magnetic objects.

I didn't like the idea of the two of them texting again, but based on how red Emily's face got, I think I won this battle. Throwing salt in the wound, I took Parker's hand and led her out of the auditorium. That little stunt gobsmacked the remaining onlookers into silence, letting Parker and me leave in peace.

"It's time for a dating review," I said when we were in the hallway on our way to the student parking lot. I dropped her hand and gave her a look so she knew she was in trouble.

"Oh?" Parker sputtered a little, way too amused. Sometimes I couldn't decide whether I wanted to smack that look on her face off or kiss it. "What's that?"

"Well, this is all about learning how to be better girlfriends, right? We've been dating for a week. It's time for a performance review."

"I love how seriously you take everything," she said casually, trying to dismiss the task at hand. "Let's hear it. What did I do?"

"Guilty conscience?" I raised a brow.

"No, I'm psychic. Sorry you had to find out this way. Don't worry." She held her hands up. "I only use my powers for personal gain."

I laughed.

"Give me your worst, Elizabeth."

"Maybe," I started, and couldn't stop myself from sounding irritated. My annoyance took over like a poltergeist. "When you're dating someone don't openly flirt and talk with someone else. Don't adore your ex-girlfriend in front of your current girlfriend?"

Parker whirled her head back, nearly losing her eyes they popped out so fast. "What? I wasn't—?"

I stopped and crossed my arms, glaring at the ginger giant. Waiting for her blathering to stop, I finally saw the realization flicker across her eyes. She flushed, shrinking like a berated puppy dog. "Em and I aren't like that anymore. She can't stand me."

"Em, huh?"

"*Emily* and I are done. We're overdone. We're burned to a crisp. Honestly, I've been so wrapped up in the trial, I'm focused on you and me," she said casually, despite making my heart flutter. Either she was a master at telling me what I wanted to hear or that sweet smile was sincerely for me. "I'm not sure what Emily and I will be in the future, it's complicated. I'd rather spend time with you and make the most out of these thirty days."

I raised my brow. "But you're going to text her later?"

"Only for her journalism thing," Parker assured me, raising two fingers in a Scout's honor salute. "If she even dares to start some small talk, I will remind her that I have a girlfriend and I'm hoping for a raise in my next performance review, so I can't talk to her anymore."

"Again. I'm not paying you." My brow lowered.

"There's other ways to pay me." She grinned, leaning nice and close, and my tongue nearly flopped out of my mouth. She needed to start warning me before she did that, before she ruined me forever. It was getting hard to breathe.

I forced myself to roll my eyes so she wouldn't figure out that she'd gotten me good this time. I said, "Okay, it's your turn."

"My turn?"

"Yeah, I'm not just going to give you shit and leave it at that. We're in this together. Give me a performance review too."

"Okay." Parker nodded. She crossed her arms and let her eyes wander to the ceiling in mock consideration. "Your texting productivity is up. Flirting with me has been down."

"I like your . . ." My eyes narrowed at her bell-bottoms. ". . . pants."

"Oh wow, we're way back up again." Parker grinned, amused by the whole conversation. "I don't really have anything negative to say." Parker shrugged, and a little pang of guilt took me by surprise. "I think you were cool standing your ground like that. Not a critique but should be said. The Lizzie I knew before the trial would've never been that forward."

"I don't only have negative things to say."

"Do tell." She nudged me.

With that sweet little smile that was becoming my weakness, Parker needed to know she wasn't all bad. I told her as earnestly as possible, "You make me laugh."

Parker smiled and opened her mouth to say something, but I wasn't finished. "Parker, I've never felt this confident in my life and I know it's because I decided to change, but I wouldn't have made it this far without you. You bring out a lot of the good in me that I didn't even know I had."

She looked at me, searching my face for the punchline that was never going to come. I slipped my hand into hers and dragged her a few steps before she remembered we were walking. We strolled quietly. Every now and then, I would lightly bump into her shoulder, and she'd bump into mine.

We took the long way to my van and when we finally got there, I had to make up a reason why it was so important that I had to grab some random notebook from underneath the seat. She didn't question me. She waited, her eyes lingering on the back of my neck and my body as I stretched into the van. My face warmed, feeling her eyes bore into me. It made my nerves swell up inside the middle of my throat. I cooked up a million things to say, to joke about so all this tension could fizzle.

When I finally turned around, after slamming the door shut, all the words disappeared. Parker took a step closer to me and I could feel again the long stringed note slicing through my chest. Parker lightly touched my arm against the fabric of my coat, but it made every single hair on my body stand on edge. There was so much power in her touch.

"You're way too good for me," Parker whispered, her eyes ripping through my soul. "How would you feel about kissing practice now?"

With her other hand she slipped her fingers along my jaw, and I raised my chin automatically, as if following her lead in a dance. She tilted her head, and I tilted mine. My hands stayed firmly clutched around my notebook, as if her eyes had turned me into marble.

She brought her lips to mine and my eyes fluttered closed. I savored the softness of her mouth and the warmth of her body as she pressed it into mine. It was like stepping inside my home after spending hours outside in the cold. The cool layer over my skin melted and I was a warm, mushy marshmallow softening inside a hot mug of cocoa. Her fingers ran over the back of my head and I thanked all the gods of the world that I cut my hair so she could do *that*.

We kissed.

I kissed Parker.

Whoa.

I dropped the notebook and it clattered to our feet. I touched Parker in all the ways I had always dreamed. I explored the length of her arms, touching those elusive little freckles like a kid who wanted to drag her hand through wind chimes and hear the sweet music they created. I greedily ran my hands through her hair, caressed her back and her soft vintage clothes. I was drunk off the taste of her mouth, a fever breaking out in my head, making me dizzy and hot.

"You're not doing anything important at practice, are you?" Parker grinned between kisses.

"Not in the least," I said and opened the door. I climbed into the backseat, dragging Parker on top of me. I grabbed her neck, pulling her against my lips as if claiming a new foreign territory. Who would have thought this obnoxious mouth was good for something other than arguing with me?

Kissing Parker was like screaming. It was like letting loose every bottled-up emotion and every worry, so it didn't bother me so much anymore.

Was Parker enjoying herself? Have I ever kissed like this before? Who was the better kisser? Me or Emily? I craved Parker's thoughts, desperate to know if she was freaking out as much as me.

Parker

Oh wow.

Oh my god.

Oh my god.

Lizzie

I was jealous of the confident way Parker touched me and how she knew all the little patches of skin that could make my knees weak and my skin tingle. She did this crazy thing of dragging her teeth down my bottom lip. It made the blood in my veins hot. Even the weight of her body pressed against mine awakened a strange new feeling in the bottom of my stomach. My mind was everywhere, partly obsessed by the way Parker's tongue led me in this symphony and partly freaking out that we were kissing at all.

The car echoed with the sounds of our heavy breathing and my needy gasps because I forgot to breathe through my nose. All my thoughts were heightened, every feeling amplified. I've never multi-tasked anything better in my life than while I slobbered all over Parker and freaked out. I pulled back, catching Parker's dreamy expression. With her freckled face flushed and the soft velvet nature of her eyes, she never looked more beautiful. My heart ached. I couldn't help but smile like a huge dork. Relief flooded my veins and my mind slowed down.

She smiled back, laughing to herself, and I joined in. Reaching up, I smoothed her hair around her ear as I basked in Parker's beauty. This look, this moment, I wanted to burn into my memory to keep forever.

TWENTY-FOUR

OCTOBER 9

Parker

Yesterday, I could've spent all day in Lizzie's car. Closing my eyes, I could remember her soft lips. I could recall her calloused fingers connecting the dots of my freckles, forming pictures of flowers and stars. If she wanted to do it, she could use any part of my body as a canvas and paint me to her liking. One afternoon of kissing and I was *weak*. Elizabeth Hernández surprised me more and more every day. It was mind boggling to me that someone could possibly break up with that beautiful creature and survive to tell the tale.

Checking my phone, I noticed that not much time had passed since the last time I checked the clock, which turned out to be two measly minutes ago. Stupid slow passage of time. Stupid me for getting ready an hour early for our date. I've been meandering around the house wearing my tapestry coat with matching maroon bell-bottoms and a fluffy burnt-mustard turtleneck. I was saving my fake snake boots and my long tassel earrings for a special occasion too.

Staring at the front door, I double-checked my messages with my mom. I had filled her in on our kiss and also told her we were going on a date today and that my status of "the one-date wonder" needed to be put to rest.

No reply.

Not yet, anyway.

"She's not going to get here faster if you watch the door," said my dad from some obscure corner in the house.

"I'm not watching the door!" I lied, but loudly, so it sounded more convincing.

"Remember when you were a kid—" he shouted back, which earned us both a curious peek from Debbie, popping her head out of her home office. We locked eyes and she sighed, rolled her eyes with a smile, and closed her door as my dad went on "—you used to look out the window and wait for the mailman to come! He was your first crush! Trevor Wright! Do you remember? You said you liked him because he always had presents!"

"No! I've blocked it out!" But my face did get warm, as I vaguely remembered something about smelling envelopes a lot.

Then there was a knock, and I jumped up, flinging myself at the door. As I opened it, my dad started shouting about a love letter I once wrote to the garbage man, and Lizzie squinted at me as she intently listened to my father's ramblings. She grinned. This was a date. Without being able to help myself, I leaned down and pecked Lizzie's soft lips. She jumped and immediately her face burned with a deep-red blush. I panicked.

"Sorry!" I spouted as a matching blush appeared on my cheeks. We looked like a pair of strawberries hanging off the same bush. "I should have asked. I guess," I admitted, awkwardly rubbing the back of my neck. "I got a little excited—to see you, I mean!"

"No! No!" Lizzie waved her hands. "No, I liked it! I was just surprised."

"Surprised by the attack?" I asked, unable to help myself. "Or surprised by how much you liked it?"

She rolled her eyes, biting down a smile and turned for her car. "Let's go before I change my mind." Watching her walk down my porch, excitement overcame me as I realized she hadn't denied my accusation.

Walking the streets of historic downtown, I held Lizzie's hand. She looked up at me with the biggest grin and the cutest little dimples I've ever seen.

Setting my eyes forward, I took a huge gulp of coffee that was too hot, and possibly burned my taste buds forever, but it was worth it to not look like a major dork on the outside.

Hand in hand, we passed the Bad Advice booth on our way to our restaurant destination. Crissy Jensen waved from across the street and called from underneath her pink muffler, "Lookin' good!"

"Thanks," Lizzie yelled back. "I think I'm done with bad advice for a while!"

"Suit yourself!" Mitchell shouted, but he didn't look up from his phone. I chuckled as I admired Lizzie's haircut again and the peek of her neck between her hair and her collar. My fingers tingled, thinking about reaching out and touching her velvety skin again. If we were going to do any more lessons, I think I'd like to teach Lizzie how to make hickeys with a hands-on technique.

Lizzie shook my arm, nearly jerking it out of the socket, and elbowed me, too, causing a splash of my coffee to fly out, spilling over my fingers. "Whoa!"

"Parker, Parker!" She motioned across the street. "Look at Miss Patty's Salon! It's different from yesterday!"

I was so consumed with staring and drooling all over Lizzie that I'd forgotten all about Miss Patty's Salon. Lizzie was right. For the first time, the three mannequins were dressed in Halloween costumes, one as a wicked witch, one in a skintight skeleton suit, and the other one wore huge angel wings. They held plastic champagne flutes filled with glitter. Mini candy bars, more chunky glitter, and plastic carved pumpkins littered the table.

Letting Lizzie's hand go, I pressed my face into the glass and fogged it up with my coffee breath. The way I looked at Miss Patty's Salon might be the same floating feeling people feel when they're walking up to Cinderella's Castle at Disney World. If I died, if I suddenly keeled over from a lightning strike, behind the gates of pearly heaven would be this salon, but the doors would be open and Miss Patty would be inside.

Or I'll die and come back as a ghost and haunt the fuck out of this place.

I could feel the touch of the tiara on my fingertips. It was so close.

"I'll be right back," Lizzie said, and ran back across the street to the coffee shop. I patiently waited in my despair until she came back. "So the owner of the coffee shop said the window display has been different since Monday, which means Miss Patty has to be changing it every Sunday night."

"Elizabeth," I said, getting serious but also refusing to take my forehead off the glass, still hoping for the spontaneous superpower of walking through walls and making this situation easy to fix. I told Lizzie, more like a threat than a promise, "No more games. We've gotta stop messing around and get serious. We have to come back Sunday before Miss Patty changes the window dressing and stake this place out, even if we have to stay up all night and wait without food or sleep."

"Okay, Parker," Lizzie said, tinged with amusement. She pulled her hair behind her ear and my heart punched a hole through my chest and flew into the sky. This ignited a fire in the pit of my stomach.

"You know," I said, pushing off the glass. At least, if anything, I'd left my mark on this place with my sticky, grubby little hands and greasy face. Crossing my arms, I leaned against the glass, attempting to come across like a cool James Dean type. I lowered my voice, wiggling my eyebrows. "I've never asked anyone out on a stakeout before."

"Aren't I a lucky girl." Lizzie laughed, no longer stifling her amusement. This was the Lizzie I liked, bursting with emotions. Her eyes shone. Maybe because she'd cried earlier. Maybe because my own happy glow hit her eyes like the sun's reflection on the top of the ocean. "How will anyone else compete with that?"

I hoped nobody could.

TWENTY-FIVE

OCTOBER 10

Lizzie

Parker's tarantula-like legs bobbed underneath her kitchen table. Starting in her hands, her head slowly slipped farther and farther down until she laid her cheek on her forearm. Her hair was slumped in defeat, too, tied loosely in a messy bun. She stared at her math homework like it was speaking Spanish, and I stared at her because, well, I've picked up a new hobby of staring at my girlfriend.

I had never realized how often Parker changed expression, how well she could manipulate her eyebrows and quirk her soft pink lips. I didn't want to miss a single second.

Her brother and I locked eyes for a second and I jumped, dropping my attention back to my chemistry homework (even though I wanted to work on a different kind of chemistry). We had settled on doing homework at Parker's house because if Parker came anywhere close to my parents, I worried they would take one look at us and know we've been making out every single day since we first kissed.

"Quit it." I bumped Parker's leg with my foot.

"I'm not doing anything," Parker insisted, and kicked back.

My competitive nature flared up and I retaliated, shoving her knee. That finally perked Parker up, and she burst with a new energy. A devilish glint sparkled in her eyes as she kicked me with her fuzzy, pink-socked foot. I struck back and Parker's knee slammed the top of the table and she unleashed a scream of anguish. She crumbled, sliding off her chair and I couldn't stop laughing long enough to help her live.

Hayden muttered, "I'm not caffeinated enough for this."

He got up from the table and moved away from us, as if being weird was contagious. As I watched him start a pot of coffee, Hayden became my favorite Parker in the family while Ashley Marie rolled across the floor moaning about unfair things from her knee to her homework and the price of *Hamilton* tickets. Jumping up, I walked over to kneel beside my wounded girlfriend.

I patted her head. "There, there."

"Life's so unfair." Parker faked a sniffle.

"I know."

"I found a leather jacket once at Goodwill that was perfect for me, but when I went back for it the next day, it was gone."

"You can't walk away from anything in Goodwill."

My phone buzzed as Parker kept rambling. "I want a leather jacket. I don't want diamonds or flowers. I want a cool leather jacket."

"That's gay," I said.

"It'll become significantly less cool when you wear it," Hayden added.

On my phone, a text from Camille popped up:

Camille: Hey! We haven't hung out lately. What are you guys doing today?

I was texting her when Parker lifted her hand. "What are you doing?"

I lied. "I'm documenting how pathetic you look."

Her arm straightened, striking my hand like lightning, and I dropped my phone. It did such a great somersault that it would've received tens across the board. Parker snatched it with her long mutant arms before I could and dashed out of the room. I screamed, chasing her through the house.

"Sorry, Debbie!" I yelled as we ran by her office.

But while Debbie laughed, Hayden sighed. Loudly.

After lots of running and wrestling, I managed to pin her to the floor by her hands and acted on the first idea that sprang to my head. Parker's usually pink face was extra rosy as she grappled with trying to breathe. The fading adrenaline caused my skin to buzz and I tilted my head as I continued to push back on her hands. Leaning down, I kissed Parker's lips. She jumped, and I liked that her reactions could be cute too.

The tension in our arms relaxed, and Parker stopped fighting me. She loosened her hands so she could wrap them around my neck. I held myself up with one hand while the other tiptoed across the carpet to clutch my fallen cell phone. I whispered against her lips, "I win."

"Huh?" Parker asked, her face contorted into a question mark. She snapped a look over her head as I jumped up, running for the kitchen. I used Hayden as a shield, which he didn't love, but didn't hate enough to stop me either. Eventually, we settled down with our coffees and Parker's dad came home and made us all burgers and potato wedges.

I finally remembered Camille's text, realizing it had been well over an hour since I'd opened it. She had a point. It's been a minute since the group was all together.

I finally replied:

Lizzie: Hey! Sorry!

Lizzie: I got held up. We're busy tonight. What about Friday?

Camille: Well . . .

Camille: If you guys still loved me you'd remember I'm putting together a party on Friday

Lizzie: Right! Of course! I remember now. We'll totally be there 🫶

It wasn't long before Camille texted back:

Camille: You know you guys are becoming that couple who doesn't hang out with their friends

My stomach tightened. I glanced at Parker, wondering if she'd caught the guilty look on my face. She was too busy trying to steal potato slices while her father tried to tell her about his day. I quickly typed a reply.

Lizzie: Oh. Sorry. I didn't realize. It's all so different with Parker. I didn't notice. Sorry

Camille: Yeah okay

Camille: Can I be honest with you?

My gut's intention was to text No.
But instead:

Lizzie: I guess

Camille: I'm worried about you. I know you and I know you get your heart wrapped up into things pretty easily. I don't want to see you get hurt by the end of the trial

Lizzie: I'll be fine

I typed some more, then thought about it more and erased it. I typed something else.

Lizzie: We're just having fun

That wasn't a lie. We were having fun. I didn't really have any friends. Not the kind of close friends you see on TV or in movies, where a group of girls would die for each other. I had Camille, who was my cousin. I had Andrea, but we really didn't hang out outside of school, unless you counted band competitions or football games during marching band. Parker. Parker didn't start off as a friend. She belonged to Camille, but, so far, I've never been close to anyone outside of my family, except for Parker.

At this point, I feel like I could tell Parker about the worst part of myself.

And she'd still like me for me.

I looked up from my phone and told Parker, "Hey! We're going to Camille's house on Friday."

"Sweet," she said, finally kicked out of her father's cooking space. "How come?"

"She's having a scary movie marathon. Do you remember her talking about it?"

"No?" she questioned back, probably wondering if she was supposed to remember.

We sucked.

One more buzz from my phone surprised me.

Camille: Remember it's not real

I glanced up in time to catch Parker looking at me. She smiled and I couldn't help it, I mirrored the happy expression. Every inch of my body tingled, eager to grab her arm, yank her down, and smash another kiss on her lips.

Remember it's not real.

After dinner, Parker walked me to my car, but before I could get in, I blurted, "Can I ask you something?"

"Yeah, of course. What's up?"

"After the trial, after we fix our bad dating habits, what are you going to do? Is there someone you still have your eye on?" Saying it aloud curdled my stomach acids.

Please don't say Emily.

Please don't say Emily.

Please don't say—

"I haven't thought about it." Parker shrugged and her neck disappeared. We both stood under the lamplight on the street, watching our breaths disappear into the chilly air. Her family had spun some cobwebs into their bushes, where plastic purple and orange spiders lived and twinkled. I wondered if after all this I'd still be invited over. "We still have a long way to go."

I forced a tight smile. "You're right. Twenty more days."

"Twenty more days," she agreed.

I got into my car and watched her walk back into her house. The tightness in my chest didn't relax. If she'd asked me the same question, maybe I wouldn't have asked for an extension. Maybe I would have said I wanted to break the trial altogether and see what really dating her could mean. Maybe I would've admitted that my hate had turned to like, which was dangerously turning into something as serious as a heart attack. Maybe this. Maybe that. *Maybe* was becoming my least favorite word.

I drove home in silence.

TWENTY-SIX

OCTOBER 11

Parker

I had to remind myself that Lizzie wasn't at practice today. Her mom had pulled her out of school early for a doctor's appointment, so I was left unattended and girlfriendless.

Ian waved his hand. "Over here, Red."

He sat in the front row with the script as he jotted down his lightening cues and other adjustments. I dropped into the seat beside him to finish hand stitching a few feathers onto headbands.

The play was two weeks away and I had all the ensemble costumes done, but Mrs. Donnelly still wanted to wait for a proper dress rehearsal. Glancing at the stage, our Prince Charming, Jordan, walked right into a fake tree. A handful of the girls screamed as it careened down and slammed against the side of the stage. The fake tree snapped in half, also taking out a few light bulbs outlining the stage.

A few awkward beats went by until Jordan said, "Sorry."

"You need glasses, man!" I shouted.

"No, Taylor, I don't!" Jordan snapped back at me.

"I'm Parker, you dunderhead!"

"Oh." Jordan squinted, trying to catch the difference.

"We can't keep doing this!" I shouted, throwing my hands up in exasperation. Jordan jumped, looking around like he thought I'd actually thrown something.

"Everyone calm down," Mrs. Donnelly said, her words bogged down with the kind of exhaustion that could only be created by a cast of hormonal teenagers in a musical. "Let's clean this up." She could not go on without sighing. "And we'll start back at the top."

In the corner Norah started singing again, which annoyingly sounded as good as Phillipa Soo. Camille and Kara Harris (one of Norah's many thespian lackeys) practiced their lines as stepsisters, but they couldn't look more different. In a pretty pink floral dress, Kara clashed with Camille's long black dress and leather harness.

"Parker, how do I look?"

I jumped, ripped from my daze, and saw Emily with her curls managed into a bun. Only a few curls escaped to frame her face. My face burst into flames and I was suddenly aware of every hair out of place and every wrinkle on my person. This was too soon. I wasn't ready to face her again.

"Hey, Emily," I said, like a loser. I cleared my throat and held my hands behind my back, hiding my nervousness. "How are you? It's been a hot minute."

She shrugged a little, her eyes studying me. I wasn't sure what I needed to hide, but something about the smirk on her lips told me she had already found what she was looking for. "I'm doing good," she said, calmer than I ever would to an ex who'd ruined a party for me. "Thanks." Nudging me, she laughed a little. "Well? You didn't answer me. How do I look?"

She did a little twirl, showing off her matching set of gray sweatpants with black stripes down the sides and a sweatshirt, and I had to pull myself together again.

"On top," I started, testing the waters between us to make sure it wasn't too hot or too cold, "you look like a village wench, but on the bottom you look like you're ready to Netflix and chill, but actually watch movies."

"You nailed it," Emily said with a twinkling smile. "You're too good at that."

"Are you joining the musical?"

She sat beside me and I glanced at the paper in her hand. "No, I came to show my samples for the show's poster and they asked if they could practice on my hair. Donnelly hasn't found enough replacements for the ensemble, so I thought I'd help out."

My brow furrowed at the paper. "A casting call? Two weeks before we go on?"

Emily shrugged. "Apparently, a couple of the girls from the ensemble were undercover cops and don't have to attend school anymore now that they busted the big drug ring led by the science club kids."

"Really?" I blinked.

"No!" Emily burst with laughter. "They got jobs and can't come to practice anymore."

"This place is so lame," I grumbled, and after a few beats of silence, my awkwardness got the better of me. Casually, I asked, "So, uh, are you going to go to Camille's party tomorrow?"

"I got an invite," she said, "but I wasn't sure if we'd be able to share the same space."

"Oh." I nodded, realizing that made sense. A thought rolled around in my head. Lizzie was making actual changes, and it felt like this was my time to do the same. Emily was my freshest wound, and I wanted to feel healed for once.

"Hey, Em," I said, trying to get her attention.

"Hmm?" she hummed, marking up the stuff she wanted to fix on her poster.

"I wanted—" I had to lick my dry lips. "I wanted to say sorry."

Emily froze.

She looked up, her eyes wide, even mystified, as if I'd transformed into a magical creature. Ian slunk out of his seat, evaporating in the tension and mumbling about going to the tech booth.

I continued before I lost my nerve. My courage was already shaky and I could feel my face get embarrassingly hot. "I'm sorry for being such a dick to you when we were dating. I ignored you and I know I was hard to get along with sometimes—well, maybe all the time. I'm sure there were a few instances when you were having problems but I didn't even pay attention well enough to notice, so I'm sorry."

"You've never apologized to me before."

"Yeah." I rubbed my neck. "My bad. Should we say all's forgiven then?" I winced, guiltily raising my hands in a shrug.

"Yeah." Her smile fell. "You're different, you know?"

"Am I?"

"Yeah, you're sweeter."

Those two little words alone could soften all my edges. "Oh, thanks."

She stood up in front of me. Determination burned behind her big brown eyes. "You know, I think we can handle being in the same room. Let's hang out. You owe me a fun party, right?"

"Huh? What? Wait—" I reached for her legs but toppled over, my fingers missing the fabric of her sweats. My knees hit the floor and I wobbled to get back up, flinging myself on the stage and waving my hands until Camille noticed me. Her attention didn't last as Emily appeared in front of her. They chatted for a while, laughing and catching up like the old friends they were. Leaning around Emily, Camille flashed me a smile and a thumbs-up.

I dropped my head on the gritty floor. This was bad. I wasn't ready to rekindle the old flame. Not when I was still learning from Lizzie. Not when I'd promised her a month.

Lizzie was going to kill me.

TWENTY-SEVEN

OCTOBER 12

Lizzie

As I rolled up to Parker's house late Friday afternoon, she walked outside. A light fluttering sensation made my body weightless. My posture perfected as all the ache in my muscles melted away like a fallen dollop of ice cream hitting the hot summer pavement. We were perfectly in sync. She knew how long it took me to drive to her house from mine. Catching my eye, she grinned proudly at her cute accomplishment.

Her ginger mane was braided around her head into a crown, and her black sweatshirt read this witch didn't burn. She'd paired it with black and white grid pants. Meanwhile, I wore my usual wardrobe, but with the addition of cat ears on a headband. She hurried down the porch and hopped into my car.

"You look cute," I told her, to watch her eyes sparkle.

"So do you," she said, leaning over our armrests. I tilted my head. My heart worked like a magnet to hers, pulling out of my chest the closer she loomed. We kissed, and like every kiss before, I took a deep breath, as if I had never captured a proper breath in my life.

"If we keep kissing in here," Parker muttered, between cherry-flavored lip chap, "your car is going to become my favorite place in the world."

"Is that a bad thing?" I asked.

"It's an *I'm never going to want to leave it* thing."

I hummed, not really seeing the problem, but caught the time on the dashboard, and a little guilt flicked me in the back of the head. After a few final pecks, I leaned away. She moved closer again and I laughed, lifting my fingers as a shield. "We have to go. If we're late Camille is gonna be pissed."

"Fine." Parker sighed, her body deflating. She leaned back in her seat and I put on a playlist with all of the Halloween classics.

Lizzie's "Let's get spooky" Playlist

It didn't take long to get to Camille's house, but I honestly could've stayed and jammed out a little longer. I turned off the car, but when I reached for the door, Parker cursed.

"Shit."

Glancing around, hopefully looking as confused as I felt, I watched all the color leave Parker's face as she looked at her phone, and I supposed it was glaring back. Parker looked at me and cringed, her face getting smaller and smaller the more it scrunched together.

"What?" I asked.

"I gotta warn you and I'm sorry I didn't do it sooner." She raised her hand like all she needed was a bible to be sworn in and then she'd only say the truth and nothing but the truth, so help her. "Emily is here—"

I gasped. I couldn't help it. Being betrayed made me dramatic.

"I know! I know!" Parker shrank, throwing her arms up to avoid my wrath.

A sigh rattled out of my throat. "I don't like being the bigger person."

"Neither do I."

"I'm going to have to play nice."

"Because you're so nice."

I shook my head. It was amazing. Before I started this trial I didn't think I had ever even met Emily, and now I couldn't get her out of my life, no matter how hard I tried. She was the pimple on my chin that refused to die. I finally caught what was on Parker's phone. Emily's Instagram was pulled up and she was posed by a skeleton wearing a top hat. She was making a kissy face to the camera. God, she was so pretty.

"Let's go," I said, and got out of the car. Parker ran ahead of me to open Camille's gate for me. I rolled my eyes as I walked by and headed for the door covered in over a dozen fake bats. I knocked and then finally said what I couldn't shake from my head. "How did she even know about the party?"

"I might have mentioned it at practice. She already had an invite but wasn't gonna go until maybe I encouraged her by accident."

"Parker!" I gasped again. My entire girlfriend review really went in one ear and out the other. Shouldn't have kissed her. Mom always said kissing led to losing brain cells.

"I'm sorry!" She raised her hands again. At least she knew when to surrender. "We started talking and—"

"About what?"

"It's embarrassing." She dropped her arms. I could tell she wasn't lying by the way she wouldn't meet my eyes. She scratched the back of her neck and admitted, so quietly I almost missed it, "I told her I was sorry for being such a dick when we were dating. You've helped me realize that sometimes I'm not as nice as I should be, but I'm trying to be better. You've made me want to be better."

Now I made a face.

"What?"

"I hate that I don't mind it," I grumbled, and crossed my arms. It was difficult to get mad when she was being so sincere. It was my own fault for introducing the concept of apologizing into her vocabulary. A smile broke through my defenses, and I rolled my eyes, shaking my head. I took her hand and said, "I do like you. The you right here."

"Good," she said, and tilted her head, leaning in front of my face, but before she could kiss me, the door swung open. We jumped, and out of panic I dropped her hand. Camille stood on the other side, cheering and jumping.

"You're here!" She threw her arms around us like we were home from the war. She stepped back, threading her arm around Parker's and showing us the way inside as if we hadn't come over a million times before. Though, to be fair, I couldn't remember the exact last time.

A Halloween Spotify playlist took up the television screen, while the house was littered with faux cobwebs, flickering plastic candles, a caldron or two full of a mysterious liquid, skull throw pillows, and bowls and bowls of candy. Glancing at Parker, I started for the stairs. "Hey, Parker, I'll be right back."

"I'll miss you!" she yelled after me.

"You'll live!"

I made a quick pit stop in Camille's parents' room to say hello to my auntie, going through the usual line of dialogue about school. It wasn't long before she mentioned she was sorry to hear from my mom that I wouldn't be returning to music in my senior year and how she missed me around the house.

I only answered in one-word affirmatives: Yeah and Yes.

That was it. I still hadn't told my mom about orchestra, so there was no way my aunt would be the first to hear about it.

A knock on the door saved me and Camille poked her beautiful goth face into the room. Her eyeliner was gloriously thick, and she was in her element. She had her face all painted up to look like a skull, and she was rocking a baggy skeleton onesie. In Spanish, she asked for my safe return. Her mother rolled her eyes but shooed us away so she could get back to watching old episodes of *Law & Order*.

I expected to return to the commotion of the girls, but from the muffled conversation dulled further by the music, I guessed they were all gathered in the kitchen. Landing on the last step, I finally laid eyes on Emily in the living room. She was staring right at me, which distracted me almost more than her gigantic orange jack-o'-lantern sweater.

"Here, quick, take this," Parker said, appearing in front of me with drinks and a plate full of little Halloween goodies. I could still see Emily in the background, and as I accepted my drink, Emily's face hardened. Her brow twisted, turning her angelic appearance into something more monstrous than what was hidden underneath my bed.

"Uh, thanks," I said and gathered the treats wrong, slowly losing a cupcake with a witch hat, until Parker quickly grabbed the edge and waited patiently until I found a better way to hold the plate.

"You got it?" Parker checked my stability.

"Got it," I said as Emily's eyes tore a hole through my skull.

"All right. I'm gonna go back and help Camille in the kitchen a little bit." Parker touched my arm and I didn't even look at Emily, but my face still suffered third-degree burns. Parker asked, "Or do you want me to find a spot in front of the TV with you?"

I rolled my eyes. "I can handle finding a spot."

"Us a spot." She corrected me with a wicked little smile. I nudged her with my foot to get her to go already. Laughing a little, Parker got the message and walked back to the kitchen. I let out a breath, which gave me a little bit of slack in my chest. The relief didn't last long.

I was trying to leave the steps when Emily appeared, bright and shiny again, like a diamond I couldn't tell was fake or not. I jolted back so as to not bulldozer her.

"Lizzie, I've been looking for you," she said, and I held my goodies close, readying myself for the looming battle. Her smile was so sugary sweet that I debated skipping the Halloween candy this year.

"If you're looking for Parker—" I started to say, but she shook her head.

"You and I have a mutual friend." Emily paused a beat. "Kind of." She laughed at her own joke. "Do you remember Jenna? Jenna Miller?"

Nausea formed a tight knot in the back of my throat.

Jenna Miller and I dated a full week before she dumped me. She told me I was boring and she was therefore not interested in me. Curling my lips, I bit down so I wouldn't say anything that would make me regret speaking at all for the rest of my life.

"Sure," I said, pretending not to care.

"Yeah, she started dating this really cool guy like a couple of days after you guys broke up. I saw his promposal the other day. How long has it been since you've seen her?"

"Gosh, off the top of my head? *Long*," I said, wishing she would get to the point already.

"And do you remember Katelyn?" she asked, even though she must have known that I did. She was bringing up my exes for a reason. There were plenty of choice words I wanted to say to convince Emily to get on with her point, but they shriveled and died on my tongue. I hated being put on the spot.

"I remember," I said, and attempted to step off the stairs and around Emily, but she bobbed in front of me, her mood still gooey and sweet.

"Well, she's been dating her girlfriend for months."

"Okay."

Again, I wasn't sure how I was supposed to react to this line of questioning, which was going nowhere but spiraling down the drain. Emily explained, "I find it interesting that the girls you date end up in long happy relationships right after they dump you."

My stomach double knotted.

"So?" I asked, pretending to not understand her line of thought, pretending not to care a whole lot about it.

"I sort of hope I'm the next one Parker sees after you two break up. It's almost been two weeks, right? Time's ticking."

"Get a life, Emily," I huffed and finally shoved her out of the way with my shoulder, acting like a wrecking ball. She might have laughed at me, but my ears were already buzzing like angry bees. My body ached for the door, my car, and a really good mixtape that understood me better than any actual person. I wanted to throw myself on the couch and screech into the cushions.

But I wasn't leaving.

Emily wanted that.

Then it hit me that history was going to repeat itself at the end of the month. I would be the one who got left alone again, abandoned by the side of the road as cars drove by. I was always the last girl standing at the end of the movie. Roll credits. It was a tragedy all along.

TWENTY-EIGHT

Parker

Originally, I was only joking that I'd miss Lizzie, but standing in the kitchen, surrounded by Camille's friends, I craved her company. All these girls were from another planet, speaking a language that didn't register. It hit me that Lizzie might be my best friend, and I wasn't sure what to do with that revelation.

I grabbed a black and orange cupcake and stuffed it into my mouth in one go, and the sugar hit my stomach like a nuclear bomb. I didn't want to think about the future with Lizzie. I wanted to enjoy what we had now.

"Parker! There you are!" someone called, and my whole body cringed the moment I recognized the voice. The way this girl practically sang my name really tipped me off.

Gulping down the rest of the cupcake, I still had to cover my mouth as I turned around. "Norah." Norah appeared in an admittedly adorable skeleton onesie, and I refrained from rolling my eyes. Norah and Camille matched. Then the questions started rolling around my head:

Did they plan this together?

Was this an accident?

When did they become so close?

"You've got some . . ." Norah said, pointing to the side of her own lip.

I used my whole palm to wipe away the rest of the icing. "Thanks. So, uh, you come here often?" I half joked.

"Yeah, all the time," she laughed, but my nerves only grew as I imagined her here all the time. It was obvious, the sudden lack of Camille's art-class friends and the burst of the thespian crowd.

My aggravation pricked my face like hot needles. The situation drove me crazy. It was like being shouted at to think fast but my mind wasn't quick enough and I got a softball to the mouth. Clear thoughts burned to a crisp inside the dumpster fire that inhabited my brain.

"I'm guessing you've picked out a Halloween costume already, right?" Norah asked, standing at my side. She smiled, picking at the spread, pinching small portions of everything. Her plate was a mountain of sugar. "I'm sure yours is going to be amazing, but I might have you beat."

My brow furrowed. "It's not a competition."

"Oh." She blinked. "Uh, yeah, I know. I didn't mean it like that—" She flopped like a fish on the dock that didn't know how to make it back to the water.

"How did you mean it, then?"

"I—not like in any way."

"I'm messing with you," I said, forcing a laugh, not because my joke didn't really exist, but because for once in my life I didn't want to be the stupid person in the conversation. Besides, my smile wasn't any faker than any other time Norah has smiled at me. Two could play this game.

She smiled uneasily and made a sad, puttering laughing sound as Camille finally arrived and announced, "Okay, grab some snacks—" At that, Norah grabbed a drink and ducked through Camille and me on her way to the living room. Her voice softening, Camille's eyes tailed Norah as she disappeared around the corner. "We're gonna start the movie soon."

The remaining girls grabbed their food and drinks, filing out of the kitchen while I debated if Lizzie would be down to share a snack plate with me. Then Camille jabbed her little fists into my side and I convulsed, half tickled, but mostly from the ache.

"Hey! Hey!" I hollered, bobbing and weaving from her wrath.

"I told you to be nice!" she seethed through clenched teeth. Now wasn't a good time to tell her, but there was some black lipstick on her front tooth and I couldn't stop staring at it. God, why was it so hard for me to be normal?

"That was like forever ago," I insisted, recalling my promise.

"It didn't have a time limit, Parker."

"Fine. I just don't get why you're so obsessed with Norah."

"I'm not *obsessed*." Her face flushed. "We're friends. I can have other friends. I think you're afraid of not being the most important person in the room."

My ears started burning. My fists clenched at my side as our once fun little game took a dark turn. "Well, I think you're afraid of not being able to control everything."

"I think you're afraid of having to share."

It wasn't about sharing.

It was about losing her completely, the way people tended to walk out of my life so easily. I was such an easy person to ditch. Unlovable. Unknowable. Gone. Camille would be trading up from me to Norah, like from a broken-down jalopy to the newest smart car.

Venom coated my tongue as I lashed back. "I think you're afraid of being alone."

"Yeah." Camille nodded. Her eyes bore into mine. "Aren't we all, Parker? But what I don't think you realize is sometimes we end up alone because we refuse to let anyone in. It's not easy being friends with someone through a closed door."

We would've stood there forever but Lizzie walked into the kitchen, stopping cold in her tracks when she spotted us. The worry lining her face made my chest tighten. Tonight was supposed to be fun.

"I think you're afraid of really trying to change. I don't think you like change," Camille stated, ripping the last word right from under me. "I'm starting the movie in five."

She left the room, trailing an exasperated sigh. In a wordless explanation, she looked at Lizzie with an eye roll and joined the rest of the party. Lizzie focused on me. "What did you do?"

I frowned. "Why do you assume it's me?"

"Well, did you do something?"

"Maybe."

"*Parker.*"

"Hey!" I threw my hands up in a desperate plea. "You should be on my side no matter what!"

"Uh, no. If you told me you celebrated the complicated plot of *Cats*, I wouldn't be on your side. If you for some reason said coffee was swill, I wouldn't be on your side."

"If any of that were to happen, you have my complete permission to take me out. I've been compromised and must be destroyed."

She laughed but it wasn't like her normal laugh. It was a bit lackluster, like a light bulb I knew was going out. My brow furrowed and I took a step closer, putting my hand on her shoulder. "Everything all right?"

"You're asking me?" she asked with a tight smile. "You're the one fighting with Camille."

That fact toppled on top of me like a pile of bricks. Feeling my face grow hot, I shook my head and tried to bury it six feet under. "No. We're not fighting."

"It looked like fighting to me."

"It's banter."

"Okay, Parker," Lizzie said and rolled her eyes.

She grabbed my hand and dragged me out of the kitchen. Quickly, I stretched my body to nab our food, and let myself be taken away. Plenty of people already crowded the couches (which included Emily, who I guess had made a couple of friends and was too busy chatting away to notice us enter) facing the TV, but there was a small enclave of the thespians on the floor, all tangled up in each other. I met Camille's eyes as she finagled the TV. Her eyes widened and her head bobbed, motioning to Norah and the others, sharing her excitement with them. Not me.

I withheld a sigh.

At this rate, I was going to be completely deflated before the end of the first movie.

"Can I sit here?" I asked Norah, pointing to the spot beside her.

"Uh." Norah short-circuited before she managed to say, "Yeah. Go for it."

"Thanks," I mumbled, and sat down, only to realize my butt was smashed into her hand. "Oh, my bad."

"No, it's fine," she said as she turned, and ended up elbowing me with her pointy arm. "Oh, sorry."

"It's cool," I said and we eventually settled down without saying another word. I could feel the awkwardness work its way through my body like overgrown weeds. Lizzie took the place next to me, piling her uneaten treats onto my plate and double-stacking the paper for maximum hold.

Camille started the marathon with a classic, *Halloween* (the 1978 version). There was a flutter of conversations, low and indistinct with a couple of uncontrolled giggles thrown in from a few of the girls. I glanced at Norah as she was glancing at me, and I had to tightly smile to keep up appearances. She awkwardly smiled back. Our eyes lingered as I desperately tried to come up with conversation, failed, and instead snuggled closer to Lizzie, resting my head on her shoulder. All my nerves fizzled enough for me to breathe easy.

Glancing up at Lizzie, I could see her going to town on some bat cookies, eating them all head first. Her eyes glazed over as the movie consumed her attention. I nudged her as the camera pulled and rose into the sky, giving us a clear shot of Michael Myers's white house and the little glowing pumpkin in the corner. "We should do that before the month's out."

"What? Murder our loved ones?"

"No." I shook my head, but not totally against the idea. "Carve pumpkins. I don't think I did it last year."

"Oh, sure," she agreed, so incredibly casual. "I've never carved one before."

My back straightened. I looked at her like she was the horror movie. "Stop. You're kidding me."

"No." She shrugged. "We never did it growing up. I don't know why. I mean, we went trick or treating, of course, but never that extra stuff."

An idea flashed into my head and my decision locked into an unmovable place. When I made a decision, I stuck with it to the very end, and nothing could change my mind. Without hesitation, I groaned, doubling over and holding my stomach.

TWENTY-NINE

Lizzie

Parker groaned, practically rolling over. Her forehead hit my knee as she tensed up, and I raised my hands in total confusion. I looked around, somehow meeting Norah Brady's eyes first. She blinked and started looking around, too, as if Parker had gone down from a phantasmal punch in the gut and she wanted to find the spectral culprit.

"Parker?" I whispered, leaning closer. She moaned, squirming around, and I softly rested my hand on her back, rubbing small hesitant circles. "You okay?" I asked closer to her face, bending my body in a mock yoga position.

Whispering low enough for only me to hear, Parker told me, *"Play. Along."*

Something in my brain clicked and this time, I spoke a little louder, "Oh no. Is your stomach acting up again?"

"What's that?" Camille jumped up. She carefully maneuvered around the girls. She crouched around me, spying Parker curled up on the floor. "Parker? Are you okay?"

"Um," I started talking, letting the words tumble out as I came up with the excuse. Every word was a little shaky, a little dumb and only a little believable. "Yeah, Parker's stomach has been hurting all day but, uh, she really wanted to come."

"Maybe she needs to use the bathroom?" Norah offered.

Parker groaned louder, growling at Norah from the floor, "I don't have to poop, you perv."

"That's not—" Norah blabbered, her eyes panicking to both avoid looking at Camille and also wishing to convey how much she wasn't trying to comment on Parker's bathroom experience. "Maybe she needs to go home?"

"I'm her ride," I said to Camille.

Camille's shoulders slumped. "Let me find some stomach medicine and then I'll send you off."

"I'm sorry, Camille," Parker grumbled, sounding downright pitiful. If I didn't know any better, I might've believed her act. My hand moved on its own, continuing to rub her back as I forced my brows to scrunch so I could look concerned.

Camille came back with gifts like the world's most underwhelming Santa Claus, handing Parker some Advil and a can of Sprite. She gave me a bottle of water for after and I thanked her, feeling a strange wormy feeling over the fact that I was in charge of taking care of another person. They all looked at me with the expectation that Parker was in my hands, that she was mine.

Quickly, I shoved us out the door because the longer we kept the ruse going, the more time Camille had to see right through it.

"So, what was all that about?" I asked, still half carrying Parker to the car even though we both knew she didn't need it. "You really give the actors a hard time, but that might have been the most dramatic thing I have ever seen."

"Just get in the car," Parker mumbled like a crazy person. It had happened. She'd snapped and she was taking me down with her. Somehow, I always knew it would end like this. Parker grunted, insisting, "Be cool for like the first time in your life."

"I will leave *you* here."

"I'll leave you here."

"That doesn't make sense."

I opened the car door for her and then climbed into the driver's seat. Parker curled herself into a little ball, groaning and moaning and bitching even though no one could hear it. She didn't stretch out until I'd driven at least three houses away, then she popped up so fast I thought I was going to scream my heart out. Swerving out of the lane and back, I smacked Parker across the arm. "You need to check your head! What are we doing?!"

"Forget that party! You and I are going on a pumpkin hunt. We're carving pumpkins tonight." She took out her phone, opening her Maps app. "Are you up for an adventure, Elizabeth Marie Hernández?"

My heart fluttered. She didn't mean to do it because how could she possibly know, but the one thing that I wanted more than anything was to be alone with Parker, free from Emily and the others. I smirked, keeping my eyes on the road. "That's still not my middle name."

"Is that a yes?"

I grinned. "Actually, I have a playlist for this."

"No way." Parker sounded legitimately astounded, and I couldn't believe she doubted me after all this time. I tapped away on my phone, pulling up a playlist I was actually pretty proud of:

Lizzie's "Spontaneous adventure" Playlist

"You're the best," Parker said, assaulting me with her freckles and her dimples and her shiny eyes. "I actually can't stand it."

"I can't stand you either," I mumbled, a smile cracking my face. At some point all this smiling was going to make my face sore. I kind of liked the ache, though, there and in my chest. I allowed Parker to lead the way out of town.

Between singing and dancing, we talked about Halloweens past, about Parker's last Halloween in New York, and I told her all about handing out candies with Camille while my brother Danny tried to scare little kids by jumping out of the bushes.

We talked about big things like dreams and the ideas desperate to escape our heads and become real things in the world. We talked about little things like the best fast food french fry and why I only had one pair of shoes (apparently, my sandals didn't count).

I found myself on the side of town at the Happy Farm's pumpkin patch.

The sky was overcast, and we were quickly reminded that we'd dressed to be inside today, not to be outside and threatened by the crisp breeze. Parker bought me a warm apple cider to make up for it. The cold was worth it, though, to watch Parker hype herself up. She walked backward down the gravel trail that led to the actual patch. The entrance was sparse of people but packed with enough fall décor to make a suburban middle-aged white woman cry out in delight, as well as a small farm-to-table market. I didn't know what the owners had sprayed all over this place, but it smelled like the inside of a Target candle.

Parker talked faster and louder than I think she realized. "There's gonna be like a huge field of little pumpkins and the other side will have hundreds of big ones. Grab whichever one you want, and I'll carry it."

"I can carry my own pumpkin," I said, trying not to look too amused, fearing she might stop this adorable behavior. I liked catching Parker off guard, when she wasn't trying to be the coolest girl in the universe. I liked this dorky Parker.

"All right, but if we get tiny ones I'll carry them. Maybe I should get Hayden one too. He might feel left out. Then we'll take them to my house. Oh shit, maybe we could try and roast the seeds. Or toast them? Which is it?"

"I don't know why you think I have that answer," I said, and sipped my cider. It was equally sweet and spicy. It warmed my entire body and my frozen muscles loosened and melted in gooey puddles. We broke through the tall grass together and I wandered a bit longer on my own, expecting to see the directions to the patch and then I noticed the lone scarecrow in a field wider than I expected. A miniature windmill stood beside a truck with only a couple of pumpkins in the bed. Out of my own awkwardness, I snickered. "You're right," I said, unable to bear it, laughing in Parker's face. "This is like nothing I've ever seen."

"What? How? Where?" Parker seemed to ask the scarecrow as we meandered to the few gourds tossed randomly on the ground. The biggest one reached up to my ankle but was just as skinny. "This can't be right. No way."

Parker took out her phone, her brows furrowed so deep I thought they'd cover her eyes. "We're carving pumpkins tonight. That's not a promise. It's a threat. I'll pay for your gas."

"Wow. My gas? I wish I'd known you were this much of a romantic twelve days ago, I would've been more inclined to date you."

Parker's anger evaporated and she looked up from the screen. Her smile cut right through my chest like an arrow through a bull's-eye. "I said I was going to get you a pumpkin, so I'm going to get you a pumpkin, even if it kills me."

"What a noble death."

"I shall perish as a saint. Chug that cider," Parker instructed as she snatched my hand. Her energy created sparks in the air that nipped at my face. "We've got places to be."

"Good, that scarecrow looks like he's about to wake up," I muttered before slamming the rest of my drink. The second I finished it, Parker yanked my arm and we ran at full force back to the car.

I really couldn't help it. I had to laugh at Parker's misery again.

At our feet at the next farm we visited was a fallen army of pumpkins. Mold covered all the pumpkins that weren't already liquefied into piles of gunk. There were more flies than people, and despite the smell and Parker losing her mind at the sky, yelling *What are the chances!* over and over again and scaring everyone around us, I laughed. Despite it all, I laughed. My cheeks burned, begging for some relief.

I bent over and did everything to keep standing. I wanted to collapse but my cushion would've been a rotted pumpkin carcass.

"I'm gonna pee," I whined.

"Another one," Parker snapped. She grabbed me and we were running again. Well, she dragged me. I was hardly capable of standing, let alone running.

"Third time's the charm, right?" I asked, looking up at the closed sign. It was in the middle of the metal chain that closed the entrance off. My van's low beams cast the entrance in a golden light now that the sun was retreating to the earth.

"I'm gonna sneak in," Parker said, already lifting one of her long flamingo legs over the chain.

"You are not!" I gasped and dragged her back to the car.

THIRTY

Parker

"At least we tried," Lizzie said with a measly shrug, like she was giving out participation trophies. But I wanted the grand prize, the real prize: an actual fucking pumpkin.

"It's not over yet. There's one place that never closes. It might be a cursed place, but we're out of options and I kind of want a bucket of cheese balls."

"Whoa. What is it, my birthday? What are we waiting for? Let's go."

We went to Walmart.

Our basket held three healthy pumpkins, a bucket of cheese balls, two packages of sour straws, a frozen pepperoni pizza, and apple cider mix. We suffered in a line of a thousand people underneath the unforgiving fluorescent light.

I caught Lizzie eyeing me. She nudged me. "Why the long face?"

Slapping my cheeks, I tried to snap out of it, but there was still a tight coil in my chest. "Sorry, it just sucks. I really wanted you to see a real pumpkin patch. I mean, it's really about the pumpkin carving, but still . . ."

"We can try again later."

"I know, but are you having fun?" I asked, realizing how big a concern that was to me. I really didn't want her to be annoyed with me. I really, really didn't want her to be disappointed in me either.

Lizzie smiled. "I'm having fun."

I let out a breath and my smile arrived on its own, outside of my control. Lizzie could comfort me with so few words because I knew from the bottom of my heart that she was telling the absolute truth. Lizzie would never bullshit me to get me to shut up or to trick me. If Lizzie said she was having fun, I knew she meant it.

"Let's check out quickly," I told Lizzie. "I wanna hop back into the make-out wagon."

Color trickled across Lizzie's face and she rolled her eyes, but she was smiling her best smile.

Lizzie

"I can help you," I offered, standing at the door in Parker's kitchen as Parker spread old, broken-down cardboard boxes across the linoleum. Fully on her hands and knees, Parker was setting up the pumpkins, the tools, and the snacks on the floor.

"No, no," Parker insisted. "We're setting you up for greatness. We're gonna bounce back from the pumpkin patch fiasco."

"Don't apologize. So far, it's my favorite part," I said, unable to help but smile. I couldn't get over it. Excitement was bursting out of me like I was an overshaken soda can. Parker was putting in so much effort for me and there wasn't anyone around to see it. This was only for my benefit.

"I'm happy I can keep your expectations low," Parker said. She sat back, leaning on her hands with her long legs spilled across the floor. She was being so cute it made my stomach hurt.

"Hey!" She suddenly shouted and I jumped, looking around to see who she was yelling at. "Hayden! Hey!"

"What?" Hayden yelled from upstairs.

Parker didn't answer. She smiled wickedly and pointed at the remote on the counter. Together, we'd stolen the TV from the guest room and had set it up on the floor with us. "Grab that for me. Let's start a movie."

Following orders, I handed her the remote and joined her on the floor, hearing Hayden clomp down the stairs. "What?" he bellowed, appearing at the doorway in a baggy sweatshirt and joggers.

"I got you a pumpkin," Parker said.

"You got me a pumpkin?" Hayden repeated. His confused look could've fooled me into thinking these two were twins.

"Yeah, if you want to hang out."

"You wanna hang out?"

"Is there an echo in here? Yes."

"No," Hayden said, and rubbed the back of his neck. "I mean, yes, but like we never—" He paused, glancing at me. It made me wonder what he'd say if I wasn't here. Instead, he simplified it. "We've never carved pumpkins together."

"Well, do you want to change that? I mean, if you're busy it's no big deal."

"Um." He nervously looked away and gave me full view of his red ears. "Let me say goodbye to my friends online and I'll be right down."

"Cool."

Then he ran back upstairs like he'd been shot out of a cannon. I glanced back at Parker. She pulled out her phone and I noticed a Pinterest board full of carved pumpkins. Curious, I slowly slid closer and snuck beside her. "That was nice," I whispered. "Are you and Hayden close?"

Parker shook her head. "Not really, but this is the first year we've ever lived together, so it's like the first year I actually feel like an older sister. I don't know. It feels like I'm always ignoring him, and I think I'm realizing I actually have to hang out with someone to get to know them."

At a loss, I hummed in agreement and tilted my head to look at the screen as she fiddled with the settings. Hayden ran back into the kitchen, excitedly offering to make popcorn to complete our floor party. Together, we scoured the internet for designs, and I debated really going for it to show off my skills, but I ended up choosing a classic happy jack-o'-lantern design, something similar to Hayden's.

He commented on Parker's choice. "You're going to regret that."

"Why?" She looked offended, looking at her inspiration again, a witch riding on a broom. "I'm an artist, okay? And I'm a gay, which means I have the audacity to do anything."

Hayden snorted but didn't argue. They argued about a movie, until I took the remote away and we ended up watching *Hocus Pocus*. My eyes were on the movie although my focus stayed on my knee pressed against Parker's. I didn't want to scare her away. Didn't want to over-whelm her. If this was all I got, this was more than enough for me.

"How's it going?" Parker asked, tilting her head to check my work. Her cheek hovered over my shoulder, and it took every fiber of my being to not close the space separating us.

"Fine," I whispered, my face burning hotter and hotter. I eyed Hayden, a worry bubbling that he wouldn't like seeing us so close, but he was either too focused on his pumpkin or really didn't care. "How are you?"

"Fine," Parker said, looking up at me with that teasing smile.

The longer we dated, the more I realized I needed to brace myself. Now, I understood the term *knockout*. Her charm knocked me off my feet. Every compliment slapped my senses silly. Her jokes put me in stitches. She would be the cause of death in my obituary. Death by Ashley Marie Parker.

Eventually, the pumpkins were done. Hayden and I had created classic pumpkins, mine smiling and his a little spookier. Parker had had to give up on her witch and so carved a big hole shaped like a small fire, which could've been worse.

Her explanation: "The creative process is always changing."

We stayed on the kitchen floor, waiting for the frozen pizza to bake as we emptied all the snacks we'd bought. I was resting back on my hands with my legs stretched out, quietly watching the movie.

Sighing, Parker leaned back with me, finding a place close to me. My brain shut down and my breathing stopped, but my heart had never beat faster. I glanced down at Parker's thumb grazing my skin. All of my senses sharpened to a single point. My eyes snapped up and though she wasn't looking at me, a bright and shiny smile hung from her lips.

All the sound was sucked out of the room. It was just me and all my fears looking over my shoulder. Taking the chance, I forced my limbs to move because if I didn't go for it, I was going to spend all night regretting it. I was tired of sleepless nights, of torturing myself over being too scared, over what could or couldn't be.

I moved my hand over Parker's and threaded our fingers together, and instantly my heart slammed bruises into my chest. Parker didn't say anything. She slowly and gently put her head on my shoulder. I wouldn't be able to recount the plot of the movie, but I could say that I loved pumpkin carving.

THIRTY-ONE

OCTOBER 14

Parker

The air was electric, and that excitement made my heart flutter and my limbs weak. It felt like the kind of magical night that would change my entire life forever, and my stomach couldn't settle. Lizzie and I were stationed in her car on a dark downtown street. Tonight we were going to go inside Miss Patty's Salon.

By two o'clock Sunday morning, we had eaten all the snacks. We had demolished the sodas. We had played Uno a million times before exhausting it.

I crawled into the backseat beside Lizzie. Too tired to make any more decisions, Lizzie let the radio play. Every now and then the connection would go all wonky and the static would fade in and out, then go back to the oldies station. We lowered the seats and casually listened to the music, and stared aimlessly at everything, the car's fuzzy gray ceiling, the dark world outside, or the lifeless Miss Patty's Salon window, still mocking me.

Groaning, I stretched my legs out and draped them over Lizzie's thighs. I wedged myself between the door and the cushion and studied Lizzie's face. "I'm bored."

She rested her hands on my legs, pinching my pants fabric. "Well, what do you want to do? Play another game?" Her round brown eyes stared back at me expectantly. "We could walk up and down the sidewalk a little."

I bit my lip, trying to play it cool and keep my grinning at bay. "Wanna make out?"

Bursting with laughter, Lizzie rolled her eyes, and shook her head toward her window. Curling my legs back toward me, I hoisted myself up. I grabbed the seat handle and yanked it, making the backseat tilt back even farther. We both wavered, and a surprised laugh flew out of Lizzie's mouth. She giggled, rising onto her elbows.

I told her, "I can't think of a better way to pass the time."

She rolled her eyes again and I realized that was the best reaction I could get from Lizzie. It meant that I'd said the best thing to make her heart flutter, the perfect thing to make her smile. I draped my arm over her head, leaning across her frame. She stopped laughing, sucking in her lips as her eyes flickered around my face.

With a warm smile, I used my free hand to caress her cheek. She was so soft to the touch. My chest tightened as the nerves set in. This part always made me nervous, but the need to kiss her beat out the fear.

"Can we?" I asked.

"Come here," she whispered and cupped my face.

I lowered my lips, pressing them against hers. Once. Twice. Three times; slow kisses that drowned out the radio playing. Lizzie took a deep breath through her nose as she arched her back enough so I could slide my hand underneath. My fingers slid to the small of her back and I traced the line of her spine. She shivered and my smile grew. This kind of thing gave my goose bumps, goose bumps.

She combed her hand through my hair, and I silently thanked the me of a few hours ago who'd decided to leave it down. My lips parted hers as I slipped my tongue inside, whirling around and back, and Lizzie followed my lead in this slow dance. Tasting her warmed my skin better than the richest hot chocolate, better than the warmest campfire.

My hand wandered around and up her stomach, brushed the edge of her bra, and Lizzie shuddered again, her surprised gasp making me jump. I retracted my hand to meet her eyes.

Flames erupted up my body as I blabbered, shouting over the alarms going off in my head "Oh, uh, sorry. I won't if you don't—"

"No!" she insisted. "I just—" She blushed, sinking against the seat cushion. "It's just no one's really . . ." She didn't need to say more for me to understand, and I wasn't so evil that I was going to make her say it.

"Is it okay?" I asked.

"Yes," she said. I smiled, before pressing a kiss to her nose.

She chuckled and pulled me back in for another kiss. Her kissing was deeper and more eager than ever before, as if she needed permission to lose those pesky inhibitions. Her teeth dragged down my lip, and shooting stars bounced against the walls of my body. As I slid my hand back underneath Lizzie's sweatshirt, her hand wandered up mine. The touch of her fingertips tickled my skin and all my thoughts went quiet as I focused only on her touch and the way it made my baby hairs stand.

My hand slipped up her shirt and I savored her warmth and her softness. A slight tremble threatened my arm, still holding all my weight, and I suddenly wished I had better upper body strength, but I was never moving from this spot.

Thumbing across the skin peeking over her bra, I tilted my head and kissed below Lizzie's ear, kissing down her neck. I nibbled the crook of her neck, sucking the skin there as her entire body reacted, pressing closer against mine.

Knock. Knock.

A pair of knuckles rattled the window and I jumped, snapping upright and smashing the top of my head against the roof. Groaning, I leaned against the far window and rubbed my poor head.

"Sorry! Sorry!" a muffled voice said from the outside of the car.

With a little wave, a man smiled and told us, "Didn't mean to interrupt your reenactment of *Titanic*. Couldn't tell if you girls were fighting or not," he admitted, and I could hear the twang of a southern accent. "But it seems like ya'll are doin' fine, so carry on. Try to come up for air once in a while."

Covering her face with her hands, Lizzie said loud enough for him to hear, "Thank you."

I glowered, more than slightly creeped out about some guy peeking into someone else's car. Sure, it was almost two in the morning and that might seem suspicious, *but still*. My eyes followed the man right up to the door to Miss Patty's Salon. I watched him rummage through his tote bags and his pockets until he revealed a key.

He slid the key into the door.

"Holy shit!" I spat out, scrambling for the door handle, throwing it open without realizing how much weight I had put on it. Slipping backward, I nearly backflipped out of the car and slammed my back into the pavement. I nabbed the side of the car in time and stepped out of the van on wobbly legs. "Hey!" I shouted for the man, running up to his side.

Closer, I realized he was actually quite tall, towering over me with a barreled chest, and while he had a shiny bald head, he also had a thick brown beard with coiled gray hairs. My eyes didn't know where to look between his flowy floral print shirt and the pink corduroy pants that matched his pink jacket.

God, it was like looking into a mirror of some alternate universe.

"I'm sorry, uh, are you opening the salon?" I asked, hearing my own desperation.

"Yeah, if the door will let me," the man said, glaring at his keys jiggling inside the lock and finding only resistance. "Come on, open for Barry."

"Barry? Um, I've been trying to get inside the shop for, uh, well, forever."

"That's a long time."

"Tell me about it."

"Well, I can only open it so fast. There we go!" He grunted, twisting the key and pushing the door open. My heart took flight. Suddenly I couldn't feel my body; it was as if my soul floated over this town. If it wasn't for my raging heartbeat, I'd assume I was dreaming.

Lizzie raced out of the car to my side. She grabbed my hand and squeezed. "Oh my god."

"Oh my god," I agreed.

Taking a deep breath, I walked over the threshold into Miss Patty's Salon. Tears pricked at the corner of my eyes as Barry found the light switches, causing lights to flicker awake one by one, lighting up a section of costume jewelry, a few small aisles of vintage clothes, elaborate costumes, and more mannequins than I ever imagined, all dressed to the nines. I walked across overlapping rugs and underneath lanterns and banners and twinkle lights and ribbons and kites.

On the far wall was a line of different pride flags from the Rainbow Pride flag to the asexual flag. My heart leaped especially at the bisexual flag.

Framed by an ornate golden frame with a draped feather boa was a portrait of the most fabulous drag queen. A queen of great stature with the stateliest curves, wearing a sparkling sequined dress of every color of the rainbow and a pink wig that was styled to the heavens. A spotlight hit the queen as she spoke into a microphone.

I recognized that queen immediately.

I looked back at Barry, who was dropping his stuff at the counter. The words formed as my thoughts did. "Are you Miss Patty?"

"The one and only." Barry gave a huge cheese-ball smile, holding his hands out as if his existence was the greatest presentation of them all. He motioned to the portrait. "I was fantastic, wasn't I? Look at me, I was stunning. They used to call me Miss Patty Cakes." His shoulders wiggled, obviously proud of himself.

"Can we call you Miss Patty?" Lizzie asked, dragging her hand down a sequined dress that changed colors depending on the direction.

"You two?" He gawked. "Are you kidding? If you call me Miss Patty, I'll slash your tires." Lizzie snatched her hand from the dress as all the color rushed out of her face, which made Barry cackle and shatter the quiet. "I'm kidding! I'm retired. Maybe one day I'll don the heels and wigs again, but for now Miss Patty is retired. I'm just Barry now."

"Barry," I said, as the last person who needed to be convinced to call someone by a preferred name.

"And you?" He pointed at me.

"Parker," I said.

"Parker, you've waited forever to get here. You're here, what can I do for you?"

"I have to know first, I'm sorry, but why do you open at two a.m.? I've been here like a million times and it's always closed. How do you even stay in business? Does anyone even know it's open?"

As if I'd summoned her, a woman barreled inside, boxes stacked in her arms. Lizzie jumped to attention and offered to help. Relieved, the woman let out a long sigh and burdened Lizzie, who was eager to help, with a box heavy enough to nearly drop her to the ground. Lizzie managed to stay upright as the new woman greeted Barry at the counter. "Evening, Barry! I've got some more envelopes, and I gave Lana a call. She says she'll bring some more sizes of the baseball tee later."

"Thanks, Kim." He smiled.

The woman, Kim, and Lizzie disappeared to the back with their boxes and left me alone with Barry.

"Sorry," I said. "I'm kind of excited."

"Don't apologize. You're curious. It's good to be curious. This place is open from two until six. Just a few hours." He came around the counter and walked the store. I trailed behind him, soaking it all in. "I got tired of the drag and stand-up comedy scene. I really found my calling with this store. I wanted to curate a safe place where queer people could find what they needed, find what made them feel like themselves, or grab something to show a bit of pride. The hours are for safety. This might be the only time someone can come here without judgment."

We arrived at a wall, and it took me a few seconds too long to notice it was a wall of binders of all shapes, sizes, and colors.

"Kim comes by and helps me package online orders. Another reason for the hours is simply that most of our business comes from online purchases. This is more like my studio. It closes at six a.m., but I'm still hanging around until nine or ten in the back. We've got a door back there, so feel free to give us a knock if you ever need somethin'."

I looked around the store again. "It's not what I expected."

"Thank you." Barry smiled. "Well, Parker, I have a business to run. I give information for free, but I'd love to sell you something. Is that your girlfriend? I sell couples' fanny packs over there."

"I'm dead," I said, imagining Lizzie and me wearing those around school. But I shook my head and tried to remain on task. I pointed at the mannequin in the store window. "I need that tiara. I'm making the costumes for my school play, *Cinderella*, and ever since I saw that tiara, I knew where it was meant to be."

Barry melted a little, sighing wistfully as he made his way to the mannequin. "Before I was a comedy queen, I threw my hat into a pageant or two. God, that must've been almost thirty years ago." He plucked the tiara off its perch and admired its sparkle. Little flecks of light danced across our faces.

"And you won?"

"Oh, hell no." Barry laughed. "I was such a mess! Really made a mockery of the whole affair! The winner, Cordelia Bedelia, was such a bitch. Pardon my language, but a cat's a cat and a bitch is a bitch. I got drunk backstage and ran off with the tiara. They had to chase after me. Imagine, over a dozen queens in ten-inch heels chasing me. Thankfully, Cordelia was actually not so bad and was pretty cute underneath all that hairspray and Vaseline. We got married last year. Not to brag," he boasted, and I had been grinning for so long my cheeks ached. "For me, it's all about the second impression, or maybe the third."

Lizzie ran back into the shop, holding a rainbow-patterned notebook over her head that said the gay agenda. She gushed, "They've got the best stuff here. It's really dangerous. You're not in a hurry are you—oh! The tiara!"

"I don't think it's for sale," I explained.

"Oh." Lizzie's shoulders lowered.

"Not for sale," Barry agreed. "But I do love donating to the arts. I'd be honored to let it take part in your production of *Cinderella*." He set the surprisingly heavy tiara in my shaky hands, trying not to breathe directly on it for fear of ruining its perfect shininess. Lizzie gushed, wrapping her arms around my waist and squeezing a squeal out of me. We jumped up and down, slightly losing our minds.

We spent another hour there as Lizzie kept me from draining my entire bank account to buy a bunch of bisexual apparel, vintage clothes, and a thousand pins and patches. Lizzie helped me narrow it down to only a few patches for my jean jacket and a bumper sticker for the glorious day I own a car.

After checking out, I couldn't bring myself to leave; even with one foot out the door, the store's gravity pulled me back. I held the tiara in my hands like it was magic, like Barry was a real fairy godmother. "Thank you," I said with a promise. "I'll take really good care of your tiara."

Barry was all smiles. "Make sure you get some tickets for me and my husband."

"Front row. Nothing but the best for you."

Lizzie and I walked into the cool Sunday morning. I collapsed into the passenger seat of her van and caught my breath. A whirlwind had blown through my life and nothing would ever be the same. I had to look inside the paper bag Barry had given me one more time. Just to make sure it had all happened.

It had.

I squealed again, hopping around in my seat. "Holy, fuck, Lizzie!"

Lizzie laughed. "I know! I know!"

"I take back everything bad I ever said about this town!"

"The town forgives you." Lizzie nodded and started the car. She drove to the more commercial side of town and pulled into McDonald's, the same McDonald's where we'd agreed to this trial. Camille still had our agreement written on that little napkin. To me, that slightly dirty napkin was a relic that would need to be preserved for future generations.

After getting our food, she found a parking spot so we could eat. I grabbed her arm. "Hey, Lizzie."

She looked back at me, still wearing the same smile she'd had back at the salon, like it was her new favorite accessory. "Thanks for coming with me. I'm really glad you were there."

"Me too."

She really had no idea how much this meant to me. I had always imagined walking into Miss Patty's Salon alone. Always imagined no one caring enough to come with me. I expected a few eye rolls and head shakes and an argument for me not to try to find Miss Patty at all. I didn't realize how much I had really wanted to share this moment with Lizzie.

THIRTY-TWO

OCTOBER 15

Lizzie

Back in the band room at school, my fingers danced along Mr. Burka's piano keys. I didn't have any friends who shared my lunch period (mostly because I had one friend and one fake girlfriend), so I hung out here.

I hummed the melody stuck inside my head. Sometimes I could hear music for a song that didn't exist. Not yet, at least. Not until I breathed life into it.

Mr. Burka sat at his desk, absentmindedly listening and answering emails. Every now and then he'd speak up and give his advice. He mimed the piano key movements and sang, adjusting his voice as he tried to nail the right key. "That again, but slower."

I did, and the sound made my skin tingle. Turning around, I grinned nice and wide to show my appreciation.

He smiled back. "I know. I'm a genius."

Playing the melody again, I burned the arrangement and the feeling it gave me into my memory. The squirmy feeling of having a crush. The sweet fluttering feeling of getting excited. And the gooey feeling of my knees going weak. A sigh slipped between my lips as I played it again.

"I don't know what's going on," Mr. Burka said over my music, "but you seem happier lately."

"Thanks."

"And since you're in a good mood, I thought I might ask you to maybe waste your summer away by being an intern for me at the Rosewood Symphony."

My hands tripped and I slammed a horrible crashing sound against the keys. "What?" I asked past my heart crawling up my throat, desperate to say yes, desperate to take the opportunity and run. "Are you serious?"

A small puff of laughter made his shoulders jump. "I'm serious. I won't lie, I was worried about letting you assist me in orchestra. I thought maybe you'd run away eventually or you'd get too overwhelmed and quit, but you've shown up and have exceeded my expectations. I always knew you were talented. I just needed to know if you cared." He smiled. "However, this internship is unpaid," he warned. "And you'll need your parents' permission."

"I'll get it," I said, not knowing how, only knowing that I must. This time I was going to look my mother directly in the eye and tell her what I wanted. Dreams didn't happen out of nowhere. Salons run by a drag queen don't open their doors and let you in if you're not knocking. Nobody walks on stage and gets the leading role. I had to make my dream happen. Or else I'd probably do something that really drove my mother crazy like get a tattoo or change my name to Lizzie Loser.

"Hey? Is Lizzie—" Andrea appeared in the doorway. The moment her eyes landed on me, she motioned me out of the room. "Lizzie! Can you follow me? Like, now?"

"Now?"

Andrea's eyes widened behind her glasses. "Now. Now."

I snatched my bag off the floor and stumbled to get out from underneath the piano. Running out of the room on Andrea's tail, I yelled back to Mr. Burka, "See ya later! And thank you!"

"Shouldn't you be in class right now?" I asked Andrea.

"Yeah, I had to go to the bathroom but I can't because your girl-friend and Camille are going at each other's throats in there."

"What?" I gasped and ran for the girls' bathroom, hearing their echoing shouts the closer I got to the door. My stomach twisted at the sound the way I cringed hearing metal scrape against my teeth. When the words became clear, I stopped dead in my tracks and couldn't go inside.

"If you're gonna lie and blow me off," Camille said suddenly—I could hear the anger in her voice, the temperature raised so high it burned my ears, "you shouldn't post about it on Instagram."

I winced. So she knew about the pumpkin carving. But how? I didn't post and Parker definitely didn't. I would've seen it.

"I didn't—" Parker started to protest, but the answer hit her hard and fast. "Hayden posted it, didn't he?" As soon as she said her brother's name I took out my phone and searched for Hayden's account. Right there. His latest post. The corner of the frame was Hayden crossing his eyes while Parker and I were in the background with my head on her shoulder, watching the same movie Camille tried to show us that night. Strange how something sweet in the moment soured so quickly.

"Man." Parker sighed, obviously kicking herself. "I'm sorry, Camille. I really am."

"Whatever. You're just sorry you got caught. I'm so disappointed. I mean, what the hell, Parker? We used to be best friends."

"Used to be? What? Have you really replaced me with Norah? Were we really best friends if you can just replace me like that? Like it's nothing? Like I don't matter?"

"You know what I mean! You'd never do that before! How do you think it makes me look to everybody if you and Lizzie ditch me and post about it?"

"I didn't post it! And it's not like anyone follows my little brother."

I had never heard Parker and Camille yell at each other, not like this. They've teased each other. They've even faked fighting over stupid stuff in the past, but it never got this serious. This dire. All my organs hardened into cement and I froze. I couldn't force myself to burst through the doors. I couldn't pull a single word out of my mouth to get them to stop.

"Oh!" Parker laughed a rotten laugh void of joy and mercy. "So that's what this is really about? You think this makes you look uncool in front of all your new friends you think are obviously better than me."

"Stop telling me what I think!"

"I said I'm sorry, Camille! What more do you want from me? God! I'm never gonna like Norah! I'm never going to like any of those people and I'm never going to change!"

A lull passed between them as tears pricked my eyes. I couldn't help it as I clutched my hands to my chest, trying to pull myself together. I couldn't handle hearing them fight. It broke my heart into jagged, messy pieces that couldn't be properly glued back together.

Finally, Camille said in a stiff voice, "You are the most selfish person I have ever met and I don't know why we were ever friends in the first place. You don't care about my feelings. You don't care about what I want. All you can think about is what's best for yourself and fuck everyone else."

"Well, I guess you have me all figured out then. It sounds like I suck. I wouldn't want to be friends with me either."

"Fine."

"Fine!"

The door suddenly flung open. Andrea and I stumbled back, out of the way. Camille's face was beet red and her thick eyeliner had smudged from wiping away a tear or two or ten. Catching me there, with my eyes watering, Camille's face scrunched together in fury. She shoved past me, her lying cousin, and ran down the hall.

I swallowed my lump of misery and held open the door to glare at Parker. "Are you really not going to chase after her?"

"No. What's done is done," Parker muttered.

She shoved through Andrea and me, stomping the other way from Camille. Two directions. Two people pulling me apart. I let go of the door and ran for Camille, all the way outside into the bitter cold and the desolate parking lot. A gray speckled sky lorded over us and the wind came with the kind of chill that sliced right through my bones.

"Camille! Camille! Wait!" I called after her, and she stopped so suddenly I almost ran headfirst into her chest. "Whoa, Camille. Are you okay?"

"No! No, I'm not fucking okay. I just broke up with Parker and, and shit! I have to go home and use a thousand baby wipes to clean my face." Her usual black makeup had melted in thick streaks down her cheeks. She shook her head at the sky. "I can't believe this is happening."

"I'm sorry. I'll talk to her."

"No, don't. This is between Parker and me."

"She really loves you, Camille, and I really shouldn't have lied to you, but I guess we were having a hard day." The more words that tumbled out of my mouth, the deeper Camille's brows furrowed. At least she'd stopped crying.

"But Parker is probably feeling lonely. She gets lonely and she's scared that you're leaving her. I think you need to assure her that nothing is changing, and she'll be fine."

"Hold on, hold on." Camille waved her hands. "Are you on Parker's side?"

The accusation hit my chest like shrapnel from the explosion.

Gawking at her, I buffered until my brain strung some words together. "No! I'm not on anyone's side!"

"Oh my god! You're on Parker's side! Lizzie, I'm your cousin! You should absolutely be on my side. We've got blood between us, and a family history of diabetes and depression."

"I know! But Parker's also my girlfriend."

"Yeah! For like another fifteen days! I'm life, bro."

I opened my mouth to hurl another defense, but nothing came out. Camille's reminder got caught in my brain and clogged my flow of thought like a deflated floaty in a swimming pool filter. Fifteen days sounded so short. Sounded so immediate. We were directly in the middle of the trial, and that scared me.

Without thinking, I said, "It might be longer than fifteen."

She laughed. "Have you asked Parker that? I dare you to ask her what she plans to do after the trial. Parker is a serial dater, Lizzie. She has to be dating someone. Always."

My spit traveled down my throat like broken glass and carved up my chest. I rubbed my face and said, "This isn't about the trial. This is about you and Parker. Are you really not her friend anymore?"

"This Camille," she said as she raised her arms to present herself, "doesn't want to be *that* Parker's friend. I miss when everything was simple, uncomplicated. Listen, I know I keep giving you shit about your relationship with Parker, but I've never seen you this confident. Ever. And I know that has a little something to do with Parker, and I understand because that's what Parker does. She's good at making you feel special, you know?"

She had to stop when her voice cracked and tears threatened to leak back out.

I nodded.

"I'm going home. You go back to class."

I nodded again but wouldn't let her leave without a hug. I held her tighter than any stuffed animal, than any security blanket. She was more precious than these things. She got into her car and left. For the rest of lunch I searched for Parker, but she'd either gone back to class or went home too.

I texted:

Lizzie: I won't ask if you're okay. You're probably not. Can I do anything?

Parker took a while to reply and I didn't blame her at all. Eventually, she texted back.

Parker: I'll be okay. I wanna go to practice and not think about it or anything. Thanks tho

Lizzie: Anytime

I took a deep breath, holding my phone to my chest. I wondered if I should've chased Parker instead, the regret rolling in my stomach like wet cement. No. Camille was my cousin. Parker would understand. It was more than just that.

At the beginning of the year, this was my dream scenario. That Parker and Camille would stop being friends. That finally I wouldn't be the third wheel. I guess I should be careful what I wish for because who knows what I might want in the future. My old wishes might turn into my current nightmare.

THIRTY-THREE

OCTOBER 16

Lizzie

"You're so cute, like revoltingly cute," Barry told me while I admired the gift I'd bought for Parker. He was kind enough to open the shop for me at a reasonable hour so I could make a purchase and still get some sleep.

It always miffed Parker that she didn't get flowers for her costumes. The crew was always an afterthought for stuff like that. However, knowing Parker like I know Parker, I had a strong inkling that an actual bouquet of live flowers wouldn't survive one night under her care, so I asked Barry to embroider daisies on the back of a leather jacket. The different colored strings were a little spaced and a little messy and not perfect, but still so pretty. Just like Parker.

Barry's studio wasn't made for aesthetics but for function; cabinets and shelves full of supplies lined the walls. Boxes of merchandise, a couple of T-shirt printers, and Cricut machines cluttered the big table where Barry worked. He was busy sewing customized binders for his online store. Underneath his sewing machine's buzzing, a rerun of *The Golden Girls* played on the TV in the far corner.

Jumping up on a counter, I kicked my legs and explained myself. "This is my plan."

"We love a plan." Barry nodded along.

"After opening night, I'm going to give Parker this jacket. Then she'll put her hand in the pocket and find a love letter from me, asking her to be my girlfriend. Officially."

I had spilled the beans about the trial to Barry without thinking in the first minute of coming here. Something about his presence weakened all my defenses and made me want to confess every dirty little secret.

"And you can't ask her?" Barry asked, leaning back in his spinning chair. "Like with your mouth parts? Like a human person?"

"No. No way. I'll crumble from embarrassment. Or worse, cry."

"Nothing wrong with crying."

My face scrunched up, feeling the exact opposite, but I was too polite to tell Barry he didn't know what he was talking about. This sentiment seemed to reach him because an emphatic laugh boomed from his mouth like a car horn. He sat back up and clapped at me. "Aren't you a performer too? Where's the confidence?"

"I have stage fright."

"You have life fright."

"Okay, if I wanted bad advice, I'd go outside and ask the Jensen twins to decide my fate. At least then I'd get some hot chocolate too."

"*Ooo.*" Barry perked up. "Grab a cup for me and ask those kids what color I should repaint my kitchen and if I should tell my husband or not?"

OCTOBER 17
Parker

My soul left my body as I read my old phone messages from Camille. The tightness in my chest hadn't lessened. The pressure to cry was like water pressing against a dam. I've had to patch too many cracks for anything more than a few leaks here and there to escape. I was a fortress.

I was sitting on the ramp between the theater seats with Ian. As if a storybook had thrown up, the stage today was littered with tech crew, their supplies scattered everywhere, including my costumes. Everyone was wrapped up in putting on a good show, except for me. Forcing myself to smile and laugh only made the hollowness in my chest grow as my misery slowly ate up what was left of me. All I could think about was Camille and how she'd tell a joke better. Her stories were better. I craved her thoughts and her feelings and her warmth. I never realized the way Camille had the power to soften me.

It was a hard way to find out I was just plain mean.

Mean.

Mean.

Mean.

I couldn't even make the argument that I didn't know I was being a jerk. The whole time I had known Camille wanted me to get along with Norah. I had known that party was a big deal to her. Camille's favorite holiday was Halloween and still, at every turn, I did whatever I wanted.

God. I was that dumb, sticky-faced kid who poured salt over a slug and watched it melt. I wished Lizzie had warned me. She used to be so good at telling me when I was breaking a record for how big of an idiot I was being.

No. It wasn't Lizzie's fault. Not when she was probably already racked with guilt over the whole ordeal.

While Ian changed the subject to some anime I'd never seen, Norah walked into the auditorium with a laugh. Whipping around, she walked backward into the room, leading Camille inside. Camille wore her Hot Topic ripped jeans with tights underneath.

The most effort I had been able to muster was to put on jeans, a sweatshirt, and the oldest pair of Vans in the universe.

We locked eyes, and my face nearly burned to an ugly crisp. I snapped my attention to the pile of fabric in my hands, and continued burning them with a hot glue gun and only sometimes actually sticking more cheap rhinestones onto the costumes instead of my hands. Camille and Norah didn't stop by my dunce corner.

While I watched them from a distance in the creepiest way possible, my phone vibrated in my sweatshirt. I slipped it out and my mom's picture flashed across the screen, that red hair like mine cut short and curled to perfection. It was my favorite photo of her; she was trying to hide her face while she was in the middle of eating chow mein and getting sauce everywhere. She was smiling so hard, every wrinkle around her face appeared. This picture lacked her usual manicured perfection, and that was why I loved it.

I hurried up the ramp and into the hallway, answering before the call dropped. "Hello? Mom?"

"Ashley!" My mother cheered and hearing her voice gave me goose bumps. The ache in my chest pounded as I realized it had been almost a full month since I'd heard her voice. "Hey, baby. How are you? How's school?"

"I'm fine. It's good," I said, feeling wildly unprepared.

"Fine? And good? Those are some sad adjectives, Ashley Marie."

"They're all I got."

A lump formed in my throat as my armpits got sweaty. It was hard to catch my breath past my nerves. A few people waved as they passed me, and I almost absentmindedly ignored Lizzie when she came up to me. I grabbed her arm and, in my panic, gave her a small shake as I mouthed, *It's my mom!*

Lizzie's eyes popped out of her skull. "Oh!"

She nearly yelled but quickly covered her mouth. She nodded and scurried into the theater to give me some space. Looking back, she gave me a quick, encouraging thumbs-up. I grinned and watched her walk back inside.

"How's work going?" I asked, dying from the quiet pause. I needed to fill it. To use it up as much as I could in these rare moments with her. "I loved the September issue. If you didn't get Paloma Young's signature for me, I'm disowning you."

My mother laughed. "That's not how it works."

"I'll make it work."

"You always have a way."

Another pause.

"Listen, Ashley," my mother said in that way people spoke when they had to give inconvenient news, like when places ran out of Coke and had to ask if Pepsi was okay. "I called because someone double-booked my schedule and I'm supposed to be on a plane the day of your play."

"Okay," I said, because her words weren't quite landing. It was all too casual. Her voice was totally normal.

"It's for a huge client and I can't say no. If it wasn't in London, I could probably make the proper arrangements to swing by, but the flights are so long."

"Okay," I said, as reality hit and my soul was leaving my body.

"I'll make it up to you, I promise."

"Okay."

"If anything, we'll see each other for Thanksgiving and I'll take you to a show, any show you like, and you can bring a friend."

A question crossed my mind and a chill passed right through me. I crossed my arms, holding myself as best as I could manage. "Does Dad know you're not coming?" I asked. Tears pricked at the corner of my eyes but I swallowed that misery, feeling it slither down my throat like cough syrup and slam into my stomach.

"I haven't told him," she admitted. "Would you mind letting him know? I don't have time to get into it with him. You understand, don't you, Ashley? He doesn't understand our work ethic."

"Right. Yeah. Okay."

"I love you, sweetheart."

"Love you too."

She hung up, but I didn't drop the phone from my ear. My shoulder crashed against the cold concrete wall as I closed my eyes and tried reinforcing the dam again and refusing to let the waterworks flow. Refusing to break. This was normal. This was what always happened.

I had to stop being so fucking surprised.

"Afternoon, Parker." Mrs. Donnelly passed me, slipping into the auditorium. Sniffling, I wiped my face and followed her inside. I pretended to still be on my phone so no one would notice my face, and sat in the back by myself. Ian and Lizzie gave me weird looks, but I looked back at my phone. First conversation with my mother in months and it didn't even last a minute.

I wanted to go back to five minutes ago. Or five days ago, when I had a best friend and I didn't have to think about losing more loved ones. Or five years ago, when I didn't have anything precious that could be taken away.

Mrs. Donnelly's voice snuffed out the voices in the room and made my skin crawl. Even hearing someone cough was enough to make my teeth clench. "Listen up, everyone. I know we've gone through the trenches during this production already, but I have some more news."

A chorus of groans answered back.

"I know, I know. This one is small. Just a small little hiccup. The advertisements we printed in the local paper announced the wrong opening day. By a month."

"It's kind of hilarious at this point." Jordan guffawed, and the sound grated in my ears. It wasn't funny. Everything had been hard. I'd worked so hard and it wasn't funny everything could be for nothing.

"It'll all be all right," Mrs. Donnelly said dumbly. "We will continue to persevere."

"Why?" I said without pause, getting up. I couldn't be here anymore. "Let's call the whole thing off. I mean, it's stupid to think we can still do this fucking play with only half a cast and no one coming to watch."

"Parker!" Mrs. Donnelly gawked at me.

Somehow, I ended up standing in the middle of the aisle, gripping one of the red seats until my knuckles turned white. "*Unless* the plan is to get laughed at? Then let me tell you we're doing the Lord's work! I hope I get nailed in the face with a rotten tomato."

"Parker." Mrs. Donnelly's voice dropped two octaves. Her stance stiffened as she stood up to match my height. "I will speak to you outside. I'm not going to take that kind of attitude."

"Wow, you're really sounding like a director now."

"Parker, I will give you one more warning and that's it."

"Parker, let's go outside," Lizzie said, walking toward me with her hands out. She approached me like I was a wild dog. I must have looked crazy. I felt crazy.

My words came out hot from the embers inside my lungs. Every word burned my tongue. "Do it. Do your worst. I'd like to actually see you do something." I stared over Lizzie's head and scowled at Mrs. Donnelly. We mirrored each other's glares and red faces. It was difficult to hear myself over my heart thrumming against my ears.

Finally, Mrs. Donnelly snapped, "Parker, you are off costumes and that is final."

"What?" Camille blurted. "But what will we do without them?"

Mrs. Donnelly snapped her hand straight at Camille, cutting her off. "We will get the costumes from donations and thrift stores like we do every year. Parker, you'll help Ian with the lighting, but if you say one more word you are out of the production entirely."

I straightened up, swallowing the lump of anger like a hairball I couldn't hack out of my throat. Keeping my shoulders rolled back and my chin in the air, I stormed back through the theater and grabbed my tub of costumes by Ian's legs, stumbling to hold it as I pushed my rack of clothes by the stage. These beautiful glimmering gowns and suits made me want to cry. Still, I had to go. My mask of pride wasn't going to hide my swollen red face or the tears welling up in my eyes.

"I'll help you." Lizzie spoke softly.

She took the rack away from me, pushing it to the exit. But the tub I grabbed popped open because like an idiot I'd overfilled it. I scrambled to pick everything up, and it wouldn't fit the same way again because of course it wouldn't and everyone was staring at me struggling to gather my useless stuff. Camille joined me on the floor and collected as much as she could into her arms without a word. She went back for a suitcase full of shoes that I almost forgot, then nudged me to follow.

We marched through the school to the parking lot. Camille was the first one to say anything. "What the hell was that?"

"I don't know," I said.

"You don't know?!"

"I don't know!"

"Let's calm down," Lizzie said, and I took a deep breath, but my entire being sizzled as my adrenaline showed no sign of slowing down. Nothing seemed like it would ever slow down. There was nowhere for me to go, but my legs still somehow brought me to Lizzie's van.

"What happened?" Lizzie asked. "Was it your mom?"

"Your mom called?" Camille softened.

"She's not coming to see the play, which is fine, right?" I grinned so wide my cheeks ached, going crazy over the rush of ache and misery flooding through me. I didn't want to cry. "It's not like I'll have anything to show anymore. No one's going to see the costumes. Not the school. You guys. Not her. She won't see—" I stopped before I could say *me*.

Camille dropped the suitcase with a huff. "I can't fucking stand your mom. Jesus!" She muttered something and kicked Lizzie's tire. "She knew how important this was to you, right?"

"Camille, cool it," Lizzie said, but Camille turned her back on her cousin.

"You can't let her do this to you. You can't stop caring about shit because she doesn't care. You care. You're allowed to care and love what you're doing."

I closed my eyes as my leg jittered on its own. Everything inside of me begged to burst. On the other side, Lizzie touched my shoulder and my bones collapsed. Camille helped guide me until I fell against the back of Lizzie's van. Camille's eyes flooded with tears. "Shit, Parker. She's letting you down and you're allowed to feel something about it. Let it out, Parker. Talk to us."

"I'm—I'm angry," I said through clenched teeth, like I was passing a vocal kidney stone. "I'm angry and I'm so sad. About everything. All the time." My voice cracked and the more I said, the harder it was to keep it all from exploding out of me. "Why doesn't she want to see me?" Tipping my head back, I thought I could hide all this misery behind my hands as my whole body trembled. If my eyes were up, the tears couldn't fall. I sucked in a sharp breath, unable to breathe. My whole body was flushed, sticky and hot, while I prayed for invisibility.

Lizzie gathered my weary body into her arms and I burrowed into the crook of her neck, my body rattling as I poured my heart out onto her shoulder. All this misery spilled out of me and washed over Lizzie.

She sniffled as she stroked the back of my head. Camille pressed into my back with so much strength I knew she'd keep us both standing. They let me cry until I became so light-headed I almost passed out.

I took several deep breaths to pull life back into this empty vessel of a body. Lizzie's hand rested on my back. She rubbed comforting circles across my rigid shoulder blades, knocking off the icicles. Camille was gone, leaving only us.

"Let me take you home," Lizzie said. Her voice was softer than velvet, kinder than a Christmas song. My arms moved on their own, pulling her into a hug.

My voice cracked like the screen of a fallen cell phone. "I really thought she'd come. I thought she'd miss me or something."

"I know. But you have to remember that there are people here for you. Your dad, your stepmom, Hayden, me."

She didn't add Camille to that list. That list used to include my mom. Used to have a lot more people, but all the names continued to fall away and disappear. I squeezed Lizzie tight, not sure what I would do if she struck her name from that list too.

Lizzie drove me home and, thankfully, no one was there to ask why Lizzie and I had brought so many costumes back inside the house. She sat with me on the couch until I was too exhausted to keep my eyes open. She pressed a small kiss to my forehead, and that was almost enough to make me cry again. I wanted to tell her how much I loved her, but I knew that might make her run.

We were too close. Too wrapped up in each other. If anyone got too close to me and started to see the real me, that was when they ran. I couldn't let Lizzie see. We needed distance. We needed to be in a position where my life didn't explode at the end of this trial.

THIRTY-FOUR

OCTOBER 18

Lizzie

Cinderella walked on stage wearing an obvious Halloween costume that must have been a child's large because the hem didn't even breathe on Norah's ankles. To avoid any slips or accidents, this Cinderella wore leggings underneath the dress and a pair of Adidas sneakers as Jordan hoisted her in the air, weaponizing her to knock the glasses right off Alex Patel's face.

Alex of course fumbled and walked into his dance partner Olivia's dress (a horrible Greek goddess costume with more holes than a pasta strainer). She fell right over on her butt. This kind of thing had stopped being shocking at this point. No one even laughed.

"Isn't she supposed to be elegant?" Andrea whispered as the actors practiced the dance routine. Mrs. Donnelly yelled the count as Mr. Burka played only the piano part. She told Alex and Olivia to walk it off and went right back into the count. Mr. Burka had fixed an awkward but encouraging smile as he watched everyone bump into each other, trip, and miss their cues.

We had downgraded from a shit show to an actual safety hazard.

Caution tape needed to be secured around the audience's seats. Warning signs should be posted in the atrium and by the snack counter that read ENJOY MUSICAL THEATER AT YOUR OWN RISK!

Andrea asked, "Cinderella is supposed to be awe inspiring or something, right? I mean, enough to fall in love with her at first sight. She's more like . . ." Andrea shrugged. "Meh."

"Yeah." I agreed. "Like she's hungover after Halloween."

"Chillin' at Walmart at three a.m."

I thought about sending Parker an update, but I hadn't gotten a reply from my last three texts, so I didn't bother trying again. I told myself it was because she probably didn't want to hear about the production she got fired from, but my gut told me she had a bigger reason to ignore me.

I didn't like it.

"And scene!" Mrs. Donnelly announced. Everyone let their partner go. Norah nudged Jordan when he looked at Mr. Burka as Mrs. Donnelly spoke. "It's better," she said, but I've seen better acting from the prop trees. "I'd like to run it from the top again, but maybe with some coffee."

"Mrs. Donnelly?" Norah raised her hand. "Are there any other dresses I can try on?" She grimaced and touched her chest. "I can't really breathe in this one." Jordan quickly unzipped Norah and she let out her stomach with a huge sigh of relief.

"I don't feel good either—" Olivia said but was cut off.

"Or!" Camille piped up, raising her hands from the seats. Any cast that wasn't part of the current scene sat behind the orchestra; seeing them all wearing their second-rate costumes from so many different time periods really made this joke kind of sad. "Maybe we tell Parker we *do* want her costumes and she can come back. Consequences for her actions be damned!"

"Yeah," Ian agreed from the tech box, the little room above the audience. His voice poured from the speakers. We all looked around as he spoke from the ether. "'Cause, like, even if everyone keeps fucking—*I mean*, messing—up, at least they'll look good."

Mrs. Donnelly spoke to the sound booth in the back. "Parker can come back as soon as she talks to me. *Personally.*"

Taylor, dressed in a knock-off princess costume that legally wasn't supposed to be Sleeping Beauty but totally was, huffed from the stage. "I don't understand why everyone wants Parker back so badly. Ever since she joined drama, she's been like superrude and so annoying for no reason. It's like she doesn't even want to be here."

Olivia raised her hand again, but no one seemed to care.

Emily shrugged. She'd joined the play because we were so desperate and would take anybody. She had to be cast as a guy and her strange hybrid costume of a pirate smashed together with a knight made a horrible screeching noise every time she moved. "I'm sorry, but do you really want to look like your clothes were dried on high? You look like you're trapped in a sausage casing, Taylor."

Taylor's face brightened pinker than her dress. Her blond hair had been stuffed inside a George Washington–style wig and she had been forced into heels one size too big. She reminded me of a startled chicken as her cheeks enflamed. "I do not! And whatever! What do you even care? You're the one who broke up with her, so don't act like she's freaking perfect!"

Emily opened her mouth, a snap at the ready, but she was cut off.

"Settle down!" Mrs. Donnelly raised her voice. With a sigh she dropped her hands and her slumped shoulders and soft words finally proved how tired she felt. "It seems evil, but I'm trying to help Parker. She needs to talk to me. Norah, let's go find something more comfortable."

"Thanks." Norah smiled uneasily and followed the director off the stage.

"Let's all take a break," Mr. Burka tried to speak up, but Emily bulldozed him.

Emily snapped at Taylor like a woken geyser. "I don't think Parker's perfect, but she's great at what she does! So if you can get over her attitude and support this production, we won't have to look like idiots."

Someone said, "I don't want Parker to come back."

Everyone stopped.

Everyone turned to me and I realized that I was the one who said it. It had meant to be an inside thought, but my feelings had a mind of their own, clawing at the cage of my teeth. The words escaped and I couldn't pull them back inside. The attention was blinding.

"Excuse me?" Emily said, walking downstage. Her attention was a sharp blade I recognized from too many encounters.

My voice trembled as I forced myself to speak up. I strangled the neck of my violin. "I don't think you deserve her. I don't think any of you deserve her."

Taylor rolled her eyes and nothing has enraged me more. "You're her girlfriend. Maybe more of us would like her if she sucked our face too."

"Okay!" Mr. Burka exclaimed. "We all need to take a second to breathe."

Anger rolled around the inside of my stomach. Glaring at Emily made it harder and harder to contain my cool. I couldn't keep my hands enclosed over my feelings anymore. Damn everyone staring and judging me. I didn't care. I needed to speak up. I jumped to my feet, startling everyone around me. "It's not about that! Parker and I aren't even actually dating!"

"Lizzie!" Camille gasped, but I didn't stop.

I couldn't stop. I was a car and Emily had cut my breaks, sending me speeding down this hill so I'd crash in a blaze of glory. "We're not really dating, but I'll still stick up for her because Parker's amazing.

She doesn't like to open up because she's scared, and hates being vulnerable. Parker has been through a ton of shit in her life, but she still makes me laugh."

The smile on my face grew a life of its own. It might be the first time I'd spoken to a crowd and not wanted to cry or run away. It was a powerful feeling. "Parker is funny on purpose and she's adventurous and she's so incredibly gentle. She'd never do anything to make me uncomfortable. She makes sure I'm good and happy all the time. Maybe you guys don't know any of that because you judged her, and the only defense she knows is to fight back. I know because she used to be mean to me. Parker is awesome, and it's stupid that you guys can't admit that you need her and you miss her."

Emily's face widened. A smile cracked from the side of her mouth and my insides withered. She asked breathlessly, "You two aren't actually dating?

"Well." I fumbled, losing a sliver of nerve. "Uh, no. But that's not the point!"

"Lizzie." Camille sighed. She held her head in her hands like she was nursing a headache. "I'm pretty sure it's against the rules of the bet to tell everyone about it."

"You told Norah!" I snapped.

"That's not the same as telling everyone we know!"

Beside me, Andrea's mouth dropped. "It was a bet? I knew something was weird. You never would've dated Parker willingly."

"I think I'm gonna be sick," Olivia announced.

Emily agreed. "Yeah! I can't believe you've been lying to us! It makes me sick to my stomach."

Ian's voice appeared from the speakers again. "That's wild, bro, but like, do you really like her, though? Does she like you? Even as a fake girlfriend, could you get her to talk to Mrs. Donnelly about coming back?"

"I'll try!" I called to him, but I wasn't really sure I could do it.

"Why were you two fake dating?" Andrea asked, and Camille sighed. Loudly. Soon she'd completely deflate.

The blush returned to my face with a vengeance, and I took up my violin again. "Um, well, we kind of wanted to fix our bad dating habits by dating each other and pointing out what we could fix." The second everyone looked at me like I'd sprouted a third head, I pointed the finger at my cousin. "Camille put us up to it!"

"Shut up!" Camille insisted and sank as low as she could in her seat. "I was kidding! You two were the ones to take it seriously!"

"Well? Did it work?" Jordan asked Andrea, but I knew he meant me. "Do you feel fixed?"

I squeezed my violin, looking at all these people. Andrea and Camille stared back at me while my heart searched for the one person who could make this jumbled mess of a feeling find peace. I missed Parker when she wasn't here. I admitted, "I do feel different. In a good way."

I smiled.

"Parker's different too," Emily said to herself. "Wow. You're not really dating."

I hated the look in her eyes, the fire that was once completely diminished bursting back with enough heat to burn me into a crisp.

"Mr. Burka?" I squeaked, and meekly raised my hand. "Can I be excused from the rest of practice?"

In the middle of rubbing his eyes, Mr. Burka nodded. "Go ahead."

"Thanks," I said, and went into a flurry to grab all my things while everyone in the cast and the band hurled question after question at me. Some people got up to follow me, when someone's groan turned into violently hurling their lunch. Olivia barreled over and threw up the entire contents of her stomach onto Alex's shoes.

Alex shuddered, covered his mouth and tried to step away. His foot hit the slick floor and he fell right into the puddle of today's lunch. He convulsed before he projectile vomited all over. Everyone started screaming and trying to run away as Olivia went on her hands and knees, making a mess of the stage. Two other girls started vomiting as Mrs. Donnelly returned.

"What on earth?" Mrs. Donnelly gasped, her hand clutched over her chest. "*Oh my lord!* Everyone calmly exit the theater!"

Panicked, we all ran out of the theater screaming. Mr. Burka instructed the light-headed kids on some breathing exercises as he pleaded for everyone to remain calm. I kept running, avoiding everyone at all costs as I escaped to my car.

As I drove home, my phone vibrated like crazy in my pocket but I didn't dare look until I arrived in my driveway. There were dozens of texts from Andrea, Ian, and some other kids from orchestra. There was even one from Norah, asking where everyone had gone.

A knock on my window nearly scared my soul out of me. It was my mother, who jumped back when I screamed. Obviously back from work, still in her Halloween-print scrubs, she held her hands up. "Sorry, Lizzie. I didn't mean to scare you."

"No, sorry." I sighed and covered my face. "It's okay."

"I figured. I'm not the boogeyman, you know. Tell me I need to go to the salon. You don't have to scream."

I cracked a smile.

"Are you coming in? Your brother will be home any minute, so you should hide your snacks."

"I will—I am. Give me a second."

My mother peered closer at my expression, and I'd die to know what she saw. I wish I knew what I was thinking. If only she could tell me.

"If you ever want to talk," she offered, "I'm here."

I nodded, feeling the pressure to cry rise.

"We don't want another haircutting incident," she joked, and it was such a relief she could joke about it now. She wasn't holding a grudge against me. "Just talk to me. I miss talking to you. I feel like you're never home anymore, and I know you're growing up, but I'll always be your mom."

"Okay."

"Okay." She smiled.

I watched her go inside the house. The dogs immediately tried to make a grand escape but she wrangled them back inside and slammed the door shut behind her. Hernández women didn't know how to politely shut a door. It was a slam or nothing.

Speaking of Hernández women.

I looked down at my phone; Camille's text stood out:

Camille: Hey dude I hate to say it but I think you lost the bet

Lizzie: Don't tell Parker. Let me do it

Camille: We're still not talking. She hasn't replied to any of my texts

Lizzie: You've been trying to talk to her?

Camille: Duh? She's going through a rough time

Camille: Stupid fights aside, her mom sucks. But Parker's only going to talk to me when she's ready . . .

Camille: which might be never. I've never seen Parker forgive anyone

I dropped my full weight against my seat, pressing my phone into my chest. Hopefully she'll forgive me.

THIRTY-FIVE

OCTOBER 19

Parker

Ever since yesterday I haven't been able to get comfortable. Even my clothes seem to hug my body awkwardly. I couldn't remember what feeling normal was like, and I wondered if I would ever stop feeling like this.

Debbie noticed something about my mood, but I shrugged it off and lied about it being period cramps. She made me some hot chocolate and left me alone. That made me cry like a big baby for at least twenty minutes. God dammit. Lizzie's crying thing was infectious. Now that I had started crying, I didn't think I was ever going to stop.

I sat outside during my break at work, freezing my fingers and toes off. There were dirty metal picnic tables bolted to the sidewalk. Nobody cool was working today, and the only other person in the breakroom was a lady named Theresa who ate chips with her mouth open, so I sequestered myself outside to die of hypothermia.

Everything had changed.

I wished there was a way I could find something more permanent. Something that wouldn't change no matter what.

My phone vibrated with a text from Emily:

Emily: Hey Parker. Just wanted to let you know I think it's fucked up you got kicked out of the play. I wanted to tell you that I still like you. I've never stopped liking you. And I don't need to be put in some challenge to date you. I would do it for free

My brain jumped off the diving board and belly flopped into an ice-cold pool of what the fuck. Quickly, I skimmed the text over again. Was this really from Emily? Did she mean that? Does she really still like me?

But she ended our relationship for good. This didn't make sense. Winning her back was the whole point of doing the trial, but I didn't know what I did to even earn this second chance. Did avoiding her make her like me again? Was this rekindling all because of one apology? My stomach was all in knots. A month ago, I'd be celebrating, but this wasn't what I wanted at all. Someone had turned off Earth's gravity and I didn't know which way was up or down anymore.

"Hey, Parker." A familiar sweater combo appeared in front of me. My head snapped up to find Lizzie. She smiled with a little shrug, and was holding a long paper bag in her hand. "I thought I'd drop by."

I couldn't help but blurt the question. "How come Emily knows we're fake dating?"

Lizzie straightened. She seemed taken aback, and for a second I thought she didn't have a hand in it at all. That maybe Norah let it slip or something, but Lizzie said, "I can't believe she told you and this fast. Wow. I'm, like, pissed, but also impressed. Emily is scary."

"So, you told her?" I could feel myself getting worked up. My heart gained a little bit of speed. "Why? I thought we were taking this seriously."

"I was, but—"

"You were? Like in past tense?"

"Hold on, hold on. No, I told everyone—"

"*Everyone?*" A horrified laugh flew out of my mouth fast enough to break glass. Thinking about Lizzie telling everyone made me want to spew my lunch. Another reason I looked stupid in front of a crowd that already hated me.

"Listen," Lizzie insisted, obviously getting frustrated too. "I told everyone because I was making a point. It really made sense at the time. If you showed up to practice, maybe it'd make more sense."

"No, it makes sense. I wouldn't want to admit I was actually dating me either."

Her face darkened as she pressed her shoes into the ground. "I'll have you know, I told them that I think you're great. That you should come back to the play because we need you, but you shouldn't come back if they don't appreciate your work."

"Well." I shrugged and tried to hurry through that little encouragement so I wouldn't have to think about how pitiful it must've been for Lizzie to tell people about her charity case fake girlfriend. "We're not really dating, so you don't have to pressure me into going back to the play." I threw my hands up in a wide flourish. "I free you."

"You think that's pressuring you?" She guffawed and took a step forward. "That's not pressuring you. God! Right now, I really do miss the way we used to be because—no, I don't miss the hating you, but I miss the way I could tell you to your face when you're being a jerk because I knew I was right—no, because I know that I'm right."

"I'm already stressed out enough as it is, Lizzie. Have I really not had enough? Did you think, hey? Everyone's been giving Parker total hell, but not me. I feel left out."

"No, obviously not!" Lizzie hissed and crossed her arms.

I grabbed at my hair, thinking I could really pull red clumps out of my head. "I have to deal with everything, including you whining about stuff that doesn't even matter anymore! Who gives a shit about the play?"

Lizzie's hands dropped. Her eyes widened like I'd just punched her in the stomach.

The word sat in the air between us, thicker and higher than the Great Wall of China. It seemed like I had the talent to say the worst thing I could possibly say.

Whining.

The exact low blow I took before I shoved her into a pool almost a month ago. That one little word changed Lizzie's entire face. Tears trickled out of the corners of her eyes, and her face flushed with anger. I was revolting to her. Despite her shaky breath, she said, "Here I thought that this trial was doing us some good, but I guess you haven't changed at all, have you, Parker?"

"Oh, whatever!" I rolled my eyes. "You think you're all that different? Because you're not. You're still the same Lizzie chasing after Camille. You act like you only have Camille and me around, but you love it, so you can cling to Camille and let her tell you what to do or you can follow me around and copy me because you don't even know how to be yourself."

"You're wrong. That's not my problem. My problem is that I'm not being very honest. I'm not telling you what I really think. You need to text Camille back. You need to talk to Mrs. Donnelly, so you can explain yourself and come back to the play."

"Uh, did you miss the part where I'm banned? Or do I have to remind you?"

"You yelled at a teacher, Parker. What did you expect? If you apologized and explained what was going on, then maybe—"

"She's not going to change her mind. I already fucked it up too much, just like I did with Camille."

"So you're going to give up? You're not even going to try?"

"They've already made their decision. People don't change their minds."

"We're not talking about them anymore." Lizzie's nose flared. Her nose always flared first when she got angry, but now I was hit by the horrible fact that it flared when she was about to cry too. My ribs splintered apart as my heart tried to bust through and soothe her emotions, but I wouldn't let her tears sway me. I had every right to be upset too. "I'm not sure what this trial is giving you anymore. You don't need a girlfriend right now, Parker. You need everything else."

My stomach plummeted to my toes.

She closed her eyes. "I have to start being honest."

"What are you trying to say, Lizzie?" I asked, venom on my tongue. It tasted like copper and bad decisions, but my head was running too hot, and like most forest fires, the destruction couldn't be contained without a few casualties. "Is this it? You really couldn't stand being around me even ten more days? I'm so awful you're really willing to lose the bet? God! Has everything been fake?"

"No!" Lizzie snapped. "Stop putting words in my mouth."

"I can't help it!" I blurted, all my anger and embarrassment inflating in my head until it exploded out. "You're so predictable. I'm sure in the next second you're going to burst into tears and run away because you can't handle your own shitty choices."

And with that, some things couldn't be unsaid.

I'd rather Norah Brady punch me in the face.

I'd rather take a pair of scissors to my favorite jeans.

I'd rather my mother abandon me all over again.

Lizzie's face hardened. She clenched her fists at her side as she forced the words out. "Thank you, Parker, for giving me one last lesson during this trial. Thanks for teaching me how to break up with someone. I'm breaking up with you."

Her voice caught like a sweater on a rusty nail. Hot tears rimmed her eyes, making them glistening and pink. "It's not because I don't like you, because I like you a lot." The tears began to fall, one after another, dribbling down her round cheeks and meeting at her chin. "I like you more than anyone. Ever. Sometimes I like you more than my own family! I like you like you're the other half of me." Lizzie's eyes looked at me like a spotlight and the expectation burned my eyes. "But." She took a step back. "I don't like what you're doing, and I don't like what you've become. I can't watch it anymore. The trial's over."

Why did everybody want to change me? Why did everybody want me to be so different? Why couldn't I just be me? Like the people I like and cut out all the people who don't like me. Everyone needed to leave me alone and let me do whatever I wanted to do. I could make new friends. I did that all the time. I could get another girlfriend. Emily wasn't asking me to change. She was the only one who didn't expect anything from me.

I scowled at Lizzie, crossing my arms so tight I cut off the circulation. "Let me give you one last tip. The next time you break up with someone, try not to break up with them while they're on break at work because now I have to go back and try not to bawl my eyes out. Great job."

"Whatever." Lizzie shook her head. She whipped around, stomping her foot against the cold pavement of the empty parking lot. She muttered, "Asshole."

"Dick!" I called after her.

She flipped me the middle finger as she stormed toward her van. The second she was out of sight I roared and used all my strength and aggression to kick the nearest trash can. It jumped only an inch, and I unleashed a roaring curse as my poor foot ached.

The last month had given me everything I ever wanted, and in one breath it had become my worst nightmare. I hated love. How it could be taken away as soon as it was given. I should've held on tighter. I should've held on until my fingers bled.

I had assumed I had done a really good job protecting myself with the thickest wall I could build but somehow one person snuck in, and like any other thief, she took my precious heart and fled.

PART THREE

End of the Trial Period

THIRTY-SIX

Lizzie

Lizzie's "I'm feeling like a garbage fire's garbage" Playlist

My fingers hovered over the phone screen, unable to hit the Play button. It was like all the strength had evaporated from my body. With my van in Park in the driveway, I couldn't even muster the strength to turn the car off or get out. *Oh god.* I can't believe I did that.

Swallowing a bit of sickness back down my throat, I let my tears bubble up to the surface. With a sniff, I changed the title of my playlist:

Lizzie's "Breakup" Playlist

I still couldn't hit Play. With my van still running, the whole structure trembled around me as car exhaust billowed in the crisp autumn air. The only light came from the motion detection light over the garage.

I changed the title again.

Lizzie's "The songs that will make Lizzie cry the quickest" Playlist

This little phone held all my secrets. I poured my heart into every playlist and right now, it read like a diary of my past few months, of all the playlists shifting from the *"Hating my friend's friends"* playlist to my *"Crush"* playlist and even my playlist all about kissing Parker.

This was my car. But Parker was all around it. I could envision her tubs of costumes and supplies in the back. I could see her long legs hiked up on my dash and how she talked endlessly with no filter. I could see her copper hair whip around like a cyclone as she rolled down the window and stuck her hand out so she could pretend to fly.

I remembered running my hands through her hair and kissing her soft lips in the backseat. Her words filled my head, telling me I was beautiful, telling me that I was too good for her, but there wasn't anything good about this. Our laughter bounced off these walls and it hit me like a pile of bricks that I was never going to hear that sound again. Parker no longer had a reason to even smile at me, let alone talk to me. My chest twisted until it couldn't twist anymore.

Closing my eyes, I let my seat drop all the way back, and the last of my resolve snapped into a thousand sharp, ugly splinters. Pressing my hands over my eyes, I sobbed, and let all my tears fall down the side of my face and wet the backs of my ears.

I wasn't ever going to leave this van.

Lots of people live in vans.

A soft knock on the window made me whine as I tried twisting off the faucet behind my face. My miserable expression tightened, and my lips quivered, fighting my desire to hide. It was Danny. He was home for the weekend. His voice sounded muffled behind the glass, but it might also have something to do with the fact that I had never heard him speak so softly before, not even to babies or cute animals.

"Hey, Lizzie," he said. "Just coming to see if everything's all right. You've kind of been in the car a while. Do you wanna come inside?"

"No!" I yelled.

After a pause, he asked, "Then, can I join you?"

Draping my arm over my face, I used my free hand to unlock the door. Quietly, Danny climbed into the passenger seat. He adjusted the heater. I hadn't realized how cold it had gotten in here until the burst of hot air melted the layer of ice across my skin. Danny lowered his seat to match mine and after a few seconds, he tried again.

He spoke the way you carefully cradle a newborn baby with so much love and care, but holding on tight enough so you'd never drop them. "If you wanna talk about it, you can. You don't have to talk, but I'm worried."

"That's the thing." I whimpered and turned away from him as I desperately used my sleeves to clean up my face. "I don't have anyone to talk to."

"That's not true. You can talk to me. I mean, I know I'm at college, but you can always call me. Always. How bad was your day?"

A miserable laugh shook out of me. "So bad!"

My heart started beating faster. I could feel my anxiety bubble up and fizzle at the top of my skin. My jaw was tired from keeping my mouth shut for so long. Danny glanced at my phone, at the playlist lighting up the screen.

"Well, this isn't gonna help," Danny said, trying to lighten the mood. "Where's your old playlist? What was it? Songs not technically about butts but are totally about butts?"

I snorted. "I made that in, like, middle school."

"You never forget your favorites."

Finally, I dropped my hands and a little wave of cool air put out my enflamed face. With a sniff, I mustered a smile that quickly crumbled and turned into another sob. "Danny."

"Yeah?"

"There's a girl I've been dating," I said, the words so wobbly on the way out. Chills ran down my arm as I tried to keep in my tears so I could say everything I wanted to say right. I thought saying it might lift the weight off my shoulders, but every word added to the weight. I only had one chance to come out to my brother. I only had one shot at not messing it up and confusing him. If I messed this up, I could lose him.

"But we broke up," I quickly explained. "But I still really like her. And I broke up with her, but I don't know if I made the right decision. I don't know what to do with all these emotions and these feelings. I feel like I'm going crazy."

"You're not crazy," Danny whispered and I let out a breath. Now the tears wouldn't stop. He sat up in his seat and motioned me into his arms. I shot up like a whip and buried myself in his chest, grabbing fistfuls of his hoodie. It had that guy smell, that spicy smell mixed with standard soap. "Can I ask why you broke up with her?"

I huffed, trying to catch my breath and also suck up at least a little of my snot so I didn't ruin Danny's shirt. "I don't think she needs a girlfriend. Not right now. Not with me. I can't—I can't explain it, but we kind of got together to help each other out, but I don't think I'm equipped to help her with this one and I don't want her to waste any time worrying about me. She needs to figure herself out."

"Oh, Lizzie." He rubbed my back. "You have the biggest heart in the world. If people were a tenth as kind as you we'd live in such a better place. I think you're more tuned in with your emotions than people twice your age are. Cry. It's not childish. I'm really sorry. You shouldn't be in this sad van."

"*Hey.*" I laughed, my nerves still frayed at the edges.

"We should be getting McDonald's or stuffing your face with ice cream."

"Not McDonald's. We started dating at a McDonald's."

He snorted. "Maybe you dodged a bullet . . ."

I shoved him and he laughed. We calmed down a little and Danny released a long sigh that made his body deflate. He leaned in and gave me the best hug he could with the dash between us. I closed my eyes and wiped away the last of my tears.

"Thanks, Lizzie," he said. "For telling me. So, does that make you gay? Bi? I mean, you don't have to decide now or whatever, but—"

"I'm a lesbian, but you can't tell Mom or Dad or anyone," I said, my stomach squirming. From the tips of my ears to my toes, I flushed.

"God, of course not," he said, shocked by my worry. We had the same parents. Of course we were on the same page. "I would never. I won't tell anyone until you're comfortable, and then, when you are, I'll tell everyone about my supercool lesbian sister who has sick playlists and is the prettiest crier I've ever seen, Jesus Christ. Give everyone else a chance."

"Shut up." I rolled my eyes.

"Do you want to go inside?"

"Yeah."

I fixed my seat and turned off the engine. By the time I climbed out of the car Danny was there with his arms opened wide. I threw my arms around him and squeezed him as tight as I could, even lifting him up a little. He kissed the top of my head and didn't release me as we walked up the porch and into the house.

When I got inside, I expected I'd want to cry myself to sleep, but I didn't. I fell asleep curled up in my bed watching TV with Danny. I didn't feel all alone in the world, like I thought I would.

THIRTY-SEVEN

Parker

The same night as my world's worst breakup, I drove downtown. I couldn't listen to any music. Every song reminded me of Lizzie, and I couldn't start weeping like a baby because I had to drive. If I wrecked the car my dad would find out I'd stolen his car keys and driven without a license, and then I'd be dead meat.

I parked right in front of Miss Patty's Salon, got out of the car, and sat in front of the door, my legs sprawled out across the freezing sidewalk. With how cold the pavement was at night, my jeans felt wet. Leaning my back against the door, I stared at all the Halloween decorations and the lights tangled up in the trees. In the distance, I could hear rock music blaring from the bar down the street. Every now and then someone's laugh was loud enough to reach me.

I glared at the vacant passenger seat. The emptiness around me matched the void in my chest. Looking down at my phone, I didn't see a single person in my contacts who wanted to talk to me. Maybe Emily, but that was because she wanted something from me. Thinking about talking to her gave me a headache.

My temper flared like a sparked match, and with all my strength I chucked my phone across the street, instant regret immediately punching me in the stomach. "My phone!" I yelped and fumbled to stand up quickly and retrieve it, honestly forgetting to look both ways before I crossed the street. I brushed off the dirt and thanked god she didn't crack my phone. I kissed my fingers and pointed at the sky.

Putting my phone away before I got any more crazy ideas, I sat back in my lone little corner, which reminded me of the time-out corner when I was a kid. Pulling up my legs, I rested my cheek on my knee. Without music. Without anything to listen to, I was left with all this empty space to think and obsess.

I replayed the last few hours over again, kicking myself for what I'd said. Why didn't I think a little first before I word vomited the first thing that came to mind? Lizzie was too honest. I wished she had lied and had told me she wanted to break up because she was taking Camille's side or she'd decided she didn't like redheads. Why did she have to tell me she didn't like *me*? The me right now. I couldn't help that.

Someone's car door slamming woke me up. Barry emerged in a checkered coat that kind of looked like my grandmother's quilt. He approached slowly with the caution of animal control. "Parker? What's going on, sweetie?"

Taking to my feet, I rummaged through my bag and quickly tried to explain. My hands shook as I tried to find that box. I don't know why they were shaking. The second I'd gotten home it felt like the right thing to do. It was the reason I'd driven here in the dead of night, still wearing my work uniform and without my dad's permission.

"I've kind of fucked up absolutely everything in my life." I pulled out an old shoe box and dropped the cardboard on the ground, holding Miss Patty's tiara in my undeserving hands. The little crystals caught the light and hit my eyes, making them well up. "So, uh . . ." I suddenly lost my breath. "I thought you should have this back because I don't deserve it, and honestly, I'm pretty sure I'll somehow break it and then you'll never wanna talk to me again, like everyone else in my life."

Barry blinked.

He dropped his bags and put his big warm hands over mine. "Keep it. It's not midnight yet. Cinderella still needs it for the ball." He patted my hand with a smile. "Come inside. I won't offer you anything strong, but the water on tap isn't bad."

Relief flooded my body as I released the breath I was holding. I guess a part of me didn't want to give up the tiara yet.

Barry brought me into the quiet salon and I sat on one of the old couches, surrounded by the mannequins and the Halloween decorations in front of the window. I had cried so much the tears were gone, but I'd traded the waterworks for a pounding headache.

"It's tea and it's not good," Barry warned me as he handed me a cup of something in a mug that read GAY JUICE. He smiled. "But you seem cold."

"That's me," I said, a shudder rippling through my body as I sucked in a needed breath. "The cold girl with no friends and no girlfriend."

"Are you saying we're not friends?" He feigned insult, pressing his hand to his chest as he plopped down on the armchair across from me. He crossed his legs, bringing his own mug to his lips. "It's rude and I won't stand for it."

I took a sip of the light-ish dark-ish tea that smelled like Fruit Loops but tasted exactly like liquified dryer lint. "*Ugh.*" I gagged, but drank again because it tickled my nose and made me feel something other than miserable.

Dropping my head, I admitted, "I said the opposite of everything I wanted to say."

"What would you have said?"

I stood up, abandoning my gross tea, and continued, "I wouldn't have brought up Emily because that's always been a bad move. Bringing up Emily was like bringing up the boogeyman to Lizzie, but if I did mention her, I'd say I don't like Emily like that anymore, not the way I like Lizzie. Then,"—I threw my arms up—"I'd say that I really don't care if people know we're fake dating 'cause like who cares if it's fake or real or not!"

"But that's not what you said."

I shrank back. "No."

"What did you say, then?"

"I got mad. I was embarrassed, I guess and I—" My lips trembled as my jaw tightened and tears welled up in my eyes again. I dropped to the floor again and hid my face with my sleeve. "I'm sorry."

"Don't apologize to me," Barry said. He grunted as he got up from his seat and joined me on the floor. "It sounds like you need to go on an apology tour, but I'm not the first stop, kid."

I sniffed, still trying to wipe the tears away, but they kept spilling out.

"You know," Barry said, and rubbed my back. His voice was so soothing after all the yelling and fighting I'd gone through. It was so gentle I wanted to weep all over again. "Apologizing is important. It lets the people around you know how you feel, whether that's guilty or bad or embarrassed, but it's just words. If you want to make things right, you're going to have to show it in your actions."

"How do I do that?"

"Now that's up to you. Sounds to me like you should first start by being honest with your feelings, especially if you're going to regret it later."

I nodded, wondering how different it might all be if I took a moment to think. He sat with me for as long as the salon was open, long after the awful breakup tea had gone ice cold. Eventually, I was gathered up and told to go home.

"Hey," Barry called before I was out the door. He raised the tiara up to me, holding it in the air between us. "Take it," he said, motioning me to it. "Don't give up. Don't give up on anything. Ever. Especially yourself, okay?"

Wiping my hand off against my pants first, I took a deep shuddering breath before I accepted the tiara. I held it in both of my hands, tilting it back and forth and playing with the sparkle. It was heavier than it was yesterday. Secretly, I wanted to first apologize to this tiara. I wanted to take it all the way to the ball, but there was no certainty I'd even get back there.

THIRTY-EIGHT

Lizzie

Letting out a breath, I adjusted my sitting position again in the café at Target. My stomach wouldn't stop churning. All the tables were filling up and I was taking up too much space all by myself. Standing up, I tiptoed out of the way and checked my phone again to avoid stares.

It was Saturday morning, and I was meeting up with Andrea. Last night I worked up the courage to finally make plans to hang out outside of school. I was so used to doing everything with Camille or Parker. I felt lonely now that they'd gone radio silent. My strategy was to invite Andrea to do an activity because if things got too awkward or quiet, we'd at least have something to do with our hands. Maybe. I didn't know.

My expertise did not include making friends with people outside of my blood relations. I found myself longing for love that was more platonic. I needed to put all this love I had to give somewhere and so far, I liked the idea of giving it to Andrea the best.

Focusing on breathing in through my mouth, I held it and then let the air escape through my nose. I did it a few times to calm down before walking over to the mugs and thermoses, pretending I had the funds for a new cup.

"Ha!" Andrea appeared, jumping in front of me with her hands stuffed inside her puffy jacket pockets. A surprised laugh jumped out of me, and I couldn't help but smile at her grinning at me. "I knew it. I knew you'd get here early."

"You're here early too," I pointed out.

She stood up straight, inflecting her words with her hands still in her pockets. "Well, yeah," she said in her gravely way. Her tone was so low and dry, she was kind of funny without even trying. "My mother taught me that being early is on time, on time is late, and late is unacceptable."

I nodded, identifying with that statement too closely. "When I was a kid, I used to make my mom drive around my friends' neighborhoods so I wouldn't be, like, embarrassingly early to birthday parties."

"Yeah, I can't help it."

If I knew I could hide it, I would be jumping up and down for joy. This simple little conversation had the power to make me so giddy. My cheeks were going to get sore from smiling. I pointed to the coffee bar. "Do you wanna get coffee?"

"Absolutely," Andrea said and walked to the end of the line. "Thank you so much for asking. So, what are we here for? Don't think I'm weird for not asking what we were doing when you asked to go out. You said Target, and that's all I needed. I love walking down aisles and pretending to buy things."

"My sister, Gina, gave me a list of skin care that I need to buy. She's probably gonna become a cosmetologist or a skin doctor or something." I cocked my head feeling puzzled. "What are skin doctors called again?"

"Dermatologists, but skin doctor sounds way cooler. Good for her.

I'll probably be an accountant, or maybe a dentist." She talked about her future like she was reading off a grocery list, and it made my jaw drop. I'd been surrounded by artists for so long, this level of practicality sounded like another language.

"Those are very, very different options. You're not interested in music?" I asked, genuinely curious. "What about the clarinet?"

Andrea snorted. "What about the clarinet? Hell, no. I wanna make money. The world is literally on fire, and I want to make enough money to like go on vacations, buy puzzles, clothes, and anything else that'll give me a sweet, sweet hit of serotonin," she said with so much passion it seemed like money would be a dream come true for her.

"Did I hear puzzles in that list?"

There was a spark in her eyes I hadn't seen before, and I'd do anything to keep it going. She raised her arms as if unveiling her true form for the first time and I had to smile, in awe of her power. "You will never meet a person better at solving puzzles than me. If that could be a high-paying job, I'd do that." I snorted as Andrea explained, "Yeah, I only joined band so I could do the yearly Disney trip. *You*, though." She pointed at me. "You should stick with music." That one little comment put a song in my heart. She wasn't being nice. She was being honest.

I admitted, "I want to. It's hard to think about colleges right now since I can't imagine auditioning for a real music school."

"Oh, you'll be fine because you want it. You'll make yourself do it because you want it. Not doing it would be worse," she said matter-of-factly, and I wanted it tattooed on my heart. Someone isn't always going to be here to push me into doing what I needed or wanted to make myself happier. I thought about Parker literally pushing me into the band room to talk Mr. Burka into letting me stay in orchestra. I needed to be the one pushing myself.

"Yeah." I let myself agree. If I could manifest a little more confidence, I think I could do anything. "I think you're right."

"I usually am," Andrea said with a nudge.

She gave her order to the barista. I followed her, creeping back to her side to wait for our coffees. I made a mental note that Andrea ordered white mochas with an extra shot of expresso. Knowing coffee orders was my love language.

Andrea took out her phone and started typing, and my stomach twisted a little. Any silence gave me the room to think of the worst-case scenarios. Ripping off the bandage, I forced myself to speak up. "Dang. I should've gotten a cake pop. I have a feeling this place is gonna make me hungry."

"Same," Andrea said. She perked up and slid her phone back into her pocket. "Hey, after we get everything, you should come over to my house. My mother will feed you whatever you want, and you don't have to spend extra money. I don't think your sister warned you how expensive skin care is, and I know you don't have a job."

Pretending to be offended, I laughed and clutched my nonexistent pearls. "Wow. Read me. *Drag me.*"

A laugh flew out of Andrea as our orders were called. Stepping up with her, I admitted, "I have to go home after this, but, um, maybe next week we can plan something."

"Totally!" she didn't even hesitate.

"Maybe you can show me your puzzling ways."

"Only if you can handle it." She winked. We walked through the store together, getting more than what we needed and straying far from our lists. It couldn't have been more perfect if I tried.

For the first time in a while, I crossed my house's threshold with ease. I'd unloaded so much anxiety walking around and talking with Andrea, it actually put me in a good enough mood to keep the ball rolling. Based on her car being in the driveway, I knew my mother was home. Taking a deep breath, I pushed myself to go upstairs and knock on my parent's bedroom door.

"Mom," I said as I peeked into her bedroom. She was under the covers, bundled up with a book as her small bedroom TV played the news. I glanced behind my shoulder at Danny's bedroom light pouring through the cracks. If I needed him, he was right there.

"Hm?" Mom hummed, before finishing one more line. She slid her bookmark into place and wriggled up to rest against her headboard. "What's up?" She paused the TV too. Her curls were down, spilling down her shoulders. More and more threads of gray were mixed with the black.

"I've been lying to you," I said, starting off strong.

My mother froze, taking an extra second to process. "Okay?" She touched the center of her forehead and I cringed, wishing I'd started out a thousand different ways. "I can feel my vein throbbing. Okay. I'm gonna try not to overreact, but you're not talking and I'm imagining something horrible like the van has exploded or you legally changed your name."

"No, no, sorry. I'm just nervous," I admitted, and walked farther into the room. I squeezed my fingers, cutting off the circulation. This had to be done. I needed her to know me. I needed the whole world to understand the things I wanted. I was so sick of being alone and caged inside my mind. It was time to get out.

If I expected Parker to start trusting people, I needed to do the same.

"The other day, when you said you missed talking to me . . ." I started again and approached the bed. Thankfully, she let her finger fall from her forehead. "I've missed it, too, but I haven't been able to talk to you." I took a deep breath and let it all come out, "Mom, I didn't quit orchestra. I want to keep making music, and my band director, Mr. Burka, offered me an internship this summer at the college where he works and I want to do it, but I need your signature. I really want your signature."

Truly, I wanted her to understand.

My mother rapidly blinked and she shook her head like I finally broke her. "I-I thought you didn't like it. I thought it made you uncomfortable. I mean, all the times I've gotten an email about you crying in class—"

"Yeah, you assumed, and you can't. You have to stop thinking for me. I love music. I'm anxious in front of a crowd, but I love to play more than I'm afraid of it. I couldn't talk to you because you'd already decided what you assumed was best for me." My voice broke.

"Oh, Lizzie." My mother held her arms out and I joined her in the bed. I snuggled against her side and let her warmth encapsulate me. She rubbed my arm. "I didn't realize I made you feel that way. I didn't want you torturing or pressuring yourself to do something you didn't want to do."

"It's why I cut my hair. I'm not a little kid anymore."

"I don't think that," she argued, and I used all of my willpower to stay calm and not get overwhelmed. I needed her to hear me, and if this escalated into a screaming match, she'd shut down. This was too important to me.

"You do. You keep telling me I'm going to be a senior next year but you don't let me make any big decisions. I want to feel like I'm growing up, but you have to let me."

"Okay, okay, I understand." She raised her hand, noticing the break in my voice. This was getting more and more uncomfortable, so she was pulling away, and I panicked.

"Do you really? You might hate this haircut, but it's the only choice I've made on my own that makes me feel like I have control over my life. I'll always be your daughter, but I'm not a little girl and I'm changing all the time."

She heard that. "What do you mean?"

"I mean—" I ran my hands down my face and took a large calming gulp of air. Letting it out, I told her, "You don't know how much music means to me, so it feels like you don't know me at all."

My mother got up from the bed and raised her arms again. "I know that I love you. I'm sorry you've been feeling this way."

Standing up, I threw myself into her hug and held on tight. She rubbed my back, whispering softly, "You need to know that I will listen. If there's anything you want to tell me, I will sit and listen to every word you have to say. When it comes to you, Lizzie, I don't want to miss a single thing." She pulled back, keeping a tight hold on my arms. "What can I do to make you feel better?"

After a pause, I tested my luck. "How about letting me bleach my hair blond?"

She closed her eyes. "Please, have mercy on your mother. I don't wanna hear about bleach, tattoos, or piercings. At least graduate high school first."

We laughed, and Danny took that as a sign that everything was safe. He ran into the room and pile-drove us into the mattress, making us all bounce. We screamed and soon Gina peeked inside, and we yelled at her to come in. She tried to run, but Danny and I chased her and brought her back to bed. Soon the dogs barreled at us, and we were officially a dog pile.

Eventually, we all gathered in the living room and watched old game shows and yelled at the screen until one by one we went to bed. It was the first time in a long time that I stayed home.

Parker

"Just tell me what to do," I pleaded, no longer caring how desperate or pathetic I looked. I was *way* past having dignity. I had both my hands on top of the Hot Cocoa and Bad Advice booth with my head hung heavily in defeat. It was Sunday, the last day before I had to go to school and see Lizzie again. My heart couldn't take it. I needed help. This morning, I'd left the house in sweatpants.

I'll say it again: sweatpants in public.

The Jensen twins sat behind the table as usual, their little faces solemn. Crissy raised her brow, eyeing her twin in a silent meeting of the minds. Mitchell nodded and poured me a whole thermos of hot chocolate, dropping two handfuls of marshmallows at the top.

"Tell me what to do and I'll do it." I groaned and turned my head up at them. Behind them, I locked eyes with their mom, who worked at the law office next door. She had a confused look on her face, but I smiled and waved, which she hesitantly returned.

I had spent the last half hour explaining my and Lizzie's entire love affair. The twins were excellent listeners, never interrupting, only asking me to wait if they got another customer, and then they'd allow me to resume spiraling. I gave them a whole ten dollars.

"Parker," Crissy started, speaking from behind her giant purple muffler. They were both bundled up as usual. Her voice was hesitant, as if she was nervous about my reaction. "Have you thought about, I don't know, actually telling everyone how you feel?"

"Yeah," Mitchell agreed. "You could try being a little vulnerable."

"What?!" I gawked, jumping back to my feet. "Are you crazy? That's your worst advice yet! You shouldn't tell people that crap. I'm calling the police." It was like they'd told me to put a gun in my enemy's hand and hold my arms up for them to shoot me.

"Take a second. Think about it," Mitchell said, the picture of calm.

"And this is nonrefundable advice," Crissy reminded me as she took their jar of cash and hid it under the table.

"What are you gonna do with all those costumes anyway?" Mitchell asked, pouring himself his own cup. Seemed like a long day for him too. "Are you going to hang them up like decorations?"

"Oh, god no. If I have to look at them any longer, I'm going to go insane. They're collecting dust in my room, mocking me for all of my mistakes."

"Then you should get rid of them."

I considered it as I took a swig of their perfect hot chocolate, then the light bulb flickered over my head. Sugar always inspired my best ideas. "That's it! I gotta get rid of them—it's not enough to throw them out. I need to exorcise them. Destroy them so they'll stop haunting me."

"That's not what he said." Crissy spoke up, but I was already gone.

Thankfully, no one was home. I stood in our backyard with its old rusty swing set and a half-dead garden as my audience. I pulled an old metal trash can from the garage and dragged it out, along with my rack of costumes and bins of accessories, excluding Miss Patty's tiara. That I put on my head.

It gave me the courage to drop Cinderella's costume inside the bin and hold up a match. The only way to get rid of these costumes was in a blaze of glory, the only glory they'd ever see. It was as close to a Viking funeral as I could manage.

I closed my eyes and said a few last words. "I'm sorry it had to end like this. You were beautiful and it's a shame no one is going to see you in your prime, but at least I'll know. That way, you won't be forced to perish without someone remembering you."

I opened my eyes and struck the match. It burst with light and heat. The wind nearly blew it out, but the little fire stayed strong. I wished I could sympathize. My stomach twisted and I lost a bit of feeling in my limbs as I watched the flame flicker.

"Here I go," I said, trying to hype myself up. "I'm gonna do it."

But my hand and arm wouldn't budge.

"*Oh my god!*" someone yelled.

Barreling across my lawn, Norah Brady in all her glory kicked the trash can out of the way and blew out my match. I yelped in surprise and stumbled back. She snapped her head at me, wearing a crazed frantic look.

"Are you an actual psychopath?!" I don't think I had ever seen Norah shout before, and it was the most shocking part of all. All I could do was stare at her, slightly scared and equally impressed. "What are you doing? That's my dress! I knew you hated me, but you don't have to burn my dress."

Shaking my head, I found my voice and fired back. "It's not about you! I was gonna burn all the costumes for me, so don't be so full of yourself—"

Norah unleashed an earth-rattling groan as she threw her head back, pressing her wrists to her eyes. Norah's black curls bounced as she moved. Over the breast pocket of her denim jacket was a patch that read hello my name is . . . and in the blank someone had sewed, THAT BITCH.

God. Why was she so cool? I hated her so much, mocking me with her awesomeness.

"Jesus!" Norah yelled, snapping me out of my daze. I felt half dead and almost completely made out of misery, but at least clothes could still cast a spell on me. "What's your problem with me?! You've been such an ass to me for no reason!"

My face went up in flames. Whoa. I never expected to be called out on it.

Flustered, I shouted, "No reason? I have a good reason." I pointed an accusing finger at her cute button nose. "You made fun of me! In front of everyone in drama! You said I was making the costumes slow for attention!"

Norah deflated and crossed her arms. "Yeah, that wasn't my proudest moment, but to be fair, you haven't been nice to the actors in the club either. I heard you went to Olivia's party, didn't remember her, and then said the party sucked. To her face."

"I forgot about that." I grimaced, seeing the trajectory of this conversation, and dreading the ending.

"What else did I do?"

"I don't know!" I gestured to her entire being. "You've just— You've—"

Norah's mouth dropped so hard I thought her jaw was going to pop off. "That's the reason you've been giving me hell! Fuck, Parker! There's more to people than your first impression of them, you know!"

"I know that!" I said, but I hadn't thought about it until now. I thought back to every moment after that, every horrible painful moment between Norah and me, which made me realize all that tension was of my own making. I had pushed that narrative onto Norah, and she couldn't do anything about it.

My body softened along with my voice. "I know. I'm sorry, but when you and Camille started getting closer, I guess I was jealous."

Norah's eyes bugged out. She stabbed a finger into her chest. "You were jealous of me? I was jealous of you! God! It's like I can't compete with you at all! You're so fucking cool! You're from New York. You make your own clothes and costumes, and you know everything about Broadway. Meanwhile, I'm just me! I've never even seen a musical all the way through!"

"Normal? Norah, you're not normal. You're a track star and you're like the best dresser at school. I mean, god, you look so cool all the time and you're nice, like genuinely nice, and I don't know how to deal with that. You're also freaking Cinderella! Norah, I am not cooler than you."

With a snort, Norah rolled her eyes again. "Yeah, sure. That's not what Camille thinks. Half the time we're together she's always talking about *you*. If you and Lizzie hadn't started dating I don't think she'd have ever given me the time of day."

Norah's eyes sparkled as she smiled so brightly I thought I was gonna go blind. This was the happiest I had ever seen her, actually gushing like she was talking about her favorite thing of all time. "Camille is fun and kind and she's doing her best. I mean, she's nervous about the play, but she's doing amazing."

As Norah rambled on, the last piece of the puzzle sank into place. A switch inside of me flicked on. "Are you . . ." I blinked. "Are you two dating?" Norah froze, and panic flickered across her face, which made me freak out. "Oh my god. Oh my god."

"Shut up! Shut up!" Norah waved her hands at me like I was a car speeding down the road to make a Norah Brady pancake. "We're not dating! Not like officially but we've been talking—" Her face burned even brighter. "You absolutely can't say anything to Camille! This isn't for me to tell you!"

"I won't! I promise!"

Norah took a deep breath to calm herself down. She looked into my eyes, maybe searching for a bit of confidence that I could keep my big mouth shut, which I deserved. If I was her, I wouldn't trust me either.

Finally, I admitted, "Wow. I probably haven't made it easy on you."

"No." Norah cracked a smile. "No, you haven't. I don't think you know how to do anything easily."

That made me laugh. "I think you're right. Damn. We could've been friends, huh?"

"We still can be." She shrugged. "As long as you promise not to burn all the costumes."

"Promise."

She laughed and helped me move all the costumes back into my bedroom. Then we moved down to the kitchen. Norah hopped onto the kitchen counter as I made us some coffee.

"Yeah, I overheard Mrs. Donnelly on the phone with someone explaining how we don't have enough people in the cast as extras and how we're basically running on empty. Plus Jordan keeps knocking over the set and our costumes are a joke without you."

"What are you guys going to do?"

"I don't know, but if we don't do anything, the play isn't going to happen."

My stomach twisted as I watched the coffee brew. The warm smell filled the house and lured Hayden downstairs. He did a double take at Norah but didn't ask questions. He introduced himself and they started chatting about school. I couldn't stop thinking about the play being canceled. If that were to happen, Camille wouldn't get to have her debut. Four years she had waited for a big role, and it was all about to be ripped away from her.

There had to be something I could do to help.

THIRTY-NINE

Parker

A knock on my bedroom door surprised me. I had been bingeing episodes of home organization reality shows to keep me from thinking about Lizzie and feeling miserable.

"Come in," I piped up from my desk.

My dad leaned past the threshold, checking to see if the coast was clear. "Hey, Parker, uh, I found this." He revealed a bedazzled shoe. "I'm guessing it's yours, or I've really lost touch with my wife."

"It could be Hayden's," I said defensively. I honestly didn't know how to turn it off.

My dad nodded. "I guess I'll go ask—"

"No! Sorry, it's mine."

He smiled and let himself inside. I got up and plopped down on my bed. He handed me the shoe. "Is this a costume thing or a Parker thing?"

"What's a Parker thing?" I scrunched my brows together, ready for a hit.

He shrugged. "I don't know. You wear very creative clothes. I wouldn't put it past you to wear anything eccentric. You're this town's very own Björk."

He was trying to compliment me, so I held back a snarky remark, though it was shockingly hard. I touched the shoe's jewels, moving them back and forth so they would catch the light and glitter.

He studied me. Maybe it was the way my lips trembled as the truth collected on top of my tongue, all the things that I hadn't told him that compiled into more of a mountain than I couldn't conquer. Tilting his head, he let out a little sigh and said, "You can tell me. Give me a chance, Parker." He shrugged. "That's all I need."

His words sank into my tired bones. We were the same. I needed to ask for one last chance. I just needed one more chance too.

Softened up, I admitted, "It's actually, um, a costume thing."

"Cool." My dad nodded and admired the shoe again. "That's really cool. Can I see the sketches?"

"Actually," I mumbled, suddenly hit with the urge to run and hide. I stood up and walked to my closet and plucked out one of my covered costumes, setting it on the bed next to him. I unzipped it, feeling my face burn red hot. My armpits suddenly pooled with sweat. "I'm doing the costumes for the school musical," I whispered, because I couldn't form the words any louder. It felt like being inside a dark basement, expecting something to jump around the corner.

My dad reached for the dress on the hanger, moving his hand over it as my entire chest tightened. I kept talking. If I didn't stop talking he wouldn't be able to totally disappoint me with his reaction. "It's *Cinderella*—um, not that dress. That's, uh, one of the other character's dresses. It's not my showstopper. I did the shoes, too, and some hats. Thankfully, they got someone else to do the makeup because you know me, or maybe you don't—but I don't wear makeup."

His smile created crinkles around his eyes as he listened to every word. "It's amazing, Parker. I can't believe you did all this work. Now I understand why your room's a wreck. If I did all this, I'd live in madness too. I promise to keep my mouth shut about the mess if it works for you." He raised his hand in a promise.

"Thanks," I said, losing all the breath in my lungs. Where was the catch?

"How long have you been working on these costumes?"

He called them costumes. Not stuff.

My eyes bubbled with tears. "Um, like a few months."

His jaw dropped. "Months? Wha—why didn't I know about this before?" His eyes widened. "Oh no. Don't tell me I missed the play?"

"No, it's not for another week. You'd come?"

He deflated, dropping his hands on his knees. "I'd love to come. Did you think I wouldn't want to come? Parker, I wanna be there. I want to be there to cheer you on. I mean, I don't know much about these plays and musicals, but if it's important to you, it's important to me."

My lips trembled and the waterworks started.

He smiled, his own eyes glistening with tears now. "I already missed so much. I can't bear to miss anything else. Hell, yes, Debbie, Hayden, and I will be there in the front row with signs and posters. I'll even print your face on a T-shirt."

"Please don't." I laughed and rolled my eyes through the tears. "Besides, it's probably not even going to happen. I really messed up and pissed off my director. She'll probably never let me back into the play."

"Should I talk to her?"

"No." I panicked, slightly horrified by the thought of my chino-wearing, couldn't-name-a-single-showtune dad talking to my drama teacher. "Don't do that. I'll talk to her."

"If you need me, I'm right here."

He was here. Right here.

"You'll always be my baby girl," my dad said as he stood, sweeping his hand through my hair. I didn't think we shared much. Only our eyes, and I swear we had the same knees, which haunted me every single day. But those were only physical things. I realized we shared other traits too: the way we liked our space, the way we got hangry, the way we fell in love with people who were much nicer than us. My dad walked out of the room and closed the door behind him, already knowing that was how I wanted it.

I wandered to my closet and shoved my hanging wardrobe out of the way, I reached down and stretched for my rolling suitcase. I pulled it out by the handle and dragged it to my bed. It was heavier than I recalled from when I arrived last year.

My last suitcase. I hadn't opened it or touched it since I moved in. This place didn't ever feel like home, so I didn't want to fully unpack, just in case.

I unzipped it, greeted by my old Broadway posters. Underneath them were my string lights, playbills of my favorite shows, some little art prints, and photos carefully stuffed inside books to protect them during travel. These were the sacred memories I had gathered over time. Everything in the suitcase had a story to tell. Everything in the suitcase was my life. And now I realized that my life hadn't ended when I left New York. It had continued.

I taped everything on the walls, including the playbill Mrs. Donnelly had printed for *Cinderella*. I added snapshots of Camille and me from a photo-booth session the summer I arrived.

Give me a chance, that's all I need, that's what my dad said.

Over the last month, I expended a lot of chances. The chance to work things out with Norah. The chance to save my friendship with Camille. The chance to make the costumes for my school's musical, the very thing I wanted to do in my life. The chance in a lifetime to be Elizabeth Hernández's girlfriend.

Stepping back, I admired my walls. For the first time since I moved into this house, they weren't totally bare. Suddenly, I was all over this room. No longer a guest.

FORTY

Parker

Mrs. Donnelly's office was filled with posters of every musical she had put on at the school. The last time I was here, I was with Emily and Camille. We were asking as a united front if I could do the costumes for the spring musical. Despite not knowing me, despite me being at this school for five seconds, Mrs. Donnelly let me do it. She warned me it was an enormous task, but once she said they were putting on *Cinderella*, I would've said anything to get the chance to help bring that fairy tale to life.

Both Mrs. Donnelly and I understood that to transport an audience, everything mattered, from the sets to the costumes. Costumes were a huge part of the storytelling, which meant I was a huge part of the storytelling.

I wanted to be a part of this wall and be a good memory for a good teacher.

"I—" I said, fighting the fist-sized lump in my throat. Mrs. Donnelly sat on the other side of her desk, patiently waiting for me to get on with it. "I took this opportunity for granted," I admitted, clutching my knees. Finally looking up, I could feel my face get hot, but I wanted to look her in the eye. "You warned me it'd be hard, and it has been, but everything in my life has been challenging lately."

Tears pricked my eyes, but I took my time and kept my voice steady. "I took it out on you and I'm sorry. You've been really great to me and I'm so sorry."

Mrs. Donnelly handed me her box of tissues and I unloaded a baseball-sized wad of snot into the soft white cotton. I told her everything about my mom and my drama with Camille, and I even spilled the entire trial with Lizzie and how Lizzie saw me like she did last month, with hatred and remorse.

Now, it was Mrs. Donnelly's turn to form all these little imperfections into little bullets that she could fire against me. I closed my eyes, waiting for the attack. It was what I deserved.

"I can't speak to the Lizzie situation," she said tactfully, "but when it comes to *Cinderella*, we'd be happy to have you back in our production."

"Really?" I asked, my tears welling up again.

"Of course. We're a family. We fight. We have our troubles. We apologize. Parker, if I lost you, I'd mourn you for years. You are a huge part of this production. When you win your first Tony Award for costume design, I expect to be thanked."

I laughed and another cement block tumbled off my shoulders. There was still some weight there. I still had a little work to do.

"But I don't want to disappoint you," Mrs. Donnelly spoke carefully. She folded her hands with her ten rings, one on each finger. "By the end of the week, I must decide whether or not to cancel the production—"

"What?" I gawked.

"I'm leaning toward cancellation."

"You can't. My dad's coming to the show." I stuck my thumb out at the door behind me. "Norah's gotta play Cinderella—and Camille! It's her debut in a title role! And then there's everybody else!"

"I know all this," Mrs. Donnelly said. "But if we can't find enough people to be in this musical, then we can't put on the show. Not to mention Jordan takes down the sets as fast as we can build them, but we can't lose him too. No one else can learn the prince's part in time."

"So, we just have to fix these things, right? We need more people? Okay." As the words left my mouth, the idea hit me. I grinned. "I've got an idea. It's just a start, but I think the show can go on." Mrs. Donnelly locked eyes with me, not quite convinced, but with open ears. I took a deep breath and corrected myself. I shot out of her office with a thousand things to do, but only one person on my mind.

Lizzie

The last person I thought I'd see on the other side of my door was Parker. She perked up as I opened it. She wore a huge hot-pink fluffy coat double the size of her shoulders and striped pants with platform boots that doubled her height. Half her hair was up in a ponytail, tied with a matching pink scrunchie.

She stared at me.

I stared at her.

It had been days since we stood this close. My chest tightened, squeezing the breath out of my lungs. Usually I'd use that air to say something like hello or I'd ask her how she was holding up, but the only thing I wanted to know was if she also couldn't stop thinking about the breakup.

"Sorry to barge in," Parker said.

"You're not barging in, you're still outside," I said without thinking.

Parker grimaced. "I didn't mean it *like that*. I mean, like I'm sorry I didn't call first or message you, but I didn't think you'd answer."

"So you thought you'd just show up anyway?"

"No?" Parker opened her mouth to bicker back, but the question continued to hang there as nothing she thought to say helped her case at all. At least one of us was thinking. I needed to put this big mouth of mine under lock and key.

Let Parker talk first, instead of making her react to me and my hurt.

"Listen," Parker said before letting out a small little huff. She took a deep breath of the cool autumn air then unloaded everything as quickly as I could keep up. "We have to work together to save the play so Camille can have her debut and my dad can see my costumes and Norah can wear that damn tiara and you can play music. I know you broke up with me, and I know you can't stand me, but—"

Danny approached from behind me, grabbing the door to make his appearance. He narrowed his eyes at Parker, who was his height in those shoes. Parker looked at him like he was the boogeyman. Her freckled face flushed as she tried desperately to backtrack. "Uh, I mean you broke up with the *play* and you can't stand me."

I chuckled. "He knows, Parker. I told him."

"You told him?" Parker blinked. She looked between us and a smile appeared, making her eyes sparkle. It'd been so long since I'd seen Parker smile like that. I took it like a gunshot to the stomach. "Really? That's amazing. You're amazing."

"Thanks," I said, losing my breath.

Danny leaned closer to my shoulder. "Do I need to get rid of her? She's supertall, but she looks throwable."

"No, no." I patted his chest and pushed him deeper in the house. "I've got this, Danny, but thank you." Turning back around, I closed the door behind me. I braced myself against the cold by crossing my arms. "What do you mean 'save the play'?"

"Mrs. Donnelly is going to cancel it if we can't get at least ten more people to be a part of the chorus."

"But why do you need my help?"

"Why wouldn't I want your help? I can't do this without you, Lizzie. You're the only person I know who has a functional car."

I turned away. This couldn't sway me. This was a trick, and I wasn't so naïve anymore. Suddenly, Parker's voice jumped out. She sounded so panicked. "Wait! Lizzie don't go yet. I need your help to do this because everyone loves you and no one can say no to you. People *love* saying no to me."

"Parker." I folded easier than fresh laundry.

"I know I messed up, but I'm trying to fix it. I'm trying to make it all better."

"Parker, I'm—"

"And I don't want you to be left out! Because the play's important to you, too, so you deserve to be a part of the thing that saves it."

"PARKER!" I shouted and she curled her lips into her mouth. I laughed a little and shook my head. "I'll go grab my jacket and some shoes, unless you plan to carry me everywhere."

"Oh." Parker blushed.

"Stay out here or you'll have to get the third degree from Danny."

"Right, great." She gave me a thumbs-up and I hurried inside. I tossed on my coat and tied on my trusty Converse. By the time I made it back downstairs with my keys and my backpack, Parker's teeth were chattering. I hurried her to my car.

"Um," Parker said, shyer than I expected. She cleared her throat and struggled to put her seat belt on, pulling it too fast so it locked. She struggled and mumbled under her breath, "You, uh, look really pretty. By the way. Whatever. I'm cool."

With a laugh, I rolled my eyes and backed down the driveway. "Shut up and tell me where I'm going."

"We're going to Miss Patty's," Parker declared.

FORTY-ONE

Parker

An auditorium full of drag queens wasn't something I ever imagined happening, but was a dream come true. My real-life fairy godmother Barry saved the show from closing by bestowing upon us his gaggle of drag daughters to fill in the rest of the cast. Everyone was game for any chance to perform. And while everyone else was having fun, I was on the cusp of losing my best friend forever.

Despite the full cast being here, I only seemed to run into Camille. It had now been so long since we had spoken that I was out of practice and had forgotten how to initiate it. Talking to her should've been like riding a bike. Instead, I nearly knocked her down with a basket of my costumes.

"Uh, sorry, my bad," I blabbered on the top steps, trying to walk onto the stage while Camille was passing by.

Camille only glowered, unimpressed by my intelligible mumbling.

Norah tapped my shoulder. "Hey, I met Barry. He's supercool." Then Norah turned to get Camille's attention but Camille continued walking right by, her cold shoulder sending a chill down my spine.

"She's pissed," I said.

"No shit." Norah frowned and crossed her arms. "But why is she pissed at me?"

"What have you done lately?"

"Nothing. I even became friends with you, which is what I thought she wanted."

"I'd talk to her, but she's scary."

"Yeah," Norah agreed, but she seemed keener about it than me. Whatever made their relationship work, I guess. We went back to work as my true dream job began. I needed to tailor five dresses that were originally meant for high-school girls and make them perfect for an array of drag queens. All five of Miss Patty's drag daughters stood on stage wearing heels, wigs, and dresses while taking instructions from Mrs. Donnelly. They were all given a buddy, someone from the chorus who could answer any questions.

The last five extras were taken from the tech crew, including me. My main instructions were to do my best. That bastard Ian got out of it because he was one of the only people who knew how to work the switch controls.

"Which one's the girl you blew it with?" said someone named Michael in his daily life but who on the stage went by Sugar Princess. Wearing heels, he stood seven feet, and had a thousand tattoos, so I gave him the dress that used to belong to Laura, a basketball player, with long billowing sleeves and a cupcake silhouette.

I grimaced, eyeing Camille in the corner. "What girl haven't I blown it with?"

"No, no." Michael waved away my coyness. "Which one's the *girlfriend*?"

"Which girlfriend?"

"Stop bragging about all your girlfriends and point this unlucky lady out."

"That one." I pointed at Lizzie, who noticed, so I quickly waved to save face. Michael waved, too, like a real friend. Confused, Lizzie waved back, but went back to marking a few things on her sheet music. She smiled cutely to herself, and I almost started weeping.

"Wow." Michael nodded understandingly. "You really fucked up."

"Shut up," I warned him, and tightened his corset.

He grunted before unleashing a long, tortured groan, rolling his shoulder muscles around. The sound of his neck cracking reminded me of gravel crunching underneath my feet. "Come on, you can do better than that, Casanova."

It was business as usual during rehearsal as we tried going through the whole play with our new cast and our rhythmically challenged tech crew. Everybody got stuffed into their costumes, but when it was time for Camille's fitting, I panicked.

Camille's big dark eyes locked onto me like a hunter's mark, and instantly the speech I had prepared, and all my organized groveling, evaporated from my brain. A horrible thought occurred to me that maybe, no matter what I said, she'd still reject me.

"Ian," I said, whipping around with my back facing Camille, although her stare was so hot, my skin itched from the burn. "Will you help the stepsisters with their costumes, and I'll handle the ensemble?"

Ian's unamused expression didn't budge. "Fine, but you're helping me move sets for rehearsal."

"Deal."

I ran to the small handful of knights. Any time I accidentally met Camille's eyes, I looked at the ceiling. If there was a possibility we were going to pass each other, I turned and went the long way around. Eventually, Mrs. Donnelly made me go practice my part on the stage. Most of the choreographed dance numbers had been simplified to fancy posing except for the ball. The one scene I was put in still required dancing.

"Since Jordan's at the optometrist, I need a dance partner!" Norah called from backstage. Not only had Lizzie and I enlisted help from drag queens, we'd also gone to Jordan's house and bullied him into getting his eyes checked.

Despite her being nowhere in sight, my hand shot in the air. "I'll do it!"

Appearing from the wings, Norah glided onto the stage as if floating.

At last she had on the Cinderella dress. It held the classic hourglass silhouette with capped sleeves and three bountiful petticoats to make a grand statement. She drifted in this beautiful fabric that started off royal blue at the top and faded to white, as if she was floating on clouds. Working with this fade, I had added a thicker pasture of blue beading on top. The sparkles faded toward the bottom, freckling out and becoming sparse. The stage lights hit her and she was surrounded by twinkling starlight. It was magic.

I wanted to be buried in that dress.

A few curls spilled from Norah's quick bun. Her skin glistened with a sparkly skin lotion we were trying out, which added to her natural shine. My jaw dropped as she met my eyes, and despite her rolling her eyes, she still smiled.

"My lady," I said, offering her my arm. "Will you give me the honor of this dance?"

"I suppose one dance couldn't hurt." Norah succumbed to my charms, sliding her blue satin glove over my arm.

"Well, you haven't seen me waltz," I warned as I led her to the front of the stage, fixing my posture into something more princely, something more worthy of this dance.

"If my toes can survive Jordan, I can survive you, Parker."

I feigned a gasp, holding my hand over my dainty little heart. "That's the most romantic thing anyone has ever said to me."

She laughed, glancing at our feet. The orchestra swelled and Norah fell into a graceful curtsy, which I mirrored with a low bow. She smiled from ear to ear and it seemed impossible that there was even a moment when I hated her. We took our positions together and Norah whispered, "You can follow my lead."

Giggling like an idiot, I followed her in the dance, doing my best to remember all the moves. I had watched Jordan do it a million times, so my memory was decent enough. Norah did the rest. "Have you been able to talk to Camille yet?" she asked while we danced.

I shook my head. "No. I'm nervous, and honestly, I don't want to make her more angry."

Laughing a little, she nodded. "That would be bad, but you do have to talk to her."

"And you're supposed to let me lead," I said, and got her to throw her head back with laughter again. She was so smiley. I had never noticed before. We waltzed as Norah found her concrete placements and Ian debated Mrs. Donnelly on lightning up in the booth.

"Can I cut in?"

Glancing around, Norah and I spun to find Camille standing there with her hands crossed. Her big brown eyes stared back expectantly. Panic seized me, and I held on to Norah's hand and waist a little tighter. "Um, I think we should keep practicing. Norah and I found a rhythm."

Dropping her arms with a huff, Camille set her jaw tight. She shook her head. "Are you kidding me? Do I have fleas or something?"

"No, no, no," I quickly said, letting Norah go.

"Well! It feels like it. You take one look at me and you run! Are you over me now? You finally made friends with Norah and now you don't need me anymore? You two are glued together."

Norah raised her hands in surrender. "Please don't fight."

"Whoa! Whoa!" I raised my voice, my panic graduating from a tornado warning to a stage five hurricane. "You're the one who wanted us to get along!"

"Right! Like I wanted you to get along with Lizzie! I don't know how you can't fit me into your life when someone new comes along. First Emily, then Lizzie, and now, I guess, Norah. Why am I always second place? It makes me feel like I'm crazy, like I'm the only one upset here. It hurts." Her voice snagged on a small cry as her eyes sparkled with tears. "You're totally fine and I'm heartbroken all by myself. I can't even enjoy having this role because you're everywhere! I have to wear the dress you made. I wanted you to get along with people, sure, but I don't want to get left behind! I can't do this anymore."

"Camille." I tried to find my voice and think of a way to make her believe me. "I didn't mean for it to come across this way. Like, yeah, I've been avoiding you, but it's because all I do is say the wrong thing. I didn't want to make you angry."

"I've never been angrier in my life!"

The speakers crackled as the microphone inside the tech booth turned on. Mrs. Donnelly's voice boomed from the corners of the auditorium, "Girls. Girls. Please, let's calm down. We can talk it out. At the end of the day, we need to work together."

"Well, maybe I don't want to work with her!" Camille shouted.

Ian took over the mike. "But she's doing the costumes—"

"Then I quit!"

The room of drama kids gasped, dramatically and well timed.

Camille hiked up her costume and brushed past me. I was too in shock to move or to think as she walked down the steps and strutted past the audience seats toward the main lobby. Lizzie jumped out of her chair and chased after Camille. "Parker, come on!" she shouted, shaking me out of my daze. I jumped off the stage in my ball gown and ran for her like this was a rom-com airport scene.

I threw myself at the exit doors and yelled, "Camille! Get back here!"

"No!" Camille shouted, running like her life depended on it.

"Don't be an idiot!" Lizzie yelled too.

I ran as fast as I could, gathering as much of my dress as I could manage; thankfully I was wearing leggings underneath. Finally, I kicked the heels off and ran through the science department hallway, letting my bare feet slap the floor and try to catch that tiny goth, who jingled loudly with every step. Lizzie lagged behind me, immediately out of breath.

Camille quickly turned into the gym and ran down the steps that led to the basketball court. A wave of relief washed over me because I assumed all the doors would be locked. "Stop running!" My voice boomed, bouncing off the high ceiling. "Let's talk!"

Camille pulled at every door handle until she found purchase with one and we were all hit by the strong smell of chlorine and plastic. I followed her into the school's swimming pool. There was a strong echo, amplifying our labored breaths, our hurried steps, and even the sounds of our raging hearts.

Closing my eyes, I summoned the last of my strength and powered my legs to not only catch up to Camille, but also to pile-drive her five-foot body into the pool. We crashed magnificently onto the surface, creating tidal waves. The chilled water swallowed me whole. At least a pint infiltrated my nose, so I resurfaced hacking up a lung.

Almost immediately, Camille splashed me. "Why did you do that?! You're a menace, you know that?!"

"You wouldn't stop running!" I managed to get out between wheezing.

"I'm out of here," Camille grumbled, wading in the water.

Lizzie, who was trailing us in the chase, ran to the nearest ladder and slammed her feet on the top. "No, you're not getting out of here until you two actually talk."

I met Camille's eyes, her makeup running down her cheeks. It was like a couple of stray cats sizing each other up. "You can't expect me to spill all my thoughts and feelings if you're not willing to do the same. Meet me halfway, Camille." I swam toward her and begrudgingly, Camille met me.

"What's going on, Camille?" Lizzie asked. "It didn't start at the party. You've been mad for weeks."

Since the start of the trial, I realized.

Camille sighed, letting go of her tension and maybe something else too. "I've been jealous, okay?" Her face warmed with a rosy color that made her dress look cheap. "When I told you guys to start the trial, I just wanted some peace. I mean, how could my favorite people not like each other? I figured if you two really got to know each other, you'd stop fighting all the time."

She took off her play wig, along with her fake glasses, and threw them to the side. She let her black hair spill from a hair clip as she stared down at the water. "But then you guys stopped calling and I was left alone on the weekends. You guys didn't seem to care anymore. And then, when you ditched my party, I thought you guys didn't even like me. I felt so stupid." She looked up at the ceiling and sniffed. "So, yeah, I kinda wanted you guys to end the trial so I could have my best friends again." Her chin wobbled and she couldn't speak another word, not without letting the floodgates open. She did anyway. "I'm sorry, that was so selfish."

"I had no idea. Camille, I'm so sorry," I said, my chest tightening, and I couldn't bear the space between us anymore.

Lizzie slumped and without a second thought slipped into the water with us. She paddled over and put her arms around Camille. "You're my best friend. Ever. You matter to me." Lizzie's voice cracked but she pushed through the tears and said, "And I hate that I made you think anything less."

My eyes watered and I longed to be part of that group hug, moving toward them until another wave of water hit me.

"And you were so mean to Norah!" Camille started back up, splashing me again.

"Hey!" I drew back.

"When I really liked her! I couldn't believe you would be so petty even though I wanted you to like her! Even though you knew I liked her!"

"I'm sorry! I'm sorry!"

Lizzie raised her hand for another question. "What do you mean you like Norah?"

If Camille could shrink even smaller, she'd be at the bottom of the pool. She had our full attention now. She was probably regretting what she'd wished for. "I've never dated anyone. I've never been interested in dating or flirting or kissing or whatever, but you two were always dating and it felt like there was something wrong with me, like you were going to leave me behind."

"How long have you been feeling this way?" I asked.

"My whole life." Camille shrugged a little.

"We've been a couple of idiots," Lizzie said and pulled back, looking at Camille with a soft sort of smile.

"Maybe we're all too alike," Camille joked.

"We have to be honest with each other," Lizzie begged us, and her words took aim and struck right through my heart.

"I will," Camille promised, and opened her arms to me. I threw myself into them and we sank a little, making a laugh fly out of Camille's mouth. The doors to the school pool creaked opened and Norah ran over with Ian trailing closely behind, and my heart swelled. This little friend group was growing by the day.

"What are you doing? Get out of there," Norah insisted, looking at us like she regretted her entire life.

Camille smiled and turned to us. "Sorry. I wasn't honest—I never dated anyone *before* Norah. Norah!" Camille piped up and, looking sweetly at Norah, slapped the water. "Jump in!"

Horrified, Norah took a full step back. "No way!"

Lizzie's jaw dropped. She looked up wide eyed at Norah and then back at Camille. She had the answer to the equation, but not the math to get there. "Dating? Cinderella—I mean, Norah? Really? But when—" Lizzie looked down at her hands. "I thought I was the gay cousin."

"Come on, Norah!" Camille insisted. "Show them your commitment to me and jump in."

"Can I please do anything else?" Norah refused to join us, so we eventually gave up. She coaxed us back out and led us to the theater. Everyone watched Camille walk back up to the stage with her head held high.

She stood center staged, dripping wet and teary eyed. "I'm sorry for freaking out. I'm committed to the play." Her nose flared out. "If you'll still have me, I'd be honored to play Charlotte."

"Of course," Mrs. Donnelly agreed.

"Plus"—Ian's voice sounded from the speakers—"there's, like, no one else."

"Shut up!" I shouted at him.

We were sent away to change, and I laid out all the costumes, now twice the weight dripping wet, and googled how to make clothes dry faster. I hummed along to "In My Own Little Corner" as Norah sang on stage and Lizzie played the piano. Looking up, I caught the eyes of multiple people and found if I didn't look away I got smiles and waves. It dawned on me like sunrays in summer that this was all so much fun.

FORTY-TWO

Lizzie

Backstage on opening night was magical. Girls and guys crowded every mirror, fixing their hair and makeup inside of clouds of sticky sweet hairspray. Parker sat with her little travel-sized sewing kit in the corner with a line of actors in front of her getting last-minute alterations or details stitched. Some were humming or doing warm-ups. The ones who'd gotten ready the fastest were lounging around in full costume, laughing and talking over each other. The buzz in the air alone made things surreal, as if nothing would ever be better than this—we were all together.

Losing myself, I watched Parker sitting cross-legged on the floor with pins in her mouth as she fixed the drooping hem of one of the knight's pants, readying him for "Me, Who Am I?", Prince Topher's first song. For now, she matched him in the costumes repurposed from *Once Upon a Mattress*: short tunics belted in the middle and brown tights, but with pieces of armor around the shoulders, breastplates, gauntlets, and some helms spread out between the actors. Get rid of the armor and they were suddenly peasants. The swords and shields really sold the look.

For a split second Parker did a double take when she noticed me and dropped the pants. She waved, and my heart and my hand waved back in unison.

That look in her eyes could make me fall in love with her all over again.

The playing field had changed. This wasn't about a bet anymore. This was about two real people with real feelings. Feelings with the horrid potential to get beaten, battered, and bruised, but still liking each other anyway. I prayed Parker would take it easier on my heart this time.

"You look snazzy," someone said.

I spun around, finding Emily dressed as a peasant, with a bit of fake dirt on her jaw. Underneath her wool bandana hid perfect little ringlets for the ball later. She had attached her microphone, which looked like a little bean in the middle of her forehead.

"Thanks, you look poor," I said.

Emily forced a small puff of laughter. She sized me up in my concert uniform, a long black skirt with a matching black short-sleeved top that had a weird square-shaped neckline. After curling my hair and putting half of it up, Gina had showed me how to apply eyeliner and let me borrow her red lipstick. My mom also let me wear her pearl necklace and matching earrings.

"What's in the bag?" she asked, referring to the paper bag from Miss Patty's shop in my hand. Tonight, I planned to give Parker the leather jacket as a gift for doing so well with the play. No other reason. Not at all.

"It's nothing," I said, hiding it behind my back.

"Relax. I come in peace. Taylor sent me to remind everyone that the opening night party is going on at her dad's house. Not her mom's house. Do you need her passcode to get through the gate?"

"Oh, um, I'm probably going to pass."

"Really?" Emily's eyes sparkled.

"Okay, you don't have to get so excited." I gripped my bag and stormed off, yelling over my shoulder. "Why don't you break your leg, Emily!"

"It's break *a* leg."

"I know what I said!"

The show started with Mrs. Donnelly's speech. She expressed how this might have been her hardest production as a drama teacher, but she wouldn't change a thing. She thanked Miss Patty's Salon and even Parker. She said, "Without Parker, this production would've never been possible, but as we all know,"—she smiled—"impossible things are happening every day."

I was sure that made Parker cry. Her family was sitting near the orchestra, and Debbie even noticed me. She nudged Parker's dad, and they both waved. From my chair, I could hear him bragging to the other parents that his daughter made the costumes.

Mine were on the other side, taking turns using my father's reading glasses because my mother refused to admit she needed them. They sat with Camille's parents, our *abuela*, a few cousins, and my auntie Gloria. Meanwhile, Gina was probably in the back with her friends, giggling over how cute Jordan was going to look as Prince Topher.

Then the curtain lifted and the show began.

The arrival of the peasant drag queens got a round of applause out of the crowd. It was a good way to start. Miss Patty herself swept the stage, coming out of retirement to help the crew with scene transitions. She was a showstopper with her gorgeous makeup and a blond beehive wig. Her costume was peasant meets flower girl. She had a huge basket of flowers with matching ones trailing up her wig. Miss Patty wore a smile like she knew she looked good.

"Look alive, people," she announced as she scanned the crowd, offering flowers as the stage crew set up the market behind her. She gave dainty little waves and tossed the crowd flowers, entertaining them with little comments like:

"Welcome. Love those pearls, ma'am. I hope they make it back home with me."

"Which kid is yours? Oh, I'd keep that to yourself."

"Thank you. I do take cash, credit, and applause for tips."

Locking eyes with me, she winked, before throwing a flower backward to one of the crew. That got another good laugh.

The play continued. The newer ensemble members forgot a few cues, but the moment Jordan started singing, no one cared. He ran around the stage as charming as a prince, wearing his new round black glasses. He didn't run into a single tree.

When Camille graced the stage, our family started a round of applause that almost broke her completely out of character, but she gathered herself and sang like a little songbird.

Since we didn't have the Broadway budget for Cinderella's transformation, Ian played with the lights, and as the orchestra music swelled, Norah performed the quickest costume change this high-school stage had ever seen. Parker threw Norah back on stage among swirls of fake mist surrounding her, and the audience roared with thunderous applause.

Cinderella danced with the prince. Jordan swept her off her feet and spun her around and around the stage. I could've listened to them sing that song forever, but the curtain fell for intermission. That was the funny thing about loving musicals. The wait to see one took forever but consuming them with your very soul only took a few precious minutes.

The band played into intermission until the music switched to overhead speakers and the house lights brightened. A soft buzz rumbled from the belly of the theater as people got out of their seats, shuffling to the bathroom and the little concession stand.

Jumping up from my seat in the orchestra, I pulled the paper bag from Miss Patty's from underneath my seat. The time was right. I was giving Parker this jacket. I took the long way around the auditorium to sneak backstage, slipping through the ensemble and searching the crowd of ball gowns. Everyone was buzzing, hurrying to go to the bathroom, to get snacks, or change into their next costume.

Miss Patty's drag daughters were high-fiving their friends while Mr. Burka awkwardly laughed. A queen named Miss Fortune tried to figure out if our music teacher was available for private lessons. Among them, Miss Patty stood out the most. Her peasant flower-girl costume was gone, replaced by a bountiful purple ball gown and a shimmering pink wig. Out of everyone, her chunky rainbow of jewelry sparkled the most. All smiles, Miss Patty was cooling herself with a fan of matching purple feathers when she caught my eye. Standing tall, Miss Patty tapped the bottom of her chin and I rolled my shoulders back in response, keeping my head held high.

Her smile was infectious. She blew a kiss, which I caught and pressed into my heart to keep forever. I mouthed, *I love you*.

She motioned me to go off with her long, manicured hand. Maybe she read my mind, telling me to find the person I was looking for, the person I'd been looking for my whole life. It was stupid to wait any longer.

"Lizzie!"

Spinning around, I saw my mother in the shuffling crowd, waving to me. Surprised, I glanced around for Parker once more but still couldn't find her. I hurried over to my mom, who instantly swept me up in a hug. I melted into her arms, squeezing her tighter. She pulled back, letting out a relieved sigh.

"So, this is what you like?"

I smiled. "It's what I love."

"I love it too." She hugged me again. Running her hand through my hair, she said, "I'm so proud of you. You're doing such a good job."

"Thanks." I could only whisper back, trying to keep myself from crying. "It gets hard sometimes, but I still love it."

"I guess I just had to see it," she agreed, and let me go again. Her eyes snagged on the paper bag in my hands. "Oh? What's that? Did someone get you a present?"

"What?" I jumped a little, having totally forgotten about the bag in the moment. Pulling it back from her curious eyes, I opened my mouth to lie, but stopped. Her soft brown eyes, framed with wrinkles because she was smiling, looked so welcoming. A part of me wondered if I could tell her the full truth. But another part of me wasn't ready, so I told her a half-truth. "It's a gift for someone else. Um, I'm actually looking for them now."

My mother nodded. "Go. Your father and I are going to have dinner at Gloria's after the show, so feel free to go out with your friends afterward. When your brother comes home this weekend, we'll celebrate together."

"Thank you." I quickly side-hugged her and pecked her cheek. "I love you!"

"Love you too!" she said, and I was off again, holding my hand over my heart. I was really putting her through the wringer lately.

Checking the time, I noticed I only had a few minutes to do this. Practically running, I headed toward the dressing room that was just the drama room with curtains covering the windows and doors, searching for Parker. My excitement was bubbling to the surface, and I was about to burst with all the things I wanted to tell her. My hands shook, holding not only a jacket, but also my confession. Emily was still walking around, reminding people where the after-party was being thrown. I purposely ignored her presence. No Parker in sight.

Going back to the theater, I struggled through the crowd walking against me. My heart pounded as the top of my skin tingled. I was bursting with all the things I desperately wanted to say to her, all of it tap-dancing on the tip of my tongue.

As I returned backstage through the curtains, someone yelped and a splash of little plastic beads scattered across the floor. "Oops," a girl said, holding up her dress. She caught some of the beading before it fell to the floor. Everyone around immediately dropped to their knees, scooping up the tiny walking hazards. The girl smiled sheepishly at Parker and said, "I'm guessing it's not supposed to do that."

No wonder I couldn't find Parker. She'd traded in her knight's costume for a pink ball gown that made her look like an overiced cupcake with about a dozen bows too many. She had stuffed her hair into a blond beehive of hair too.

My heart expanded and I almost called out to her, when Parker responded, "Of course it's not supposed to do that! Go outside. We'll shake you off and then I gotta do something about the rip. Let's go," she said, and shuffled the girl through the mess while I watched until she fully disappeared through the back exit doors. The last thing Parker probably wanted to hear during a clothing disaster was me pleading to get back together. It wasn't about us. Not yet.

With a sigh, I walked back to the drama classroom. I was jolted to see Emily still lingering, and stuck my nose in the air. Coolly, I breezed right by her and moved to the other side of the room, but that wasn't even far enough. If this was the last day I saw Emily, it'd still be one day too many. Creeping into the corner, I found Parker's emptied clothing rack, some bins, and her large sewing kit. This was it. Letting out a breath, I placed the bag on top of Parker's kit, fixing it so it sat perfectly upright to greet her.

She'd find it and we'd be able to get right to talking. This forced a conversation. I couldn't chicken out. Smiling to myself, I kept my head held high as I breezed past Emily without a single look.

Parker

The warm, gooey emotions welled up in my tear ducts, but I couldn't cry past the huge smile on my face. Taking a deep breath, I clutched the collar of my shirt as the entire cast of *Cinderella* took to the bottom of the stage for their final bows.

The crowd applauded, certain audience members whooping and hollering for their friends and loved ones as the orchestra played "Impossible" again. At the end, the entire cast motioned me on stage with them. With a push, I shuffled out and took my bow hand in hand with Camille.

From the wings, Miss Patty appeared wearing the fairy godmother's wings and walked out on stage, handing roses to Jordan, Camille, and finally one to me. The tears threatened to break through as I threw my arms around Miss Patty. Her tight squeeze made me truly believe she had magical powers. She whispered, "Look around, kid. You've earned it."

Taking a step back, Miss Patty continued to applaud. The entire cast's opened hands stretched toward me. They all looked so beautiful. Jordan walked to my other side, and we all took a final bow together. I looked back at the cast, remembering the long nights, the soreness in my joints, the pain in every knuckle on my finger, every prick from the needle, and the absolute torture of drying off the stepsister's gown. Tears welled up in my eyes, threatening to burst like a geyser as I couldn't help but smile. It was worth it.

I wasn't meant to do anything else.

I found Lizzie in the orchestra and waved, mouthing the words *We did it!*

She grinned from ear to ear and looked back down at the piano keys.

The very second the curtain hit the floor and the music faded to a stop, I bolted. I wasn't going to stop for anybody. I knew some people would need more help to get out of their costumes than others, but I hadn't seen Lizzie all night and my heart was going through withdrawal.

Hurrying down the steps, I almost went headfirst into a bouquet of roses. "Whoa!"

I stumbled back to find my dad, Debbie, and Hayden, who offered me the flowers. "Hey."

"Parker, everything looked so beautiful!" Debbie cheered and brought me into a side-hug that felt nicer than I expected. This was our first hug that I could recall, and I think I liked it. She rubbed my shoulders, still brightly smiling. "You're so talented."

I looked at my dad, and he just kept nodding, tears rimming his bloodshot eyes. He nodded as he pulled me into an even tighter hug, like it was a who's prouder of Parker contest. Debbie laughed, her hands on her hips. "Your father has not stopped crying."

"I'm pretty sure the family behind us thought we brought a toddler," Hayden grumbled.

Dad sniffed and wiped his eyes with a crumpled napkin. "I'm sorry. I'm really proud of you. Lots of people, you know," he said, needing to take another breath, "they'd like to do something like this, but you actually did it and it's hard work. That should be recognized." The nodding returned as his lips thinned into a line trying to keep another sob at bay.

"Thanks, Dad." I laughed deliriously or else I'd get choked up too. Any minute everyone was going to sprout wings and fly, or else this wasn't a dream. This was real.

Hayden nudged me again. "Good job."

"I know." I could barely get it out, and threw my arms around him, making him sway with me back and forth. I got a little squeeze back, then let him go. He handed me the flowers and I cradled them like I'd won Miss Universe. It suddenly dawned on me that my mother had never crossed my mind tonight. I was too busy with the cast, friends, and seeing my dad in the crowd to check for my mom's text. For once, I didn't care. My family was right in front of me. Not making me wait by the phone.

"Um," I said, "there's an after-party tonight. Is it okay if I stay out a little late?"

Dad could only nod, so Debbie answered. "Sure. Remember to text us when you're on your way home, but if it's too late, try to sleep over, okay? Have fun. Be safe."

I couldn't contain it. I hugged them all again before bolting into the drama classroom to shed this ball gown and find Lizzie. I figured it'd be better to confess my feelings dressed like myself. Setting my roses down by my sewing kit, I pulled off my wig and my hair net, so my hair could fall back down.

"Hey, Parker," someone said.

I spun around to find Emily, dressed in smiles and her purple gown with pink trimmings from the finale. There was a glint of eagerness in her eyes. Something about her was off; maybe it was the energy from the performance still making her adrenaline bubble.

"I know you want to greet the masses so everyone can drown you in compliments," Emily said, teasingly rolling her eyes.

I grinned. "Then you know why this can wait until later—"

"Slow down so I can give you this."

She raised a brown paper bag, and I straightened. "Lucky for you I like presents as much as I like praise," I said, and she handed me the bag. I shoved my hand inside, touching cool rough fabric, and my fingers recognized the distinct feel of leather I yearned to own. I couldn't take it out fast enough.

As I dropped the paper bag, my jaw also dropped as I admired the shiny metallic buttons and the zipper outlining the lapels. I flipped it over and my heart jumped up my throat in total glee. A scribbly threaded bouquet of daisies. My dream gift.

"Wait, wait." I did a double take, scrunching my brow at Emily and asking, "Where did you get this? How? When? Is this seriously for me?"

"Of course, it is," Emily said, playfully shoving my shoulder. "I felt pretty guilty ruining your coat at Olivia's party, but I think this suits you better anyway. It's a big night for you. You deserve it."

"So I can have it?"

"Yes," Emily insisted, pretending to be exasperated with a smile.

"Em! This is amazing! I love it!" I threw my arms around her, tightening my hold around her, despite how rigid her form felt. "I can't believe this. You know I wanna die and—"

"And come back to life as a leather jacket, I know." Emily smiled tightly and nodded. "Do you have a ride to Taylor's party? I can drive you."

"Really? Yeah, that'd be cool," I said offhandedly, too consumed with stuffing the ball gown's sleeves into the jacket sleeves, so I could now start my new life as an owner of a leather jacket. Who doesn't want to be a woman with a leather jacket? I stretched my arms, admiring the leather.

"Great." Emily rubbed her hands together. "Um, I'm gonna get changed. Do you wanna meet me by my car?"

"Sure."

"Okay."

"Thanks again!" I cheered and hugged her one more time. I hadn't realized how much Emily truly knew me. Right down to my very soul.

She turned for the other side of the drama room to grab her stuff, glancing behind her shoulder to check if I was still there. She still had a strange, unreadable expression, but I needed to get out of this gown and now. The best part of wearing high heels was taking them off. I kneeled down and detached from the shoes. Down there, I was shoving a stray playbill into the paper bag and some of my jewelry when I recognized a pair of leggings pass me.

"Andrea!" I called, snatching her sleeve before she could get away. "Hey, where's Lizzie? Have you seen her?"

"Lizzie?" Andrea raised her brow. She glanced down at my hand touching her and I promptly dropped it. I jumped to my feet as she explained, "Lizzie already left. I saw her bolt out of here. Maybe she's trying to avoid someone."

She walked away with her stink eye, so I shouted after her, "One day you'll love me! Everyone succumbs to my charms eventually!"

"HA!" Andrea threw her head back.

That didn't sound like it boded well for me, but I quickly changed into my comfy street clothes. I kept my eye out for them, but there was no sign of Camille or Norah either. I checked my phone but there weren't any new messages or missed calls. An uncomfortable nervous feeling festered inside my stomach like energetic gnats whirling like cyclones in the humid summer.

Something wasn't sitting right.

FORTY-THREE

Lizzie

I shoved the exit doors open, my eyes burning white hot with tears. This misery landed in my skull like a nuclear bomb, instantly giving me a headache. Rushing through the parking lot, I avoided the stream of cars trying to leave. My stomach churned in agony, seeing the line to escape was the length of the parking lot. Before I could drive, I was going to have to sit in my car with the seat down so no one could see me crying, giving me enough time to pull myself together and drive away from this hellscape. The tears poured down my cheeks anyway.

It had all happened so fast.

When I found Parker, I watched in slow horror as she threw her arms around Emily. She smiled my favorite smile. She laughed. She even hugged Emily again. My heart splintered into tiny shriveled needle-thin pieces that struck the inside walls of my body.

Emily asked to take Parker out.

And Parker said yes.

Before Parker could turn and spot my horrified face, I ran. She was wearing the jacket I got her, but her arms were wrapped around

Emily. Because of Emily, she was smiling and laughing. The best she'd looked in ages. Not because of me. But I guess heartbreak trumps a cool jacket every time. I was the one who broke up with her in the first place. Emily had been spending half of this trial trying to get Parker back. Sucking up my tears, I could feel the weight of my choices bury me. I couldn't believe that I'd actually trusted Parker when she said she and Emily were done.

"Lizzie!" Camille called.

I only glanced behind me but did a double take seeing Cinderella's evil stepsister chasing my heels. It was a surreal strange moment, a break from reality crushing me into a paper wad that had the great destiny of being garbage.

"Where are you going?!" Camille huffed, trying to catch up to me.

"I'm going on tour to say sorry to my exes."

"What?" Her voice cracked in surprise. "Why? It's not Halloween. You two still have time."

"I have to pay my debt from the trial. I have to shut the door on this forever and leave it behind. Officially." I pulled out my keys, rubbing my face with the sleeves of my jacket. Like rubbing sand across already raw skin. "I can't let the present pass me by. I have to move on like everybody else. Finishing this bet is the only way to do it, the only way I can let go."

"Um, *I'm* supposed to be the dramatic one. Lizzie, are you really giving up on Parker?"

I whirled around. Maybe Camille was a figment of my imagination. But she just stood there in this crazy reality, mirroring my stupefied look. "I thought you were against our relationship."

"I mean," She shrugged her glittery shoulders and crossed her arms. "At first I was a little worried. You were falling for her so fast and hard that I thought you were going to fall flat on your face."

"Don't you dare tell me I told you so."

Her eyes bugged out. "No! I was worried at the beginning until I noticed that Parker was falling too. We already discussed that I was being a jealous hag, okay? So, we don't have to go through that again."

"You don't know that."

"What?"

"That she fell for me. We're friends now and you know what?" I stormed around my car and hopped into the driver's seat. "I asked for this. I broke up with her, so I'm going to deal with my self-imposed consequences."

"Wait!" Camille knocked on the glass. "Let me come with you! I'll get changed really quick!"

I started the car and revved the engine, forcing Camille to quickly back off as I zoomed to join the exit line and waited my turn to pull onto the road. Fifteen excruciating minutes of pretending Camille didn't exist and that she wasn't staring at me and calling my cell phone.

Hanging up on her, I went to my text messages instead. One step at a time, I was going to walk away from Parker. I've never been the end goal for her and tonight solidified that.

Lizzie: The costumes were amazing. You're amazing. I'm so lucky to be your friend

Parker

The nerves in my stomach bubbled. My little worries refused to settle down, like a bag of hot popcorn still popping even after the microwave deemed it finished. Glancing over my shoulder, grazing the faces at Taylor's party, I tried to find the reason for these worries. I felt as if some unearthly being was standing outside my vision, watching me and waiting for the perfect opportunity to pants me in front of the entire drama department.

I looked at Lizzie's cryptic message again.

Lizzie: The costumes were amazing. You're amazing. I'm so lucky to be your friend

The friend comment made my hunger disappear. I'll never have an appetite again.

"Have you seen Lizzie?" I asked Jordan and Ian, who were sitting together on the couch. Despite there being an entirely unoccupied sectional, the boys sat snuggly, wedged into the corner. Ian rested his elbow behind Jordan with a look that told me I wasn't welcome. The placement was casual enough not to raise too many questions. Intimate enough to keep people away. But not me; I'm the best at purposely not taking a hint.

"No, we haven't. Go away," Ian deadpanned.

"Is everything okay?" Jordan asked, his puppy-dog eyes welling up with worry.

Ian groaned and detached from Prince Charming's side, sinking into the back cushion. "Have you asked Camille?"

I shook my head. "I can't find her either. Or Norah"

"I'm sure they're fine," Emily insisted, returning to my side with two ice-cold sodas. "Can you, like, relax for two seconds? Just have fun."

"Yeah, but I need to talk to her."

"It can wait, I promise."

Emily grabbed my wrist and pulled me from the boys. We wandered around the party; she talked at me about something, but I wasn't listening. My eyes were looking through the crowd. My heart skipped a beat every time someone walked into the room. Every time I caught the end of someone's short dark hair. But my hopes were always shattered to see someone other than Lizzie. I needed to find Lizzie and strike the word *friend* from her vocabulary.

"So? Do you want to?" Emily asked.

"Want to what?" I turned, gracing Emily with my full attention. We leaned against the wall as everyone else stood crowded around the living room. Behind us was one of Taylor's dad's photos of an icy forest, sparse of life and covered in snow.

"Do you want to go to the art museum with me next week?" She turned to me, her hand grazing up the side of my arm. "I miss hanging out with you. It's been lonely. My life has been quiet without you. I didn't realize how much I liked the noise. How much I liked . . ."

Her warm brown eyes flicked up to mine and I recognized that heated look. Those eyes were a warning. Emily wanted to kiss me. My chest squeezed in a familiar way, but I wrestled with that knot and let it loosen and fall limp.

"Emily." I tried to stop her.

"I think we should try again. We haven't fought at all. Not since we became friends again, and you're different now. I can see that. I think it could work."

She touched my cheek, and I knew what came next in this dance. A month ago I would've done anything to kiss Emily again. Tonight, I grabbed her wrist and touched my forehead with hers. "I'm sorry, Em." I lifted my head. "I don't want to get back together. We weren't good for each other."

"But we could be." Her chin trembled, but her jaw fought back and tightened. Her emotions were a splattered mess across her face, shocked widened eyes, a fierce anger straightening her lips while her nose flared "Things have changed. You've changed! And you don't even want to try again with me?"

"You're right. Everything changed, and I'm the kind of person who doesn't want this anymore. I'm sorry—"

"I can't believe this!" She shoved me and I took a stumbling step back. "You don't even want to try! It's not fair and it's so mean." The tears began to fall in fast streams. "You changed for Lizzie. Why couldn't you change for me? Why her? What's so great about her? Do you know what it's like? Getting treated like garbage and then being forced to watch you be so sweet to another girl? Why couldn't you be that sweet to me?"

"I'm sorry. I know you're mad, but—"

"You think I'm mad? I'm not mad, I'm—" Emily tried to open her mouth to say more, but only a sob fell at my feet. "Don't make me say it! It's embarrassing! I'm not the girl you're willing to change for so what does that say about me?"

"Emily," I whispered. "I'm sorry—"

She threw the last of her drink at me before running out of the room. A wave of déjà vu nearly took me out. She zoomed past Taylor, who immediately locked eyes with me. She threw her hands up as if asking what on earth I had done. I lifted my arms in innocence, which earned me an eye roll and a huff. Taylor chased after Emily for me.

Thank god.

It was too great of a punishment to ruin this jacket. And now I was going to have to give it back. *Dammit.* I knew it was too good to be true. As I shrugged the jacket off to give it a good wipe, something flew out of the pocket, and a little, folded-up piece of paper flopped onto the floor.

Dropping down, I rested on my legs as I picked up the lined notebook paper. I unfolded it to find a message:

Do you want to be my girlfriend? (For real this time)
Please check yes or no.
Lizzie

And then, at the bottom, there were two little boxes for me to decide.

I read it again. Looking at the leather jacket again, with its perfect bouquet, it hit me.

Lizzie got me this jacket. Or why else would there be this note.

"Fuck."

I scrambled to take out my phone as I put the jacket back on. I tried dialing Camille yet again, and as if I summoned her, I could hear her voice inside the house. Frantically, with my heartbeat vibrating through my veins, I trailed Camille's voice and the trickle of laughter, and found her and Norah in the kitchen. Camille was popped up on the counter, wedged inside of Norah's arms.

"Stop making out!" I shouted, my voice wrung tight in panic. "We gotta go!"

Camille jumped and Norah threw herself back, holding her hands up and freezing as if I'd stop seeing her if she stopped moving. Reaching with both hands, I grabbed Camille and dragged her out of the house.

"Whoa! What's going on?" Camille yelped, grabbing Norah because no girlfriend gets left behind.

"We have to go right now," I shouted over the chatter, with only the exit in my sights. "We have to find Lizzie. There's been a huge misunderstanding and I need to talk to her right now. I can't let her go another minute thinking I'm not in love with her."

Camille threw her hands up in sweet relief. "Finally!"

I raced to Camille's car, throwing myself in the back. I beat my fists against the front seat. "Go! Go! Go!"

"I'm going! Do you think I want Lizzie to talk to her exes? No! I'm going to end up being financially responsible for her therapy," Camille yelled back, flooring the gas pedal. I was knocked back by the force and nearly did a flip into the back window. Scrambling to get back up, I held on to the headrest for dear life and looked back at Lizzie's note.

"I'm so stupid!" I told them.

Camille snorted. "I've been telling you that for ages."

"Nice jacket," Norah said.

"Lizzie got it for me," I said, finally looking at the back of the note and finding something else.

Lizzie's "Lizzie x Parker" Playlist

"Why does Taylor live in fucking nowhere?" Camille yelled, and her engine growled as she tested the speed limit.

I lunged for Camille's aux cord and desperately searched for Lizzie's Spotify playlist, my data plan be damned. My finger nearly cracked the screen as I slammed the Play button. Soft music poured from Camille's speakers and my heart swelled up, stuffing the entirety of my chest with the fluff of crisp white clouds.

The playlist went on and on with the sappiest, sweetest love songs from decades ago. It was like she was saying our relationship was classic, the stuff people had fantasized about having since the dawn of time. Her playlist ended with Elvis Presley's "Can't Help Falling in Love." I couldn't believe I almost missed this. I couldn't believe I almost missed everything. From falling in love with Lizzie, to making friends with Norah, to meeting Miss Patty, to using the tiara, to creating the costumes, and even forgiving my dad.

I smacked Camille's headrest over and over. "Come on! We have to find Lizzie. I need to see Lizzie right now."

Camille snapped back, "What do you think I'm doing?!"

A *ding* from Camille's phone surprised us all. Norah glanced at it and her brows shot up. "Lizzie is already making the rounds." She turned Camille's phone to me and there was a picture of Lizzie looking more miserable than when we broke up.

Tears had obviously washed away her makeup, leaving her eyes a little swollen and a lot sad. She stood next to Jenna, her ex, and my chest squeezed, realizing Lizzie was probably putting me in the same category. Right now, I was any other ex.

"Katelyn must be next. Let's hurry before Lizzie has a psychotic break," Camille said, and slammed on the gas, causing a whirlwind in her car, whipping around our hair and clothes. "Roll my windows up."

"Wait!" I said and opened her car's skylight. "I've got an idea. Roll all the windows down."

FORTY-FOUR

Lizzie

The last time I saw Jenna Miller, she dumped me after a single week of dating. She was taller than I remembered, and her brown hair was full of highlights. All she wore was purple silk pajamas and slippers, but she still looked more put together than me, sniffling on her doorstep like an absolute wreck. I was still wearing my orchestra costume underneath my puffy coat, and sweat from the performance still soaked my short hair in the back.

"So, anyway, I wanted to apologize," I said, a sigh leaving my body. It sounded like the last of my sanity disappearing in the wind. "I was a bad girlfriend and I have no plans to get better."

Jenna's brow stayed narrowed. She raised her hand and stopped me. "Wait. Wait. Wait. Go back to the whole trial thing. You were fake dating a girl? Like actually?"

"Yep." I nodded. Every time I said it out loud, it became more ridiculous. "And I couldn't last thirty days because I haven't changed at all. I'm sorry I stopped putting in effort once we were officially dating. You must have been hurt."

Jenna shook her head. "Lizzie, it's all in the past."

From the living room, a guy called, "Jenna! Babe, you're letting the cold in! What's going on?"

"Don't worry about it!" Jenna called back. "I'll be back in a second."

Right. Emily had said something about Jenna finding a boyfriend. People in this world were actually date-able. Not me. I glanced at the ground, pressing my feet into Jenna's porch, and wondering if the world could swallow me whole.

"First of all, Lizzie," Jenna said, her arms firmly crossed against the cold and probably me. "It's wild that you came to my house without calling first. I mean, what if I wasn't home?"

"I kind of wanted to get this over with. Like ripping the trauma bandage right off."

Jenna sighed. "And second, don't say you didn't change."

I finally looked up, meeting her big brown eyes. Jenna smiled at me, and I realized my type must be pretty, confident girls with great smiles. "The Lizzie I dated would've never made it to my front door. The Lizzie I remember didn't understand why we broke up, but you seem to have figured it out."

Raising my brows, I was taken aback. I didn't expect Jenna to actually talk to me. Once she saw me, I assumed she'd shut the door in my face. "But I did know why we broke up."

"No," she corrected me. "You told everyone that we broke up because I thought you were boring, but that wasn't true. It was the opposite. I thought you were tired of me. I figured if you liked me more, you would've wanted to see me."

"I'm sorry, Jenna," I said and this time, it wasn't about the trial. I meant it.

"It's all right." She smiled.

Wincing at myself, I remembered the next step to all of this and forced the words out. "I'm also sorry about this, but we need to take a selfie, so I can prove to Camille that I did it."

With a snort, Jenna shook her head and let me pull out my camera. She smiled like someone was holding her at gunpoint. "Sorry again," I said.

"Hey, it's whatever. But I am sorry about your fake breakup. Sounds like you've had quite the adventure. Whoever this fake girlfriend is, she must be something special."

Her words punched me right in the gut and I was trembling, holding a sob at bay. It wasn't Jenna's fault. She had no idea how much she was kicking me while I was down. "She was."

"Who are you going to next? Katelyn?"

I blinked. This must be another dimension constructed by my worst nightmares and everyone else was in on it. "Yeah. How did you know?"

Jenna shrugged, coyly. "Maybe I cared about who you dated after me. Maybe I kept up with you a little. Katelyn's at a Halloween party. I can give you the address if your phone number hasn't changed."

"It hasn't. Thanks, Jenna."

"You're welcome, Lizzie. Take care of yourself," she said.

We didn't hug or shake hands, even if I felt we did in my soul. She closed the door, closing that part of my life as well. Despite things not going as planned, I felt different. Maybe it all meant something. Not that I cared about that today, when all I wanted to do was throw myself on the ground and sob.

Choosing maturity, I turned my back on Jenna's door, let myself go just enough for my vision to blur with hot tears, and walked off her porch.

The memory of Parker and Emily hugging wouldn't stop torturing me. Images of Parker's beautiful face smiling at Emily's incredibly gorgeous face haunted me when I closed my eyes, and I'd remember the last time Parker had even seen me was when I was wearing my stupid orchestra uniform. I sighed with my whole body, losing a piece of my soul.

Tonight was quiet.

The stars weren't even out. The inky black cold consumed me, and I shivered for the millionth time. My tearstained face had frozen over for new tears to ice skate across. I looked around at the weeping willow in Jenna's yard, slumping in solidarity. Little handmade ghost dolls had infiltrated her yard and hung from the tree limbs.

After this month, I certainly felt haunted.

My phone buzzed, and I glanced at Jenna's message. She'd sent me Katelyn's address as promised. Great. At least the party was close to my house, and once I had finished destroying the last of my dignity, I was going to crawl into bed and never resurface again.

FORTY-FIVE

Lizzie

The fact that my ex-girlfriend Katelyn was dressed as a sexy Cinderella was a level of irony that had the power to destroy the last shred of my mental health. The realization struck me that the movie, the stage musical, and all the adaptations would be ruined forever. I would always associate sparkly blue gowns, lost heels, and tiaras with Ashley Marie Parker.

Destroyer of my life.

"Uh, hi?" Katelyn squinted at me in pure confusion after a nice drunk person had gone inside and brought her out for me. The thought of trying to push my way into that sea of strangers and having to call Katelyn's name like a crazy person sounded worse than death.

Whoever's house party this was, it was happening at a scale I had never experienced. Everyone here was older, drunker, and so much louder than I expected. The house was shaking from the hyperpop music. It was pitch black outside, but the lawn and house were lit up with purple and orange string lights. There were cobwebs in the bushes and trees, while fake skeleton bones were scattered across the lawn.

"Hi, Katelyn," I said, while she looked at me like I was a lunatic. Katelyn was definitely debating whether or not she was going to pretend to not know me, which was fair. It'd been over a year, and our last interaction was us fighting over the fact she cheated on me and if I deserved it or not. Jury was still out.

"This isn't going to take long," I promised more to myself than her.

"Okay?" Katelyn still treaded with caution.

"I lost a bet and I need to let you know I was a bad girlfriend and I make no plans for getting better," I said again, and this time hurt my own feelings.

Her face twisted into a mean scowl. "Are you trying to embarrass me?"

I sighed, more embarrassed for myself. "No, not at all. It's a long story and I don't think I can tell it again." This was me begging, but my heart really wasn't in it. "Can you take my word for it? And take a selfie with me?"

"No," she said, like she was offended she even had to respond. "Lizzie." She kept her voice low as she tried to find the words. "Why would you have to apologize to me? When I cheated on you? Either start making sense or get out of here."

"But you cheated on me because I was a bad girlfriend," I insisted, but hearing myself say it out loud suddenly put everything into focus.

"Some relationships aren't meant to work out. I'm not going to say we wasted our time on each other," Katelyn said. "I don't believe in wasted time, but you weren't a bad girlfriend. I'm sorry for cheating on you. I should've broken up with you sooner, especially because I did like you."

I softened. "I liked you too."

"Listen, if you want to come in—" Her words were caught in her throat. She picked her head up, turning her head toward the front of her neighborhood. "Do you hear that? What is going on?"

"What?" I asked, but I heard it too. Something strange was creeping into the darkness. There was music playing from down the street, and nothing like the music pounding inside. Slowly, I walked down the driveway onto the sidewalk, and if I hadn't known any better, I'd swear Camille's car was speeding down the road, past the partygoers' parked cars.

In the distance, Camille's headlights flickered on and off to catch my attention, as if the car honking and the music weren't enough already. From the skylight, Parker poked out. Her red hair whipped wildly in the wind behind her, making her look like the asteroid that killed the dinosaurs. Now hurtling toward me.

"Lizzie!" Parker yelled, waving her arms.

It was then I realized what song was playing and where it must have come from. Number ten on my playlist declaring my love for Parker: "Only You (And You Alone)" by The Platters.

"Are you crazy?" I yelled back at her, totally flabbergasted. Suddenly, I couldn't tell if I was awake or asleep. I pinched myself and the pain sobered me up. This wasn't a dream. Freaking out, I waved them down so they'd come to me. "You're gonna wake up the entire neighborhood!"

Camille made a sudden stop in front of the house party and Parker jutted forward into the side of the roof. She made a tortured noise before dropping back inside the car and then appeared again as she opened the rear door. She stepped onto the street in all her glory and my chest tightened. I wanted her to come find me, but I had zero clue what she came here to say.

"I've been looking for you all night," she said.

"Really? Why?"

"What do you mean why? I'll always try to find you."

"But Emily—"

Parker grabbed my hands and squeezed. "Emily and I are over. We've been over. We didn't have a chance the very second you and I started the trial."

"But—" I tried to stop her again because my hopes were soaring and I desperately wanted to avoid getting burned.

"There is no but, Lizzie," Parker insisted.

"But there is! We broke up. We couldn't finish the trial. I don't know what you're thinking."

"Just wait a second!" Parker yelled back, like she'd scream it from a mountaintop if one was available. "I have to say this. I have to say it right now because I can't go another second without letting you know that I'm in love with you."

My lips parted.

"I'm tired of all the confusion and the mixed messages. I wanna be real with you. I want to be honest." Parker let go of my hands and I watched her stalk off to the car and grab something. She wriggled around, struggling to do something, and I couldn't figure out what until I heard the click of a pen. Turning, she revealed my note and showed me her answer.

She checked *yes* to be my girlfriend.

And she grinned, all teeth and dimples.

"Say it again," I begged, needing to hear it one more time so I knew it was true. "Tell me again."

"Lizzie," Parker said, dropping her arms. She strolled back up to me and declared, "I don't want another trial. I don't need one. I know what I want. I want a year-long subscription to be your girlfriend. No." She shook her head. "Even that's not long enough. I want five years. Ten. My whole life. Tell me where to sign and I'll be all yours."

"All mine?"

"If you want me."

I reached up, cupping her cheeks. She touched my waist, and the impressions of her fingers burned through my fabric to warm my skin. "I do. I want you. Parker, I love you too." An uncontrollable smile appeared as I rose on my tiptoes to plant a kiss on Parker's lips. My hands slid down to her neck, the thrum of her heart tickling my palms.

This was too good to be true. A part of me couldn't believe this was my life. Usually things like this didn't work out for me. Not this well. Not this perfectly. But this moment had everything. All my favorite things tied up in strings, music, written agreements, and kissing Ashley Marie Parker.

Camille and Norah applauded and hollered, but Norah was grinning the widest, shaking two thumbs-up in the air. "Finally!" she cheered.

"No one's happier than me that you two are finally dating!" Camille yelled again. "But can we go get something to eat? You can be in love anywhere!"

Grinning, I rested my head on Parker as we soaked in this happy moment. Parker snatched my hand and we jumped into my car, letting Camille follow us. We laughed, zooming out of my neighborhood, driving to nowhere in particular. Eventually, we settled on McDonald's. The entire time I wouldn't let go of Parker's hand. I talked to Camille and Norah, but Parker's thumb and mine were having their own conversation. Every now and then Parker would lift my hand and place a kiss on my knuckle.

I settled into one of the seats at McDonald's and took out my note. Right by where Parker agreed to be my girlfriend, I made my own check mark and signed it. Parker grinned, scribbling her own signature. Before she finished, I kissed her cheek because I wanted to do it. Because I could do it. Because I could kiss Parker as many times as I wanted.

This marked day one of Lizzie and Parker officially dating.

Day one of many to come.

I'm told after thirty days something can become a habit. Whether that's brushing your teeth every night or feeding your cat around the same time. It could even be thirty days of making a beautiful girl laugh and then you'll do it every single day after that. It could be thirty days of sending a girl a good morning and a good night text until it becomes clockwork.

Sometimes all it takes to fall in love is thirty days.

It certainly worked out for me.

Playlist

Flirting With Her
Sir Babygirl

You Were in My Dream Last Night
Babygirl

Bad Ideas
Tessa Violet

Girls make me wanna die
The Aces

What if I love you
Gatlin

Ordinary
Amber Ais

Drain Me
Towa Bird

Golden Hour
Kasey Musgraves

Bags
Clairo

Honey
Kehlani

We fell in love in October
girl in red

Pretty Lips
WINEHOUSE

Sick of Losing Soulmates
Dodie

Girlfriend
hemlocke springs

Washing Machine Heart
Mitski

Breaking News
Flowerovlove

Nice to Know Ya
Carlie Hanson

Vertigo
Griff

Frequent Crier
Future Teens

Birds of a Feather
Billie Eilish

Cinderella: Impossible; It's Possible
Cinderella (Original Television Cast)

Build me up Buttercup
Lara Anderson

Love Me Anyway
Chappell Roan

Only You (And You Alone)
The Platters

Acknowledgments

By nature, I am an introverted, anxious little creature, so I could not have done this without so much love and support. I was worried about writing my first ever acknowledgments because I would be so sad if I missed thanking someone, but now my thanks are pouring out.

First, I have to thank all the Wattpad readers who could've read any book on the platform but chose mine. Thank you to every reader who has offered me encouragement, praise, musical theater gush sessions, and jokes that are usually funnier than mine. Without your push, I wouldn't have been able to do this. And if you saw yourself in this book, you're not alone.

And a thousand thanks to the Wattpad Team who saw something special in my book and gave me a chance! To Delaney, Sun, and Fiona for your much-needed encouragement and your trust in me that fought my imposter syndrome into silence. A monumentally huge thank-you to my editor, Rebecca Sands, who basically shared half of my brain and helped me turn my story into an actual book. Thank you for all of your ideas, our brainstorming sessions, and most of all, your kindness. I couldn't have asked for a better experience.

Being a writer is a solitary experience, unless you stumble upon the coolest people on Wattpad and they welcome you with open arms. This truly wouldn't have happened without Philline Harms, who did this first and always provided advice if I needed it. You are so cool, and I can't wait to join bookshelves with you, even if it doesn't make sense alphabetically. Thank you, Olivia Vaughn! If I could switch writing styles with anyone in the world, it'd be you. You're so talented, funny, and kind that it makes me want to shake every reader I know to make sure they read your books. I need the world to discover who you are!

An extra special paragraph of their own to Natalie Cook. My CP, friend, fellow swiftie, dog mom, cool girl, and incredible writer, you deserve an ocean full of my thanks. I've had a roller coaster of a time during this process, and no matter how much I pull away or close up, you're always there to welcome me back. It means more to me than anyone can understand. You're awesome. Thank you for showing love and care for this book before I sent it away. Thank you for letting me read your books (they're so good!). I get to say I read Natalie Cook's books before they were cool, so HA! Let's continue this journey together.

Thank you to the wonderful people in my life who have never once doubted me. Writing this actually makes me emotional. You all have never, ever questioned my dreams. You guys always assumed it would happen to me. I'm relieved you're right, haha. Thank you, Molly. I miss you all the time and can't wait to see you again. Thank you to the entire Crupi crew, Reese, Watson, and my fellow reader, Lilly. Nice people exist! And they're the best! Thank you to Johnathen, who has been my unlikely friend. Please let me win at *Mario Party*.

Thank you to Adam, RJ, and the group chat who were unknowingly my co-workers while I worked on this book. Thank you for the laughs, references, your thoughtfulness, and for introducing me to K-pop. Thank you to all the people who listened to me talk on and on about my books at Publix. Thank you to Travis, Aiden, Sarra, Viola, Helena, Kat, and Nicole. I would have gone absolutely insane by now if it weren't for you guys. Let's have barbecue again soon.

I waited for this moment to thank my family because I am a big crybaby and I'm already tearing up, so let me get my tissues. Our family isn't big, but the love I receive is more than enough. I couldn't ask for more when you guys make me feel special. I must be a good person because you guys love me so much. Thank you to my mom, who read this book first and listened to the audio version. I want to tell you all my stories because your excitement excites me. Thank you for showing me art, musicals, books, and more. Thank you for writing my first book with me and Rebecca. Thank you for showing me I could do that. Thank you, Duke, my little brother. I can't believe how lucky I am to have my best friends in the world be related to me. I am more and more proud of you every day. Thank you for showing me what you love and sharing it with me. Thank you for letting me hear your stories. Thank you for making me laugh so hard I could scream. You're the best. I love you.

Thank you to my older sister, Rebecca. I've spent my entire life with you, so I have never once been alone. Thank you for traveling around the country with me. Thank you for all the adventures that were spontaneous or planned, and for trying new things with me, but also sharing what makes us both so cozy and comfortable. I'm worried I'm going to forget to thank you for something because that's how much you mean to me. Thank you for this life I have! It's a really wonderful life. Let's grow old together.

Also, thank you to Rebecca for my best friend, Rhyland. RHYLAND! You're the best boy in the world and I'm obsessed with you. Look! Your name is in a book!

And, finally, thank you to the reader who picked up this book. Thank you for reading *The Trial Period*. It means so much to me and I deeply appreciate that you gave me a chance! If you came from Wattpad and picked up this book again, thank you. I hope you receive all different kinds of love in your life. Thank you!

About the Author

Auburn Morrow is a nonbinary asexual writer who dropped out of college for English but ended up becoming an author anyway. When they're not writing, they're learning new hobbies, playing video games, or crying over their K-pop biases. Together with their best friends (their sister and nephew), they live in Georgia and dream about writing more queer stories.